Statement required by the Act of August 12, 1970, Section 3685, Title 39, United States Code, showing the ownership, management, and circulation of *Reader's Digest Select Editions Large Type*, published five times per year (February, April, June, August, and November) at Mt. Kisco, Westchester County, New York 10549, as filed October 1, 2017. Annual subscription is $20.00.

The name and address of the publisher and owner is Reader's Digest Partners for Sight Foundation, Inc., a New York not-for-profit corporation, Mt. Kisco, New York 10549. The Editor-in-Chief is Jim Menick of White Plains, New York 10601.

There are no bondholders, mortgagees, or other security holders. Tax status, N/A.

The average number of copies of each issue during the preceding twelve months, and of the single issue (August 2017) nearest to filing date, respectively, are as follows: Total number of copies printed (net press run) 54,781—52,898; paid circulation—sales through dealers and carriers, street vendors, and counter sales—none; mail subscriptions 52,663—50,000; total paid circulation 52,663—50,000; total distribution 52,663—50,000; copies not distributed 2,118—2,898; total 54,781—52,898; percent paid and/or requested circulation 100%—100%.

I certify that the statements made by me above are correct and complete.

(signed) Susan Olivo, Executive Director

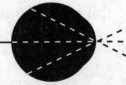

CONTENTS

THE
MISTLETOE
PROMISE

RICHARD PAUL
EVANS

A SUCCESSFUL businessman offers a woman who works in his building a most interesting proposition.

Prologue

IF YOU could erase just one day from your life, would you know the day? For some, a specific date comes to mind, one that lives in personal infamy. It may be the day you lost someone you love. Or it might be the time you did something you regret, a mistake you wish you could fix. It may be a combination of both.

I am one of those people who would know the day. There is one day that has brought me unspeakable pain, and the effects of that day continue to cover and erode my world like rust. I suspect that someday the rust will eat through the joists and posts of my life and I will topple, literally as well as figuratively.

I have punished myself for my mistake more times than I can remember. Each day I wake up in the court of conscience to be judged guilty and unworthy. In this sorry realm I am the judge, prosecutor, and jury, and without defense, I accept the verdict and the sentence, a lifetime of regret and guilt to be administered by myself.

I'm not the only one who has punished me for what I've done. Not by a long shot. The world has weighed in on my failure as well. Some people I know, more I don't. And there are those who have learned to use my mistake against me—to punish or control me. My ex-husband was an expert on wielding my mistake against me, and for too long I offered up no defense.

Then one day a man came along who was willing to plead my case. Not so ironically, he was an attorney. And for the first time since that black day, I felt joy without the need to squash it. I met him around the holidays just a little more than a year ago. And that too is a day I'll never forget.

Chapter One

November 1, 2012

I HATED the change; the commercial changing of the seasons was more obvious than nature's. It was November first, the day after Halloween, when orange and black gives way to red and green. I didn't always hate the change; I once looked forward to it. But that seemed like a lifetime ago.

I watched as the maintenance staff of the office building where I worked transformed the food court. A large, synthetic Christmas tree was dragged out to the middle of the room, strung with white lights, and draped in blue and silver tinsel. Giant corrugated-styrene snowflakes were brought out of storage and hung from the ceiling, just as they had been every year for as long as I'd worked in downtown Salt Lake City.

I was watching the transformation when I noticed him staring at me. *Him*—the stranger who would change everything. I didn't know his name, but I had seen him before. I'd probably seen him a hundred times before, as we ate pretty much every day in the same food court: I near the Café Rio with my sweet pork salad and he, fifty yards away, over by the Japanese Food Emporium eating something with chopsticks. *Why was he looking at me?*

He was handsome. Not in your Photoshopped Abercrombie & Fitch catalog way—women weren't necessarily stopping mid-sentence when he walked into a room—but he certainly did catch their attention. He was about six feet tall, trim, athletically built. He was always dressed impeccably—in an expensive, custom-tailored suit, with a crisp white shirt and a silk tie.

I guessed he was a lawyer and, from his accoutrements, one who made good money. I, on the other hand, worked as a hotel and venue coordinator at a midlevel travel wholesaler, booking educational trips for high school students. The company I worked for was called the International Consortium of Education, but we all just called it by its acronym, ICE, which was appropriate, as I felt pretty frozen in my job. I guess that was true of most of my life.

THE lawyer and I had had eye contact before. It was two or three weeks back when I had stepped on an elevator that he was already on. The button for the seventh floor was lit, which was further evidence that he was a lawyer, since the top two floors of the tower were occupied by law firms.

He had smiled at me, and I'd given him an obligatory return smile. I remember his gaze had lingered on me a little longer than I'd expected, long enough to make me feel self-conscious. He'd looked at me as if he knew me or wanted to say something; then he'd turned away. I thought he had stolen a glance at my bare ring finger, though later I decided that it had just been my imagination.

After that, the lawyer and I had run into each other dozens of times, each time offering the same obligatory smiles. But today he was staring at me. Then he got up and started across the room toward me, a violation of our unspoken relational agreement.

At first I thought he was walking toward me; then I thought he wasn't, which made me feel stupid, like when someone waves at you in a crowd and you're not sure who they are, but you wave back before realizing that they were waving at someone behind you. But then there he was, this gorgeous man, standing five feet in front of me, staring at me with my mouth full of salad.

"Hi," he said.

"Hi," I returned, swallowing insufficiently chewed lettuce.

"Do you mind if I join you?"

I hesitated. "No, it's okay."

As he sat down, he reached across the table. "My name is Nicholas. Nicholas Derr. You can call me Nick."

"Hi, Nicholas," I said, subtly refusing his offer of titular intimacy. "I'm Elise."

"Elise," he echoed. "That's a pretty name."

"Thank you."

"Want to see something funny?" Before I could answer, he unfolded a piece of paper from his coat pocket, then set it on the table in front of me. "A colleague of mine just showed these to me."

I know a guy who's addicted to brake fluid. He says he can stop anytime.

I didn't like my beard at first. Then it grew on me.

He pointed to the last one. "This is my favorite."

I stayed up all night to see where the sun went. Then it dawned on me.

"Is that what you do at work?" I asked.

"Pretty much. That and computer solitaire," he said, folding the paper back into his pocket. "How about you?"

"Candy Crush."

"I mean, where do you work?"

"On the third floor of the tower. It's a travel company. ICE. It stands for International Consortium of Education."

"What kind of travel do you do?"

"We arrange educational tours for high school students to historic sites, like Colonial Williamsburg or Philadelphia or New York. Teachers sign up their classes."

"I wouldn't think there was a lot of travel on a teacher's salary."

"That's the point," I said. "If they get enough of their students signed up, they come along free as chaperones."

"Ah, it's a racket."

"Basically. Let me guess, you're a lawyer."

"How could you tell?"

"You look like one. What's your firm?"

"Derr, Nelson, and McKay."

"That's a mouthful," I said. "Speaking of

which, do you mind if I finish eating before my salad gets cold?"

He cocked his head. "Isn't salad supposed to be cold?"

"Not the meat. It's sweet pork."

"No, please eat." He leaned back a little while I ate, surveying the room. "Looks like the holiday assault force has landed. I wish they would take a break this year. The holidays depress me."

"Why is that?"

"Because it's lonely just watching others celebrate."

It was exactly how I felt. "I know what you mean."

"I thought you might."

"Why do you say that?"

"I just noticed that you usually eat alone."

I immediately went on the defensive. "It's only because my workmates and I take different lunchtimes to watch the phones."

He frowned. "I didn't mean to offend you. I'm just saying that I've noticed we've both spent a lot of time down here alone."

"I didn't notice," I lied.

He looked into my eyes. "So you're probably wondering what I want."

"It's crossed my mind."

It's taken me a few days to get up the courage to come over here and talk to you, which is saying something, since I'm not afraid of much." He hesitated for a moment, as if gathering his thoughts. "The first time I saw you, I thought, *Why is such a beautiful woman sitting there alone?* Then I saw you the next day, and the next day . . ."

"Your point?" I said.

"My point is, I'm tired of being alone during the holidays. I'm tired of walking through holiday crowds of humanity feeling like a social leper." He looked into my eyes. "Are you?"

"Am I what?"

"Tired of being alone during the holidays."

I shook my head. "No, I'm good."

He looked surprised. "Really?"

"Really."

He looked surprised *and* a little deflated. "Oh," he said, looking down as if thinking. Then he looked back up at me and forced a smile. "Good, then. That's good for you. I'm glad you're happy." He stood. "Well, Elise, it was a pleasure to finally meet you. I'm sorry to bother you. Enjoy your salad and have a nice holiday." He turned to leave.

"Wait a second," I said. "Where are you going?"

"Back to work."

"Why did you come over here?"

"It's not important."

"It was important enough for you to cross the food court."

"It *was* important. Now it's moot."

"Moot?" I said. "Sit down. Tell me what's moot."

He looked at me for a moment, then sat back down. "I just thought that maybe you felt the same way about the holidays as I do, but since you're *good*, you clearly don't. So what I was going to say is now moot."

I looked at him a moment, then said, "I might have exaggerated my contentment. So what were you going to say that is now moot?"

"I had a proposition to make"

"Right here in the food court?"

"We could go to my office if you prefer."

"No, here in public is good."

"I'll cut to the chase. Socially, this is a busy time of year for me. And, like I said, I'm tired of being alone during the holidays, going to all my company and client dinners and parties alone, enduring everyone's sympathy and answering everyone's questions about why a successful, nice-looking attorney is still single. And, for the sake of argument, we'll say that you're also tired of doing the holidays solo."

"Go on," I said.

"As one who would rather light a candle than curse the darkness, I say that we do something about it. What I'm proposing is a mutually beneficial holiday arrangement. For the next eight weeks, we are, for all intents and purposes, a couple."

I looked at him blankly. "Are you kidding me?"

"Think about it. It's the perfect solution. We don't know each other, so there's no deep stuff, no pain, no bickering. The only commitment is to be good to each other and to be good company."

"And being good company means ending up back at your place?"

"No. I'm proposing a purely platonic relationship. Maybe we publicly hold hands now and then to sell the facade, but that's the extent of our physicality."

I shook my head skeptically. "Men can't have platonic relationships."

"In real life, you're probably right. But this isn't real life. It's fiction. And it's just until Christmas."

"How do I know you're not a serial killer?"

He laughed. "You don't. You could ask my ex, but no one's found the body."

"What?"

"Just kidding. I've never been married."

"You're serious about this?"

He nodded. "Completely."

"I think you're crazy."

"Maybe. Or maybe I'm a genius and everyone will be doing this in the future."

I slowly shook my head, not sure of what to think of the proposal or the proposer.

"Look, I know it's unconventional, but oftentimes the best solutions are. Will you at least consider it?"

I looked at him for a moment, then said, "Allright. I'll think about it. No guarantees. Probably not."

"Fair enough," he said, standing. "I'm leaving town tonight, but I'll be back Monday."

"That will give me some time to think about it," I said.

"I eagerly await your response."

"Don't be too eager," I said.

"It's been a pleasure, Elise." He smiled as he turned and walked away.

THE encounter left me A little dazed. I didn't tell anyone about it. Actually, I didn't really have anyone to tell. The person at work I spent the most time with was my colleague Zoey, and I definitely wouldn't be telling her. You don't know Zoey, but you do. Every company, every school in the world, has a Zoey—the kind of girl who attracts male attention like a porch light attracts moths. She was naturally beautiful, skinny without starving or Zumba, born with a body that designers design for. She even looked good without makeup, which I knew for a fact since she usually spent the first hour at work applying it.

Even worse than being beautiful was that she knew it. A few months after I started at ICE, before I really even knew her, she offered to give me some makeup, which sounded like her saying that I could be pretty if I tried. I think what hurt the most about her offer was that, whether she meant to convey that message or not, it was true. I didn't take care of myself. After Dan, my ex-husband, divorced me, I sort of let things slide. Not completely, but enough to change. I put on a little weight and stopped spending time at the mirror or buying clothes. I guess I was treating myself the way I felt—undesirable.

At the opposite extreme, Zoey was in her prime with a perpetually full roster of men, with someone always up to bat and someone always on deck, ready to fill in when she tired of the current player. She was the one our company's airline and hotel reps, mostly balding, middle-aged men, would plan their office visits around.

What I had said to the lawyer about eating alone at lunch was true, mostly. One of us was supposed to watch the phones, but that's what voice mail is for, right? The real reason I hated to eat lunch with Zoey was because all I ended up doing was listening to her stories of affairs and conquests while I sat there feeling frumpy and old. It's easy to hate the game when you're losing.

THAT WEEKEND, ALL I could think about was the proposition. *Who was this guy, and what did he want? What was his motive?* I suppose, on a deeper level, the bigger question (considering how lonely I was) was *Why was I even questioning his motive?* Why couldn't he be exactly what he claimed to be? Was that really so hard to accept?

My father used to say, "If it ain't broke, don't fix it—but if it's already broke, it don't matter what you do." My life was definitely broken. So why not? What did I have to lose? I even asked myself, *What would Zoey do?* I knew what she'd do. She'd say, "You only live once, girl," and she'd buckle up for the ride. I suppose that my mind was somewhere in Zoeyland when I decided to say yes.

THE next Monday, Nicholas arrived in the food court about a half hour after I'd started eating.

"Hi, Elise," he said. "How was your weekend?"

"The usual," I said, even though it was definitely anything but.

He sat down across from me. "Did you come to a decision?"

"Right to the point," I said. I set down my plastic fork. "So, hypothetically, let's say that I said yes. What would this arrangement look like?"

He smiled. "First, we write up a contract."

"Why, you don't trust me?"

"Contracts are not always so much a matter of trust as they are a matter of understanding. This way we'll be more likely to meet each other's expectations."

I should have had one of those before my marriage, I thought.

He leaned in closer. "Let me tell you what I had in mind. I'll pay for all meals, transportation, and admissions. We'll have lunch together when possible, and in addition to the social functions, I'll take you to dinner or some holiday-themed event at least once a week, and I'll send you something, a gift, each weekday up until the end of the contract. Then, at midnight on Christmas Eve, the agreement terminates and we go back to our lonely, pathetic lives."

"If I agree, how do we start?"

"We'll begin by going through each other's calendars and determining what events we can attend. It's two-sided, of course. If you'd like, I'll attend your events as well."

I thought a moment more, then, with his eyes locked on to mine, said, "All right."

"All right, let's do it?" he asked.

I nodded. "Yes. Let's do it."

"Are you sure?"

"Why not? Lunch every day?"

"When possible. At least every workday. We're two days in on that now. It hasn't been too painful, has it?"

"It's definitely been interesting. I don't know about you sending me things."

"Why?"

I shrugged. "I don't know."

"You'll get used to it."

"Do I have to send you things too?"

"No. I expect nothing but the pleasure of your company."

I took a deep breath. "Okay. Get me a contract."

"Great," he said, standing. "I'll see you tomorrow."

"You're not having lunch?"

"No. I have a deposition in an hour that I still need to prepare for. I just came down to see you."

Something about the way he said that pleased me. "All right, I'll see you tomorrow."

"Thank you, Elise. I don't think you'll regret it."

A minute later, a food court worker said to me, "You have a cute husband."

"He's not my husband," I said. "He's . . ." I paused. "He's my boyfriend."

"Lucky you," she said.

THE next day, Nicholas walked into the food court carrying a leather Coach briefcase. I was sitting at my usual table, waiting for him. He smiled when he saw me. "Shall we eat at Café Rio?" he asked.

"Sure," I said.

We walked together up to the restaurant's counter. "I've never eaten here before," he said. "What's good?"

"The sweet pork salad is pretty much my mainstay," I said.

"Two sweet pork salads," Nicholas said to the woman who was rolling out tortillas.

"Pinto beans or black beans?" she asked.

Nicholas deferred to me. "I didn't realize there would be a quiz. I'll let you take over."

"Pinto beans," I said. "With the house dressing. Cheese, no pico."

"I'll have the same," he said.

"Drink?"

"The sugar-free lemonade," I said.

"One sugar-free lemonade and a Coke," Nicholas said.

He paid for our meals, then carried our tray over to a table.

"This is pretty good," he said. "I can see why you have it every day."

"It may be the most delicious salad ever made," I replied.

After we had eaten for a few minutes, he reached into his briefcase and brought out some documents. "Here you go," he said, holding out the papers. "The contract."

"This looks so *official*."

"It's what I do," he said.

I looked it over.

MISTLETOE CONTRACT

"Why mistletoe?"

"You know how, at Christmastime, people show affection under mistletoe to people they're not necessarily affectionate with?"

"That's clever," I said. "Can we change the word *contract?* It sounds too . . . formal."

"What would you prefer?"

I thought a moment. "How about *promise?*"

"Done," he said, striking a line through the word *contract* and penning in the rest. "Mistletoe Promise."

I looked over the agreement.

MISTLETOE ~~CONTRACT~~
PROMISE

This service agreement is made effective as of November 6th by and between

Elise Dutton (Lessor) and Nicholas Derr (Lessee).

"How did you know my last name?"

"I'm a lawyer," he said, which didn't really answer my question.

1. DESCRIPTION OF SERVICES.
Lessor will exert due effort to provide

to Lessee the following services (collectively, the "Services"):

a. Lunch together each weekday as schedules permit.

b. At least one evening activity per week through duration of contract.

c. Best effort to demonstrate a caring relationship.

I couldn't help but think how every relationship would benefit from such an agreement.

2. PAYMENT. In consideration of Lessor's services, Lessee agrees to pay for dinners, joint activities, admission fees, travel expenses, etc., for the duration of Contract.

"Travel expenses?" I asked.
"Gas money," he said. "Mostly."

If Lessee fails to pay for the Services, Lessor has the option to treat such failure to pay as a material breach of this Contract and may cancel this Contract but not seek legal redress.

3. TERM. This agreement will terminate automatically on December 24, 2012, at 11:59:59 p.m.

4. LANGUAGE. Lessor and Lessee shall, for the duration of this agreement, refer to each other as boyfriend or girlfriend or by any term of endearment, including, but not limited to, *sweetie, sweetheart, love, dear, babe, beautiful, cupcake,* and any term found acceptable by both parties.

I looked at him incredulously. "Really? *Cupcake?*"

"I wasn't planning on using *cupcake.*"

"Then why did you put it in the contract?"

"In case you were. It's just an example," he said. "Granted a poor one. But I don't know your preferences."

"I would rather not be called after any food or animal. Actually, avoid any noun."

"Consider all nouns, especially *cupcake,* stricken from my vocabulary. Does that include *honey?*"

I thought about it. "I guess *honey* is okay. It's gone mainstream."

"*Honey,* okay," he said to himself.

I went back to the contract.

5. PLATONIC NATURE OF ARRANGEMENT. This agreement does not constitute, imply, or encourage, directly or indirectly, a physical relationship, other than what would be considered expected and appropriate public physical contact.

"What does that mean? *Expected* physical contact."

"Nothing exciting. Hand-holding in public, that sort of thing." When I didn't respond he added, "Things real couples do. For instance, we might hold hands at a company party, at least when walking into the party, but we wouldn't be holding hands when we are alone, since that obviously wouldn't be necessary to convince others."

"I get it," I said.

6. CONFIDENTIALITY. Lessor and her agents will not at any time or in

any manner, either directly or indirectly, divulge, disclose, or commu-
nicate in any manner any information
that is proprietary to this agreement
and agrees to protect such information
and treat it as strictly confidential. This
provision will continue to be effective
until the termination of this Contract.

7. BREACH OF CONTRACT. If any
of the above stipulations are not met,
Contract will be considered null and
void. No recourse is available.

ADDENDUMS
1. No deep, probing personal
questions.
2. No drama.

"Talk to me about these addendums."
"The first is self-explanatory. We do not
ask each other any deep, probing personal
questions. It's irrelevant to our objective and
will only cause problems. Do you really want
me asking deep personal questions about
your life and past?"

I tried to hide the effect the question had on me. "Nope, I'm good."

"Exactly. This relationship should be so shallow there's no possibility of drowning."

"Agreed," I said. "And the second?"

"No drama. Life's too short."

"Agreed."

"Then all that's left is your signature."

I looked at the signatory line. He had already signed the contract. "Why do I feel like I'm signing away my soul?"

"It's not an eternity. Just forty-nine days."

I breathed out. "All right. Do you have a pen?"

"I'm a lawyer. That's like asking me if I have a lung."

"As opposed to a heart," I said.

"Another fan of lawyers," he said. He extracted a pen from his coat pocket. I took the pen from Nicholas and signed the document.

"There are two copies," he said. "One for your own files. Please sign both."

"Now you're really sounding like a lawyer."

"I am one."

"So you keep reminding me." I folded the contract in half and put it in my purse.

When I'd finished eating my salad, I said, "I better get back to work."

"I'll walk you to the elevator," he said. As we waited for the elevator, he said, "Don't forget to bring your calendar tomorrow so we can work out our schedule."

"I'll be ready."

As the elevator door opened, he leaned forward and kissed my cheek. "Have a good day, dear."

"Thanks for lunch," I said. *"Cupcake."*

He smiled. "This is going to be fun."

Chapter Two

ZOEY screamed. Cathy, our company bookkeeper, and I rushed out of our offices to see a florist deliveryman standing in the middle of the office holding a massive bouquet of yellow roses. It was one of the largest bouquets I'd ever seen, the kind people were more likely to send to the dead than the living.

"They're gorgeous," Cathy said. "Who are they from?"

"I don't know," Zoey said. "Probably Paul. Or Quentin. Could even be Brody. So many men, so many possibilities."

I rolled my eyes at her theatrics.

"Where would you like them?" the man asked.

"Oh, just set them there," Zoey said, motioning to her desk.

"And if I could have you sign right here." He handed Zoey an electronic clipboard.

Her expression abruptly changed. "They're not for me." She looked up at me. "They're for you."

"Elise?" Cathy said, not masking her surprise.

Just then, Mark, our boss, walked into the room.

"Those are pretty . . . massive." He looked at Zoey. "Who now?"

"They're not for me," Zoey said. "They're for Elise."

He looked at me. "Someone's got a fever for you."

I walked over to my flowers. There was a

small unsealed envelope attached to the vase. I extracted the card.

Dear Elise,
    Happy Day 1. I hope the flowers brighten your day.
    —Nick

"Who are they from?" Cathy asked.

"Just . . . a guy."

"What guy?" Zoey asked.

"My *boyfriend*." The word came out awkwardly.

They looked at me with expressions of bewilderment.

"You have a boyfriend?" Zoey asked.

"It's new," I said. I lifted the heavy vase and carried it to my office. *Thank you, thank you, thank you,* I thought. I couldn't wait to thank Nicholas.

FLOWERS are complicated. The last time I had received flowers from a man was a nightmare. I was in the hospital, and I'd just come out of intensive care after almost dying from a burst appendix, but the pain I remember most wasn't caused by the operation. It was caused by my husband. But I'll share more of that later.

I debated over whether or not I should take the flowers home but finally decided to leave them at the office. I told myself that they were so big I doubted I could get them into my apartment without damaging them. But really I think I left them in the office in defiance of my coworkers' incredulity. Driving home, all I could think about was that it had been the best day I'd had in a long time.

THE next morning at work I was making copies of a travel itinerary for a group of high school students from Boise, Idaho, when I heard Zoey greet someone.

"I have a delivery for Elise Dutton," a man said.

I walked out of my office. "That would be me."

"Here you go," the man said, handing me a box.

"What is it?" Zoey asked.

"I don't know." I opened the box and smiled. "Oh. Chocolate cordials." I wondered how he knew that I loved them. There was a card.

Happy Day 2, Elise. So far so good?
—Nick

"What are cordials?" Zoey asked.

"Chocolate-covered cherries," I said.

"Why don't they just call them chocolate-covered cherries?"

"Because they're cordials," I replied. I took one out and popped it into my mouth. It was delicious. "Want one?"

"Sure." She looked a little injured as she walked over to me. "Tell me more about this guy."

Even though it was the first time she'd ever asked me about my personal life, I didn't want to share. "He's really just more of a friend."

"Guys don't send chocolates and massive flower bouquets just to be friends. There's always an agenda. What's the lowdown?"

"His name is Nicholas."

"What does he do?"

"He's a lawyer on the seventh floor."

"Nicholas what?"

"Derr."

She puzzled a moment, then said, "As in Derr, Nelson, and McKay? You're dating one of the partners?"

"We're just . . ." The truth was, I didn't know whether he was a partner, but Zoey's incredulity made me angry. "Yes. Of course."

"Oh," she said. "Well done."

"Don't look so surprised," I said.

"It's just that you've never showed much interest in dating."

"Maybe I just hadn't met the right man," I replied.

"Nicholas is the right man?"

"Maybe." This was already more fun than I'd thought it would be. "I've decided to at least give him until Christmas. I think that's enough time to see if I like him."

She looked almost stunned. "Okay," she said. She started to turn away, then said, "Oh, could you trade me lunchtimes today? I met this guy last night, and he's coming to meet me."

"I'm sorry," I said. "I'm meeting Nicholas."

You have no idea how good it felt saying no. It was the first time I'd ever turned her down. It was the first time I'd had a reason to.

A LITTLE after noon, I went to the food court. Nicholas wasn't there yet, so I ordered my usual salad and sat down at my usual table. Nicholas showed up about ten minutes later.

"I'm sorry I'm late," he said, looking stressed. "Long-winded client, antitrust stuff. Too dull to discuss."

"It's okay," I said.

He sat down across from me. "How's your day?"

"Good," I said. "Thank you for the flowers. They're beautiful."

"Like you."

I smiled a little. "And the chocolates."

"Do you like chocolate?"

"All women like chocolate. It's like female catnip."

He grinned. "I hoped as much."

"You don't need to spend so much, you know."

"I know," he said simply.

"Are you going to get something to eat?"

"No, I'm sorry. I know we were going to go through our schedules today, but my morning fell apart and I have to get back to that meeting. I just didn't want to leave you hanging down here alone. Is tomorrow okay?"

"Same time, same place."

"Thanks. I'll see you tomorrow. Bye, Elise."

"Bye."

He got up and walked away.

Maybe it was a small thing, but the fact that in spite of his busy schedule Nicholas had come down to meet me meant even more than the flowers and chocolates.

Back when I was still married, my husband, Dan, invited me to lunch, then forgot about it. I waited alone for almost an hour before calling him.

"Sorry, I forgot," he said. "I got distracted."

"Am I that forgettable?" I asked.

"Don't talk to me about *forgetting*," he said.

That shut me up. I hung up the phone, then broke down crying.

THE next morning I was booking rooms at a New York hotel when Zoey walked in carrying a silver box from Nordstrom and set it on my desk.

"It's from the lawyer," she whispered. Then she just stood there, waiting for me to finish the call. As soon as I hung up, she said, "Open it." She looked even more eager to see what was inside the box than I was. I opened the card first.

Day 3. It's been a cold winter. I thought this might help.
—Nick

"So what did Lover Boy send today?" Zoey asked, sounding incredibly jealous. I'd be lying if I said that I didn't enjoy it.

"Let's find out," I said. I untied the ribbon, then lifted the lid. Inside was a piece of light tan cloth. I lifted it out.

"It's a scarf," I said. "It's soft."

Zoey touched it. "It's cashmere." She instinctively went for the label. "Pashmina from Bottega Veneta." She looked up at me. "You realize that's like six hundred dollars."

I tried not to look impressed. "Really?"

"This guy's made of money. What does he drive?"

"I don't know."

"How do you not know?"

"I haven't been out with him yet."

"Amazing," she said, shaking her head as she walked out of my office.

I wore the scarf to lunch. Nicholas was

waiting for me near Café Rio. He stood, smiling, as I approached. "I see you got it," he said, looking at the scarf.

"What did I say about spending so much?"

"You told me I didn't have to, which I already knew."

"I feel uncomfortable."

"Why?"

"I don't know."

"Then don't worry about it. Just enjoy it." He looked into my eyes. "Or at least let me enjoy it, okay?"

"Okay. Thank you. It's beautiful."

"It's cashmere," he said.

"I know. Zoey told me. She's insanely jealous."

"Is a jealous Zoey a good or bad thing?"

"Definitely a good thing."

He smiled. "What are we eating today? Café Rio again?"

"Of course."

"I should have just ordered for you. Before this is over, I'm going to expand your culinary horizons. Save our place and I'll be right back. Sweet pork salad, pinto beans, house dressing."

"And a diet lemonade."

"Of course."

Not wanting to get food on my scarf, I folded it up and stowed it in my purse. Nicholas returned a few minutes later carrying a tray. "One salad with lots of sugar, and a lemonade sans sugar."

"Thank you."

He sat down.

"What did you get?" I asked, examining his meal.

"I thought I'd try the chiles rellenos with some of this rice." He took a bite, then asked, "Who is this Zoey person?"

"She's just someone I work with." A peculiar feeling swept through me. I didn't want him to know who Zoey was. I didn't want him to meet her. I didn't want her to take him. "She's, like, beautiful."

"Like you," he said.

"No, she's *really* beautiful."

His expression immediately changed. He almost looked angry. "As opposed to what?"

"As opposed to me."

He leaned back. "How long have you been this way?"

"What way?"

"Self-deprecating."

Suddenly, to my surprise, tears began to well up in my eyes. I didn't answer.

He didn't back off. "What makes you think you're not beautiful?"

"I'm not blind," I said. "I can look in a mirror."

"You have a flawed mirror," he replied. His voice softened. "Elise, anyone can open a book. Not everyone can appreciate the beauty of the writing. I want you to stop berating yourself."

"It's just . . ." I wiped my eyes with a napkin. "Around my office, I'm not the one who gets the flowers."

"Funny," he said. "I could have sworn you told me that you just got some."

What was this man doing to me? "Can we just eat?"

"I want to add something to our contract. For the length of our agreement, you will believe that you are beautiful."

"You can't just change a belief."

"People do it all the time," he said. "Besides, it's contractual. You don't have a choice. You'd be amazed at what people accomplish under contract."

"I don't know if I can do that."

"Then at least believe that I believe you're beautiful."

I sat there fighting back tears. "Can we please change the subject?"

"Will you agree to do this one thing for me?"

Finally I nodded.

"All right. Now we can eat."

We ate for a few minutes until he said, "I'm going to run out of time, so we'd better start planning our season." He reached into his briefcase and brought out some papers. "I had my secretary print out copies of my calendar for the next two months. We can use it to plan."

He handed me two pages, and I quickly looked through the calendar. Not surprisingly, he had a lot more going on than I did. I didn't need a secretary to schedule my life. I didn't even need a notebook.

"You have two work parties," I noted.

"Yes. I'm sorry if that's excessive. There's an office party for the entire firm, and then there's the partners' party."

"Gee, I wonder which one is nicer," I said.

"Actually, they're both nice. The company party is at La Caille."

"Really?" La Caille was an expensive French restaurant in the foothills of the Wasatch Mountains. "Where's the partners' party, the Grand America?"

"The partners' party is at one of our founders' homes."

I went back to the beginning of the calendar. The first event Nicholas had marked was the evening of November ninth. Tomorrow night. "What's this Hale Centre event?" I asked.

"That's the Hale Centre Theatre's production of *A Christmas Carol*. I've heard it's great. I've just never wanted to go alone." He looked at me. "I know it's sudden. If you have other plans . . ."

"No, it's okay," I said. "I'm not busy."

He looked pleased.

I moved down the calendar. "What about the following weekend? You marked an event on the sixteenth."

"There's nothing scheduled, but is there something you would like to do? We could go to the symphony, ballet, Walmart . . ."

"Let me think about it," I said. "The next week is Thanksgiving."

"Do you have plans?"

"I usually spend it with Dan's family."

"Who's Dan?"

"My ex."

He looked at me quizzically. "Really?"

"I know it's weird. But I'm still close to his parents. The way they see it, their son divorced me but they didn't."

"How does your ex feel about it?"

"He's strangely good with it. In a twisted way, I think it makes him feel like he has a harem."

"That's creepy. You don't have a better alternative? Family?"

"My parents have both passed away. I have a sister in Minneapolis. She invites me to her house every year, but it's too expensive to fly there for a day."

"You don't get frequent-flier miles with the travel agency?"

"No. I don't travel with the groups. I just do the logistics, like booking hotels and admissions at the venues."

He nodded as he took this all in. "So, back to Thanksgiving at your ex's family. I assume Dan and company wouldn't like me joining them. Disrupt the harem and all that."

"No, that might be awkward."

"Then would you be willing to join me?"

"With your family?"

"No, in that department we're in the same boat. I celebrate Thanksgiving with the family of one of the attorneys I work with."

"What's their name?"

"The Hitesmans," he said. "Scott Hitesman. Real nice family."

I wrote the name down on the calendar.

"Scott joined the firm about the same time I did. We were working over a Thanksgiving weekend on a big case, and he invited me to join them. I've been with them ever since."

"Will they be okay if I come?"

Nicholas laughed. "No, they'll be *ecstatic*. Sharon is always trying to get me to invite someone."

"Then it's a date. Will I need to bring anything?"

"I usually just pick up some pies from Marie Callender's."

"I can make pie," I said. "I make a pumpkin pie that's to die for."

"You've got a deal."

"How many pies?"

"I usually bring four. Apple, cherry, pumpkin, and mincemeat."

"Does anyone still eat mincemeat?"

"Grandma Hitesman does. She's ninety-six. When she dies, the industry will crumble."

I laughed. "Maybe you could pick that one up."

"I could do that."

We both looked back down at the calendar.

"The next week is our firm's Christmas party at La Caille," Nicholas said. "Saturday, December first."

"That's the week of my work party too. It's that Wednesday."

"Can you do both?"

"Absolutely. But I should warn you, it's not going to be La Caille. It's not even going to be Burger King, for that matter."

"I don't care," he said.

"You have no idea how nice it will be to go with someone this year. Ever since I divorced, I've been the odd one out."

"I think I have an idea," he said. "That's why we're doing this."

The next week there were two days marked

on the calendar. December sixth and seventh. "What are these?"

His expression fell. "It's nothing," he said in a way that made me sure that it was. "It's just . . . something I do." He quickly moved on. "The next week, on the fourteenth, is the partners' party. Then the week after that I have to fly to New York City to meet with one of our clients, so we won't get together that week." He looked up at me. "Unless you come to New York with me."

I couldn't tell if he was serious. "I'm afraid that would be out of my budget."

"Travel expenses are in the contract."

I looked at him. "You're serious." To tell the truth, the idea of going to New York at Christmas thrilled me. "Let's see how things go."

"That's wise," he replied.

"Then there's nothing until Christmas Eve?"

"What are your plans for Christmas Eve?" he asked.

I was embarrassed to tell him that I hadn't anything planned. "Nothing. Yet."

"How about we have dinner?"

"That would be nice. Where?"

"I don't know. We can decide that later. We have seven weeks."

"And then we're done," I said.

He slowly nodded. "Exactly. The agreement is fulfilled; the contract is terminated." He slid his calendar into his briefcase. "I better get back. I'll see you tomorrow at lunch, then tomorrow evening for the play."

"Thank you for lunch," I said. I held up the calendar. "And for all this."

He stood. "It's my pleasure. I'm looking forward to it."

"Me too."

He looked into my eyes and said, "Elise."

"Yes?"

"No more complaints about gifts. It's been a long time since I've had anyone to give to, and I'm having fun. Don't ruin it for me. Okay?"

I nodded and smiled. "If you insist."

His serious expression gave way to a smile. "I insist. Have a good day."

As he started to go, I said, "Nicholas."

He turned back. "Yes?"

"What kind of car do you drive?"

He looked puzzled. "Why?"

"Zoey wanted to know."

He grinned mischievously. "Tell her it's a very expensive one." He blew me a kiss and walked off. As he disappeared from sight, I took out my scarf and put it around my neck. It had been a long time since I had felt that warm.

Chapter Three

THE next morning was the first time in a long time that I woke happy. I followed my usual routine of shower, hair, then took extra time for makeup. I used to be good at makeup, but that was before I stopped caring. You don't take care of things you don't value.

I was a few minutes late to work, but considering all the unpaid overtime I'd pulled over the years, I wasn't worried.

"You're late," Zoey said as I walked into the office. She was applying mascara.

"I know," I said simply.

Around ten we were having our staff meeting when the bell on our door rang. "I'll get it," Zoey said, standing. She was always the first to offer. She hated meetings.

Five minutes later, when Zoey hadn't

returned, Mark said, "Elise, would you remind Zoey we're in the middle of a staff meeting?"

"Sure," I said. I walked out to the front lobby. Zoey was just standing there in a room filled with flowers. "The man's smitten," she said, shaking her head in disbelief. "It took two deliverymen to bring them all in."

There were twelve dozen roses, half white, half red. If Nicholas was making a point about sending me whatever he wanted, he'd succeeded. A minute later, Cathy walked out. "Holy florist. We're going to have to start charging this guy rent." She looked at me. "What are you going to do with all those?"

"I have no idea," I said.

"The delivery people said they'd be back to take them to your apartment," Zoey said. "Here's the card that came with them."

I unsealed the envelope.

Day 4. Next time you complain that I'm spending too much, I'm doubling it. Looking forward to tonight.
　　—Nicholas

I smiled.

"What did he say?" Zoey asked.

"He's looking forward to our date tonight."

"Where are you going?"

"We're going to see a play. *A Christmas Carol.*"

"That sounds . . . fun." I knew that a play wouldn't be her idea of a good time. She looked at me for a moment, then said, "You know what the problem with all this is?"

I looked at her. "No. What?"

"No one can keep this up forever. Someday it's going to stop. And then it's going to suck."

"It's most certainly going to stop," I said. "The trick is to enjoy the ride while it lasts."

Zoey looked at me with surprise. "When did you get this attitude?" She looked closer at me. "Are you wearing eyeliner?"

WHEN I arrived in the food court, Nicholas was sitting at our usual table. He had already bought our food. He smiled when he saw me. "I took the liberty of ordering the usual."

"Thank you," I said, sitting down. I took

a bite of my salad. He wore a funny expression, and I guessed that he was waiting for me to comment on the flowers. I decided to play dumb.

Finally he said, "So did you get anything today?"

I looked at him blankly. "Hmm. Oh, you mean like a hundred and forty-four roses?"

He grinned. "That wasn't too *excessive*, was it?"

"No. Just right. And once the delivery people return to get them, my apartment will look like a funeral parlor."

He laughed. "We're still on for tonight?"

"Yes."

"The play starts at seven, so I'll pick you up around six thirty?"

"Okay," I said.

"Then, if you're not too tired, we'll get some dinner after."

"Sounds nice."

"Anything in particular?"

"No. Surprise me." Just going out to dinner was surprise enough.

IT WAS snowing when I got home from work. My apartment was a mess, so I picked up, throwing my clothes in a hamper and loading the dishwasher. The doorbell rang. It was the florist. "I've got your flowers," the man said.

I looked around my tiny apartment. "Bring them in."

It took the man fifteen minutes to bring all the roses in from his truck. By the time he finished, it was twenty-five after. I changed into jeans and a sweater, brushed my hair, then went to put on some perfume but couldn't find any. *Girl, you've got to get back with it.*

I remembered that I had an unopened bottle of perfume in the bottom of my closet—a gift from the girls at the office for my birthday last spring. I tore open the package and was spraying it on when the doorbell rang. I hurried out past the garden of flowers.

I opened the door. Nicholas was standing there holding a bouquet of yellow gerbera daisies. I almost laughed when I saw them. "You're kidding, right?"

"I wasn't sure what else to bring you," he said.

"Let me find something to put these in. Come on in."

He laughed when he saw the flowers splayed out over my front room. "You almost need a machete to get through here."

"Almost," I said.

I filled a pitcher with water and arranged the flowers in it. When I came back out, I asked, "Shall we go?"

"Sure," he said. Then added, "You look nice."

"Thank you. So do you." He was dressed casually in a dark green knit sweater that was a little wet on the shoulders from falling snow. "I don't think I've ever seen you out of a suit."

"It's rare, but I do dress down on occasion."

I took his hand as we walked down the stairs. His car was parked out front, a white BMW sedan. He held the door open for me as I got in. The interior smelled like cinnamon. The seats were two-toned leather. He shut the door, then went around and climbed in.

"You have a nice car."

"Thank you. I just got it a few months ago. The dealer said it's good in snow. I hope he's right. I turned your seat warmer on."

"Thanks."

He started the car. The heater and wind-shield wipers came on, along with a Michael Bublé Christmas album. "Is this music okay?"

"I love Bublé," I said. "It smells good in here."

"*You* smell good. What is it? Lovely?"

"How in the world did you know that?"

"My paralegal wears it." He drove out of my complex. "Thanks again for going to this with me. I've wanted to do this for a while."

"It's my pleasure," I said. "I told Cathy where we were going, and she said she loves it. Her family goes every year."

"Who's Cathy?"

"Sorry, she's our bookkeeper."

"Are all of your friends from work?"

I frowned, embarrassed by the question. "Yes."

He glanced over. "It happens. All my friends are lawyers. Except you."

Something about how he had said that made me glad. "Tell me about this play," I said.

"Hale Centre Theatre. They've been do-ing this for a long time. I'm kind of a sap when it comes to Christmas. I watch *A Christmas Carol* on TV at least twice every holiday season. My favorite television version is the one with George C. Scott."

"That's my favorite version too."

The Hale Centre Theatre was located on the west side of the valley, about fifteen minutes from my apartment. The place was crowded. We picked up our tickets at Will Call; then Nicholas asked, "Would you like a drink or a snack?"

I glanced over at the concession stand. "Maybe some popcorn."

"Okay. Wait, it's not popcorn; it's kettle corn."

"What's the difference?"

"You'll like it," he said. "It has sugar."

"How do you know I like sugar?"

"You eat it on your salad," he said.

We got a small box of kettle corn and climbed the stairs to the theater's entrance. The theater was in the round, and, not surprisingly, we had good seats.

After we had sat down, I ate some kettle corn and said, "Picking up our tickets at Will Call reminded me of something dumb I did."

"Tell me."

"When I first started at ICE, Mark—he's the owner—sent me to pick up some plastic display holders for a convention we were doing. He said to get them from Will Call. When I got there, I went up to the sales counter and asked for Mr. Call. There were two men there, and they both looked at me with funny expressions. One asked the other, 'Do you know a Call here?' He said, 'No.' Then he said to me, 'I'm sorry, there's no Mr. Call here. Do you know his first name?' I said, 'I think it's William or Will. My boss just said to pick it up from Will Call.' They laughed for about five minutes before someone told me why."

Nicholas laughed. "I did that exact same thing once."

"Really?"

"No, I'm not that dumb."

I threw a piece of kettle corn at him.

"The play is starting," he said.

As the lights came up at the end of the first half, just before Scrooge meets the Ghost of Christmas Yet to Come, I excused myself to go to the ladies' room.

When I returned, the lights dimmed and the second half began. Near the end of the performance, I heard a sniffle. I furtively glanced over at Nicholas as he wiped his eyes with a Kleenex.

After the show, we walked out into the cold night air.

"That was really good," I said.

"I'm glad I finally got to see it."

"It affected you."

He nodded. "It's about redemption and hope." He looked me in the eyes. "Hope that we can be better than our mistakes."

His words struck me to the core. It was as if he knew me intimately.

When we got back to his car, he asked, "Are you hungry?"

"Famished."

"Do you like Thai food?"

"I've never had it. But I'd like to try it."

"Good. I know a place."

The restaurant was ten minutes from the theater. A young Thai woman seated us in a corner of the restaurant and handed us menus. I looked mine over. "I have no idea what to order."

"How about I order a few dishes and we'll share?"

I set down my menu. "Perfect."

When our waitress came, Nicholas ordered a bunch of things I couldn't even pronounce, then said, "You'll love it."

A few minutes later, our waitress returned with a large bowl of noodles, two platters of curry dishes, and a large bowl of sticky rice.

I dished up my plate with a little of everything. I liked it all.

In the middle of our dinner, Nicholas asked, "Have you lived in Salt Lake your whole life?"

"No. I was born in Arizona. I lived there until I was fourteen."

"What brought you to Utah?"

"My father."

"Work?"

"No. It's more complicated than that."

"How so?"

I hesitated. "My father was an interesting man."

"By *interesting* do you mean, 'fascinating' or a 'living hell'?"

I laughed. "More of the latter. You sure you want to hear this?"

"I love to hear people's histories," he said.

"All right," I said. "My father was fanatical. He thought the world was going to hell, and since the 'lunatic' Californians were buying up all the land around us, he sold our farm and moved us to a little town in Utah of ninety-six people. We made it an even hundred."

"What town?"

"You've never heard of it."

"Try me."

"Montezuma Creek."

"You're right," he said. "Why there?"

"Because it was about as far from civilization as you could get. And, don't laugh, because there was only one road into town and he could blow it up when the Russians invaded."

"Really?"

"It's true," I said. "He had a whole shed of dynamite."

"What did your father do in Montezuma Creek? To provide?"

"We had greenhouses. Big ones. We mostly grew tomatoes."

"How did you end up in Salt Lake?"

"I just got out as fast as I could."

"Didn't like the small-town life?"

"I didn't like my father," I said softly. "He talked constantly about the world being evil and corrupt, but the truth is, *he* was evil and corrupt. And violent and cruel. I lived in constant fear of him.

"My father was always trying to prove that he was in control. Once I told him I was excited because we were going to have a dance lesson at school, so he made me stay home that day for no reason. Some days he would keep us home from school just to prove that the government couldn't tell him what to do.

"He would rant that the police were the henchmen of an Orwellian government conspiracy, and anytime one tried to pull him over, he'd try to outrun them. Sometimes he'd get away; sometimes they'd catch him, and they'd drag him out of the car and handcuff him. I remember watching him being handcuffed and arrested, and I was afraid they were going to take me to jail too. I grew up terrified of police. Police and snakes."

"Snakes?" Nicholas said.

I nodded. "My father used to think it was funny to chase me around the house with live rattlesnakes. I remember him holding one on a stick and it trying to strike at me." I looked down.

"That's abuse," Nicholas said.

I nodded. "He was all about abuse. Only he didn't see it that way. He saw us as property, and if something is yours, you can do what you want to it. One time we had a problem with our truck. He said it was the carburetor, so he made my sister, Cosette, lie on the engine under the hood and pour gasoline into the carburetor while we drove. What kind of father puts his kid under the hood of a moving vehicle?"

"A deranged one," Nicholas said. He looked sad. "I'm so sorry."

"Thanks," I said. "When you grow up with crazy, you don't know what sane is. A year after I was married, I caught my father with another woman. They were kissing. He lied about it at first, but when he saw that I didn't believe him, he admitted that he was having an affair and told me not to tell my mother."

"Did you?"

"No. It would have done nothing but humiliate her. She found out later on her own. But she still didn't leave him. He had alienated all of her family, so she really had no place to go.

"By the time I turned eighteen, I couldn't take it anymore. I left and got a job more than three hundred miles away, at Bryce Canyon Lodge as a waitress. It was a good gig. They paid almost nothing, but there was free food and lodging, and we got to keep all our tips. I made a lot in tips. Enough to pay for my first year of college.

"Every now and then, celebrities would come through. I met Robert Redford once. He was really nice. That's when I knew that I wanted to travel and see the world. But I think it was probably more that I wanted to get as far away from my father as I could." I forced a smile. "I didn't get too far, I guess. I carried a lot of it with me."

"It's hard to leave some things behind," Nicholas said. "So how did you turn out so lovely?"

I just looked at him. Suddenly my eyes welled up with tears. He took my hand. When I could speak, I said, "Thank you."

"Is your father still alive?"

"No. He died of cancer. Both of my parents did." I sighed. "I remember going back and seeing him before he died. He was so frail and weak. I thought, *Is this really the man who filled me with such terror, who towered over my past?* He was nothing."

Nicholas looked at me. "They that see thee shall narrowly look upon thee, and consider thee, saying, Is this the man that made the earth to tremble, that did shake kingdoms? Isaiah fourteen: sixteen."

"You read the Bible," I said.

"At times," he replied. "So you went to college in Salt Lake?"

"No. I went to Snow College. My best friend from Montezuma Creek asked if I wanted to be her roommate, so I took her up on it. That's where I met my ex-husband, Dan." I paused. "Dan was from Salt Lake. He was doing his general ed at Snow. He was ambitious back then. He promised to show me the world. Then he left college to sell water purifiers. Dan wasn't very nice, but the truth was, he was my way out. I followed Dan to Salt Lake, and we got married. We were married for eight years before he divorced me."

"Why did he divorce you?"

"Wasn't there a clause in our contract about probing questions?"

"You're right. I crossed the line."

"Well, we crossed the line about ten minutes ago. It's okay. Dan divorced me because he was cheating on me with my best friend."

"Your college roommate?"

"Yes. He's now married to her."

"Remarkable," Nicholas said. "What was your divorce settlement like?"

"Not good. I didn't get anything."

"Sounds like you had a poor attorney."

"No, he had a poor client."

"Why?"

I looked down. "Some people are born thinking they're pretty important. Some aren't."

Nicholas nodded slowly as if he understood.

I took a deep breath. "So now that I've spilled all my secrets, let's talk about you."

"That's a nonstarter," he said.

"After I just shared my life history, you're holding out on me?"

"I'm only saving you from boredom."

"I think there are some answers that might interest me. To begin with, why aren't you married?"

He looked at me thoughtfully and after a

moment said, "A lot of people aren't married. A lot of people are married who shouldn't be."

"You're evading the question."

"It's complicated," he said.

"Then tell me about your childhood."

He frowned. "I was born and raised in the Sugar House area. My parents were Mormons. I went to church until I was sixteen, until . . ." A shadow fell over his face. "Until things changed."

"What happened?"

"Just things," he said. "My dark ages. It took me a few years, but I pulled myself out. I finished college and took the LSAT. I got accepted to Stanford Law School on a scholarship, graduated at the top of my class, then came back to Utah to practice law."

"You started working at the firm you're at now?"

He hesitated before answering. "No, I worked at the prosecutor's office. I kept beating them in court, so they made me an offer."

"That must be nice," I said. "To be wanted like that."

He went quiet. Then he said, "I'm sorry. That whole conversation got pretty heavy. I just wanted to get to know you better."

"Well, you know it all now."

"Do I?"

I didn't answer. He picked up the check. "Let's get you home."

It was cold outside, and our breath froze in front of us. The cars were covered with a thin veneer of freshly fallen snow.

We didn't say much on the way home. I suppose I felt talked out. But the silence wasn't uncomfortable. When we pulled up in front of my apartment, he said, "Thanks again for going with me."

"It was fun," I replied. "I'm sorry I talked so much."

"I enjoyed learning about you."

"Well, I kind of threw up on you. I guess it's been a while since I've had anyone ask me about myself."

"I'm glad it was me," he said.

I smiled at him, then said, "Me too. Have a good weekend."

"You too. I'll see you Monday."

I got out of the car and walked up the snow-covered sidewalk to my apartment stairs. Nicholas waited until I reached the door. I turned back and waved. He waved back, then drove away.

Chapter Four

Three years earlier

I COULDN'T sleep because of the pain. At first I thought it was an upset stomach. Then, as the pain increased, an ulcer. An ulcer made sense. I was a worrier. I'd worried my whole life.

While my husband, Dan, slept, I downed a bottle of Pepto-Bismol, which did nothing to relieve my agony. Finally, at four in the morning, I woke Dan, and he reluctantly drove me to St. Mark's Hospital emergency room. It wasn't an ulcer; it was appendicitis. And my appendix had burst. I was rushed into surgery and spent the next two days in intensive care being fed massive doses of antibiotics to attack the infection that had set in. On the third day I had shown enough progress that they moved me out of the ICU.

Dan came to see me that afternoon bearing a bouquet of flowers. It was only the second time I had seen him since I was admitted. I was glad to see him. We had talked for only about a half hour when he said he had to get back to work. Dan was a tele-marketer and managed a phone solicitation office. After he left, one of my nurses walked in. Keti was a Tongan woman as wide as she was tall.

"Oh, aren't you lucky," she said. "Somebody loves you."

I smiled. "Aren't they beautiful? They're from my husband."

"You hang on to him, honey. I can't tell you the last time my husband brought me flowers. How are you feeling?"

"It hurts where they made the incision."

"That's usual. An appendectomy is like a cesarean, except you don't get a baby for it."

"I feel a little warm."

She sidled up to my bed, rubbed an electronic thermometer across my forehead, and frowned. "You have a temperature. A hundred and two point four. I don't like that."

"What does that mean?"

"Maybe a little infection." As she scribbled on her clipboard, I heard the vibration of a cell phone. We both looked around to see where it was coming from; then Keti discovered an iPhone lying next to the flowers. "Is this yours?"

"No. It's probably my husband's. He must have left it." I reached out my hand for it. "I'll text his office and let them know I have it."

"How sweet," Keti said, looking at the screen. "Amore. Is that what he calls you?"

"Amore?" I looked at her blankly. "No . . ."

She handed me the phone. "It's right here."

Amore Mia
Text Message

Amore? My love? Who is my husband calling Amore Mia? I pressed the notification.

Amore Mia
Are you on your way?

I scrolled to the bottom of the thread and started reading.

Amore Mia
How is my dreamboy today?

Dan the Man
Floating. Last night was unbelievable. We need a rerun ASAP!!!!

Amore Mia
Ditto. Ditto. Please. Please. Please!!!! Can you come over?

Dan the Man
On way to hospital see Elise. I love you

Amore Mia
After. Pretty please? You'll be glad! ;-) How is Elise?

Dan the Man
She's doing okay. Made it through the hard time

Amore Mia
:(When are you going to tell her?

Dan the Man
Not now. After she is back home. Feeling better

There were more. Many more. I couldn't read them because my eyes were filled with tears.

"Honey?" Keti said.

I looked up at her. "My husband is cheating on me."

"I'm sorry."

Just then Dan walked back into the room. "Hi, babe. I forgot my phone."

I looked at him, shaking, unable to speak.

"Why are you crying?" He looked at Keti. "Is she in pain?"

"I would think so," Keti said, her eyes narrow with anger.

"Can you get her something for it?"

"Not for this pain."

He looked at her quizzically, then back over at me. "Honey . . ."

"Who is she?" I said.

"I'll check on your antibiotic," Keti said, making her way toward the door. She brushed by Dan on the way out.

"Who?" he asked, his eyes stupidly wide.

"Who is Amore Mia?"

He stepped toward me. "I don't know what you're talking about."

I held up his phone. "Who is Amore Mia?"

"Elise . . ."

"If you have something to tell me, tell me now."

"It's nothing. She's nothing."

"I read the texts. Don't lie to me."

For a moment we looked at each other; then he breathed out slowly, as if he'd resigned himself. "Okay, so you caught me. I'm having an affair."

"Who is she?"

He looked even more uncomfortable.

"Do I know her?"

"Kayla," he said.

The only Kayla I knew was my best, and only, friend, and the thought that she would cheat with my husband was so far beyond possibility that I couldn't process it. "Kayla who?"

"Kayla," he said again but with more emphasis.

My Kayla?

"Yeah."

My pain doubled. When I could speak, I asked, "How long has this been going on?"

"I don't know."

"How long?"

"A while."

I broke down crying again. He put his hand on my arm. "Elise."

I pulled away. "Don't touch me."

"Elise," he said in the condescending register he used when he thought I was being overly dramatic.

"Go away," I said. "Go to your . . . *amore*."

"I'm not leaving," he said.

"Get out of here!" I shouted.

Just then Keti walked back into the room. She looked angry. "You need to leave," she said, pointing a sausage finger at Dan.

"She's my wife," Dan said. "I don't need to go anywhere."

Her voice rose. "She's *my* patient. If she wants you to leave, you leave." She walked to a button on the wall. "Should I call security?"

He glared at her, then looked at me. "It's your fault, Elise. You're the one who ruined our lives." He turned and walked away. Two days later I was still in the hospital when Dan filed for divorce.

MONDAYS were always the hardest days at ICE. Invariably there would be some crisis that had occurred over the weekend:

lost luggage, a canceled flight, a broken-down bus.

This Monday was no different. It began with our usual staff meeting and Mark ranting about a phone call he'd received over the weekend from a parent whose daughter claimed she had gotten pregnant on one of our trips. I had to contact the teacher who had chaperoned the excursion and tell her what had happened.

I had just hung up the phone with the teacher when Zoey brought in a package and set it on my desk. All she said was "Here."

I unwrapped the paper, then opened the box. Inside was a beautiful oval-shaped hand mirror. The frame was tarnished silver that looked almost pewter. I opened the note.

Elise, Happy Day 7. Thank you for an enlightening weekend. I've sent you a new mirror. Hopefully it works better than the one you've been using.

—Nick

P.S. This is an 1807 antique. The metal is silver. The woman at the antique shop said the best way to clean it is with a cup of white vinegar, a tablespoon of baking soda, and a pinch of salt.

"So what did you get today?" Zoey asked.

I held up the mirror. "A hand mirror. It's an antique."

"It's pretty," she said simply, then left my office.

About a half hour later, I went out to use the bathroom and was in one of the stalls when Zoey and Cathy came in together. It was soon obvious that they didn't know I was there.

"So what do you think of Elise's sugar daddy?" Zoey asked.

"Good for her," Cathy said. "She needed something. Have you met the guy?"

"No. But I'm not looking forward to it. You know what they say, the amount of money a guy spends on a woman is in inverse ratio to his looks. He's probably some fat bald guy with ear hair."

"At least he's rich," Cathy said.

"Rich doesn't make a man hot," Zoey said.

"No, but it can hide a lot of ugly," Cathy said, laughing.

I was furious. I was about to say something I would no doubt regret, but I calmed myself down. I waited until they left before going back to the office. When I got to my desk, I looked up Nicholas's law firm's number and dialed. A professional voice answered. "Derr, Nelson, and McKay."

"Hi. I'm calling for Nicholas Derr."

"Just a moment, please."

A half minute later, a young female voice answered. "Nicholas Derr's office. This is Sabrina speaking. How may I help you?"

"Hi, Sabrina. I'm calling for Nicholas."

"Mr. Derr is in a meeting. May I tell him who's calling?"

"It's not important. This is Elise."

There was hardly a pause. "Elise Dutton?"

I was surprised that she knew who I was. "Yes."

"Just a moment, please."

I was on hold for less than ten seconds before Nicholas answered. "Elise."

"Nicholas, I'm sorry to bother you."

"I'm pleased you called, unless you

called to cancel lunch, in which case, I'm pleased to hear your voice, but not that you called."

I smiled. "No, I'm not calling to cancel. I just wanted to see if you would mind coming to my office today to get me for lunch?"

"I would love to."

"I'm in office three twenty-two."

"I know."

Of course he did.

"Thank you for the mirror," I said. "It's pretty."

"Like you," he replied. "I'll see you at twelve thirty. Bye."

I hung up the phone. Then I realized what I had done. He was going to meet perfect Zoey.

NICHOLAS was punctual. I heard Zoey greeting him with her come-hither voice. "Hi. May I help you?"

I waited inside my office, listening to the exchange. "I'm here for Elise," he said.

"May I tell her who's calling?"

"Nicholas," he said.

Long pause. "You're Nicholas?"

"You must be Zoey."

"Yes. I am." I had never heard her sound so awkward. "I've heard a lot about you," Zoey said.

"I'm glad to hear that," he said. "I assumed that I was just one of Elise's many men."

I walked out. Nicholas looked at me and smiled. He looked gorgeous in an Armani suit. He walked up to me and kissed me on the cheek. "I hope it's okay I came by early."

"It's fine," I said.

"Great. I was hoping you'd have time for me to take you to lunch. The owner of the New Yorker is a friend of mine, and he has a special table waiting for us. If you have time, that is."

Just then Cathy walked out of her office. She stopped when she saw Nicholas. She didn't have to say what she was thinking. "Hi."

Nicholas stepped forward, offering his hand. "Hi, I'm Nicholas."

"Cathy," she said, sounding unsure of herself. "It's nice to meet you."

"Likewise." He turned to me. "So the New Yorker is okay?"

"Of course," I said. "Let me get my coat."

I returned to my office, and when I walked back into the room, he reached out his hand to me. "Come on, gorgeous."

"Bye," I said to Zoey. "I might be a few minutes late."

"Take your time," she said meekly.

As we walked out into the hallway, I just looked at him. He was smiling.

"Is that what you wanted?"

"That was perfect. Are we really going to the New Yorker?"

"Of course. I told you I'd broaden your culinary horizons."

THE New Yorker was a few blocks from our office building. It was the kind of place where movers and shakers met and business deals were made. I had never been there before.

After the hostess had seated us at a table for two, Nicholas leaned forward. "So tell me what that was all about."

"The girls in the office have been intrigued by the gifts you've been sending. I overheard them this morning. Zoey said, and I quote, 'The amount of money a guy spends on a woman is in inverse ratio to his looks. He's probably some fat bald guy with ear hair.'"

"Did I dispel any of that?"

"I think you left them speechless."

"Good. Fortunately I plucked my ear hairs this morning."

I laughed. "Can I tell you something honest?"

"Of course."

"I didn't want you to meet Zoey. I was afraid you might want to trade up."

"No disrespect, but that would be like trading champagne for Kool-Aid."

I grinned. "That's *totally* disrespectful. And thank you again for the mirror. It's beautiful."

"Did I impress you with the cleaning tips?"

"I was *very* impressed."

He smiled. "I thought you would be. So are you ready to order?"

I looked through the menu. "No. Why don't you order for me?"

"I'd be happy to. Something to drink?"

"I'd like a glass of wine."

"Okay," he said. He ordered a glass of Chianti for me, a cranberry juice for himself, and our meal. That was the first time I realized that I had never seen him drink. I wondered if he did.

As the waiter walked away, I asked, "So what's next on our agenda?"

"You were going to come up with something for our weekend."

"There's something I've always wanted to do. Do you sing?"

"In the shower."

I nodded slowly. "That will do."

I HAD always looked forward to Fridays, but now even the weekdays were better. The whole office anticipated Nicholas's daily gifts. The FedEx man delivered my Friday gift around eleven.

"What is it?" Cathy asked as I opened the box.

"It's New York cheesecake."

Cathy read the label. "S and S Cheesecake from New York."

"I'll get some plates," I said.

"Really?" Cathy said. "You're going to share?"

"If I ate that much cheesecake by myself, I would look like our Christmas tree."

"Bless you, child," Cathy said.

Mark walked out of his office. "Did someone say cheesecake?"

"Elise is sharing the cheesecake her friend sent her."

He looked at the box. "S and S Cheesecake," he said. "I've heard of that. It's the best. And pricey. They sell it by the ounce. Like gold."

I cut the cheesecake up with a plastic knife, and work stopped while everyone ate. Mark closed his eyes as he savored a bite. "Incredible," he said. "If you don't marry that guy, I will."

NICHOLAS and I didn't have lunch that day because he was in court, but that evening he picked me up at my apartment at six.

"How was your day?" I asked as we walked to his car.

"Good. We won." He opened the car door for me, then walked around and got in. "How was your day?"

"Good," I said. "The cheesecake was a hit."

"It doesn't get better than S and S."

"How did you know about them?"

"I'm not as provincial as you might think."

"Believe me, I've never thought of you as provincial. You're the most cosmopolitan person I know."

"Well, I'm definitely not that either. I just love cheesecake, and I discovered S and S from a client who sent me one last Christmas."

The holiday traffic was heavy as we made our way downtown to Abravanel Hall, Salt Lake City's main concert hall.

The event I had chosen for us was a *Messiah* sing-in with the Utah Symphony, which basically meant that we were part of a three-thousand-member choir. To make sure we sounded good, the organizers peppered the audience with about a hundred voices from the University of Utah and the Mormon Tabernacle Choir. We were handed paper scores as we walked into the concert hall.

"I thought we were going to hear a choir sing the *Messiah,*" Nicholas said to me as we found our seats. "I didn't realize we *were* the choir."

"It's more fun this way," I said. "I asked if you sing."

"I just thought you were curious."

We sounded better than I thought we would. After the concert, we drove over to Ruth's Chris Steak House. I had the petite filet while Nicholas ordered the Cowboy Ribeye. He also ordered a seared ahi tuna appetizer (something I'd never had before) and a sweet potato casserole, which I could have eaten for dessert.

"How do you eat like this and stay thin?" I asked.

"Simple," he replied. "I don't always eat like this."

"I think I've gained a few pounds since I signed the contract. You're spoiling me. I'm not sure all this spoiling is a good thing."

"Why would spoiling you not be a good thing?"

"Because in five weeks our contract is going to expire, and then where am I?"

"I don't know," he replied. "Where are you?"

I shrugged. "Certainly not eating here."

He looked at me for a moment. "Do you know what I like most about you? How grateful you are. In an increasingly entitled world, you are truly grateful. It makes me want to do more for you."

"You already do too much," I said.

"My point exactly," he replied. "You're a beautiful soul."

"Fortunately for me, you don't really know me."

"You told me everything there was to know about you last week."

"Not everything."

He said, "I probably know you better than you think."

The statement struck me as peculiar. "What do you mean?"

He paused. "I'm just a very good judge of character."

"That may be," I said. "But you don't know what you don't know. No one's perfect. Some of us aren't even that good."

Looking at me, he said, "What I do know is that everyone makes mistakes. That's why forgiveness is so important." He let his words settle before continuing. "When I worked for the prosecutor's office, one of my first cases was a man who had shot to death a clerk at a convenience store. We had video of the crime, and I thought it was an open-and-shut case. But because of a technicality we lost. As we were leaving the courthouse, the man slapped me on the back and said, 'Thank you, Counselor.' I said, 'For what?' And he said, 'For screwing up the case. Of course I killed him. But there's nothing you can do now.'"

"He confessed?" I asked.

"Right there on the courthouse steps."

"Why didn't you just go back in and tell the judge?"

"It wouldn't have done any good. It's called double jeopardy. He can't be tried again for the same offense. It's in the Fifth Amendment to the Constitution. 'Nor shall any person be subject for the same offence to be twice put in jeopardy of life or limb.' But that's in a court of law. In our hearts, there's no such thing. People punish others over and over for the same mistake. We do it to ourselves."

I felt like he was reading my mind. He watched me silently. "Elise, you're not as bad as you think you are. Remember that."

When I could speak, I said, "So the man was never punished."

"Actually, his case turned out a little differently. He wrote a letter to the prosecutor's office, bragging that he'd gotten away with murder and stating specific details of his crime. We reopened the case based on new evidence, and he was found guilty."

"Fool," I said.

"Yes, he was." Nicholas changed the subject. "So the Hitesmans are very excited that you will be joining us for Thanksgiving. Do you still want to bake those pies?"

"Yes," I said. "Except the mincemeat."

"I've already ordered it. When will you bake the others?"

"Wednesday night after work."

"Would you like some help?" he asked.

"Making pies?"

"I don't know how much help I'll be, but I'll keep you company."

"I would love your help," I said. "And your company."

"Great. I'll be there. I'll bring dinner."

THAT night as I lay in bed remembering our date, I had a frightening realization. My feelings for Nicholas were growing bigger than the contract I'd signed. I wondered if he felt the same way. Not that it mattered. In spite of everything Nicholas had said about forgiveness and redemption, I knew there was no chance we could ever be more than friends. Not if he knew the truth about me. Not if he knew what I'd done.

Chapter Five

Five years earlier

JUNE 2007 was hot. The whole world was hot. Greece reported their worst heat wave in history with eleven heat-related deaths, and the entire European power grid nearly collapsed beneath unprecedented demand for air-conditioning.

It was equally hot in the western United States. In Salt Lake City, temperatures that normally would have been in the high eighties exceeded a hundred degrees. Our apartment's swamp cooler struggled to keep things tolerable, and the first thing I did on waking was turn it on to full before getting ready for work.

Dan never helped in the mornings. He said it wasn't his "thing." I resented him for that. In spite of the fact that I worked longer days than he did, I would get up at least an hour before him to get ready, make breakfast, then get our little girl, Hannah, fed and ready for the day. The one thing Dan did that was helpful was drop Hannah off at day care, since it was only three blocks from his office.

However, even that had now changed. I had wearied of Dan's complaints about the cost of Hannah's day care, so a week earlier I had found another place at nearly half the price. Since it was on my way to work, I would have to leave even earlier to drop her off. I wasn't used to the new routine, and one day I'd forgotten to drop her off and had had to turn around a block from my work and take her to the new place.

On this morning, Hannah was unusually quiet as I got her out of bed. "Are you tired, sweetie?" I asked.

"Yes, Mama," she replied.

"I'm sorry you had to get up so early. I made you Mickey Mouse pancakes."

She smiled. I fed both of us at the same time. Dan stumbled out of bed as I was finishing up.

"Pancakes," he said dully. Dan was taciturn by nature, at least with me, and before nine o'clock getting more from him than a string of three words was rare.

"What's wrong with pancakes?" I asked.

"Had them yesterday."

"No. I made crepes yesterday because you said you wanted them."

"Same diff," he said, sitting down at the table.

I shook my head as I carried our plates over to the sink. I filled the sink with soapy water, then looked down at my watch. "I'm going to be late. I need to grab Hannah's bag. Will you please put her in her car seat?"

"Can't you? I'm eating."

"Come on," I said.

"Whatever," he said, standing.

I quickly brushed my teeth, grabbed Hannah's bag, and ran out to the car. "See you," I said to Dan.

"Bye," he said, waving behind his back.

I threw Hannah's bag into the backseat of my Toyota. I looked back. She was asleep. "Sorry, sweetie," I said softly.

I had just pulled out of our subdivision when my cell phone rang. I checked the number. It was work. "Hello."

"Elise, it's Shirlee," my boss said. "We've got a problem. The Tremonton group. Did you book the Smithsonian for today?"

"No, they're tomorrow."

"No, we changed it, remember?"

I groaned. "That's right."

"They're standing outside the Smithsonian. They're telling them that our vouchers aren't good."

"Just call the office of direct sales. Natalie will let them in."

"Where's the number?"

"It's in my Rolodex on my desk. Look under Smithsonian."

There was a long pause. "You don't have Smithsonian here."

"Of course I do."

"I looked through all the *S*'s, Elise. It's not here."

I was puzzled. "It's got to be there."

Shirlee groaned. "There's the driver on the other line. He's got to go. He's got another pickup."

"Just tell him to wait a second. I'll be right there."

I sped into the office. I pulled into a parking place and ran inside. I had accidentally filed the Smithsonian card under *N* for Natalie. But that's not the only mistake I made.

I left my three-year-old Hannah in the car on the hottest day of the year.

I'VE heard it said that there's no greater pain than losing a child. But there is. It's being responsible for your child's death. The day it happened to me is indelibly etched into my mind. People have questioned the existence of hell, but I can tell you it's real. I've been there. Seeing my beautiful little girl's lifeless body in the backseat of my car was hell.

I don't know how long it took for the switch to connect, but after work when I got to my car I just looked at her, the sight incomprehensible. Why was Hannah in the car? Why wasn't she moving? Then reality poured in like a river of fire. I pulled her out, screaming at the top of my lungs. A crowd gathered around me. I tried CPR, I tried mouth-to-mouth, I prayed with everything I had for a miracle, for a heartbeat, for a single breath, but she had been gone for hours. The world swirled around me like a tide pool, spinning me out of control. The paramedics arrived. The police arrived.

There was talk of heatstroke and core temperatures and hyperthermia. I fell to the ground unable to walk, unable to do anything but scream and babble, to plead for my baby's life.

A police officer tried to get information from me, but it was like I wasn't there. My little girl's body was taken. I screamed as they took her away. My Hannah, my reason for living, was gone.

The press arrived with cameras and video cameras. Dan arrived after them. "What have you done?" he shouted at me. *"What have you done?"* I couldn't answer. I was catatonic.

There were discussions on whether I should be tried for murder or manslaughter. People were talking to Dan. To Shirlee. To my coworkers. To people who didn't know me well enough to speak about me. *What kind of person was I? What kind of mother was I?* No one asked me. I could have answered the latter. I was the worst kind. The kind who killed her own child.

They put me in a police car and drove me downtown to the station. I waited alone in a room for more than an hour. A few police officers came in and asked me questions. Inane questions. *Did I know she was in the car? Had I left her in the car on purpose? When did I realize she was in the car?*

Then a man about my age came and talked to me. He wore a suit. His voice was calm. Sympathetic. He asked me questions, and I mostly just blinked at him. He told me that he was from the prosecutor's office or someplace official. He finished with his questions and spoke with the police. There was a discussion on whether I should be arrested, but the man intervened. The talk of jail scared me, but nothing they could do could match the pain I already felt. Someone asked if I wanted a sedative. I turned it down. I deserved to feel the pain. I deserved to feel every barb, every hurt.

And the barbs came. My Hannah's death set off a firestorm of media. The television covered it, reducing my tragedy to four minutes of entertainment followed by a commercial for tires. Both newspapers, the *Deseret News* and the *Salt Lake Tribune*, weighed in. There were columns of letters to the editor about me. Some said I deserved life in prison for what I'd done. Some said I should be locked in a car with the windows rolled up. I agreed with the latter.

Most confusing to me was how deeply people I didn't know hated me. The attacks lasted for months. I don't know why strangers went so far out of their way to hate me. Maybe it made them feel like better people. Or better parents. Maybe it convinced them that they would never do such a thing.

I noticed stories like mine everywhere. One British lawyer called it *forgotten baby syndrome*.

A psychiatrist on TV spoke out for me. He said, "Our conscious mind prioritizes things by importance, but our memory does not. If you've ever left your cell phone in your car, you are capable of forgetting your child." He pointed out that there were scores of stories like mine. He said that this was a new phenomenon, that ten years ago it rarely happened because parents kept their babies near them in the front seat. Then airbags came, and our babies were put out of the way, where we couldn't see them.

He explained that there were two main reasons that people left babies in cars: change of routine and distraction. I'd had both. He said, rightly, that no punishment society could give could match what I was already feeling. I don't know how he knew.

Through it all, Dan's moods were as volatile as the Utah weather. He was supportive and sympathetic, then, sometimes in the same hour, angry and brooding. He was gone a lot. I didn't know where he went. I didn't care. It was easier being alone. I was fired from my job, not that I could have worked. I stayed in bed most of the time, hiding from the world, wishing that I could hide from myself.

Then, one night, I got sick with appendicitis. If I had known that my appendix had already burst, I might not have gone to the hospital. If I had stayed home for just another hour or two, I could have ended it all. Perhaps, in spite of my self-loathing and pain, some part of me still longed to live.

As I lay in bed racked with fever, I thought about my life. It came to me that one day I might see my sweet little girl again. *What if she asked me what I had done with my life?* I was not honoring her by retreating from the world—from life. At that moment I resolved that things might be different. That *I* might be different. That I might be *better*.

Then my husband divorced me.

As a rare gesture of magnanimity, Mark closed the office two hours early on the Wednesday before Thanksgiving. On the way home from work, I stopped at the grocery store for pie ingredients. It had been years since I'd made pies. I unearthed the old cookbook my mother had written her pie secrets in.

Nicholas arrived at my apartment a little before six. I had finished making all the crusts, and the cherry and apple pies were in the oven, along with a baking sheet spread with pecan halves.

"I got here as soon as I could," he said apologetically. He carried a paper coffee cup in each hand, and a large white plastic bag hung from the crux of his arm. He breathed in. "It smells heavenly." He handed me a cup. "I got you a salted caramel mocha."

"How do you always know what I want?"

"It's easy. I find the sweetest thing on the menu and order it."

"You've pretty much got me figured out," I said.

"I brought us Chinese for dinner. I got wonton soup, sweet and sour pork, walnut shrimp, and pot stickers."

"Which will all go nicely with pumpkin pie," I said. We walked into the kitchen. Nicholas set the bag of Chinese down on the table.

"So, I'm making apple, cherry, pumpkin, and pecan," I said. "The apple and cherry are in the oven. They're just about done."

Nicholas examined the latticework on my apple and cherry pies through the oven window. "Those are works of art," he said. "Where did you learn to make pies?"

"My mother. She was famous for her pies. She won a blue ribbon for her cherry pie at the San Juan County fair. It was the only prize she ever won." I opened the oven and took out the pies, setting them on the counter to cool. "I don't have a lot of happy memories from my childhood, but when she made pie, life was good."

"My mother always made pies at special times," Nicholas said, "like the holidays or special family get-togethers. But my favorite part of pie making was after she was done and she would take the leftover dough, sprinkle it with cinnamon and sugar, then bake it."

"I know, right!" I said, clapping my hands. "Piecrust cookies. They're the best. Which is why I made extra dough."

"You're going to make some tonight?" Nicholas asked.

"Absolutely," I said. "When the pies are done. I'm just getting ready to mix the pecan pie filling. Would you mind getting the pecans out of the oven? The mitts are right there."

"On it," he said.

In the end, I made four regular-size pies for Thanksgiving as well as two tart-size pies—one pecan, one pumpkin—for us to eat with our dinner.

After the last of the pies were in the oven, we sat on the floor in the living room and ate our Chinese food with chopsticks. This was followed by the small pies and piecrust cookies with decaf coffee.

As I finished my coffee, I lay back on the carpet. "I'm too full for Thanksgiving dinner."

"No, we're just stretching out our stomachs to get ready for Thanksgiving dinner," Nicholas said.

"That's a brilliant excuse for gluttony," I said. "Thanks for bringing us dinner."

"It was nothing. If I'd known you were such a good cook, I'd have added a clause in the contract requiring you to cook for me."

"I'm happy to cook for you whenever you want."

"There's an open-ended commitment," he said. "Speaking of commitments, how is the contract going?"

I wondered why he was asking. "I think it's going very well."

"So you're glad you signed?"

"Yes."

"Good," he said.

We decided to watch television as we waited for the pies to finish baking. I turned the lights out, and we sat next to each other on the couch. I handed Nicholas the remote, and he channel-surfed for a few minutes until we came to *It's a Wonderful Life* on PBS.

"Let's watch this," I said. "I love Jimmy Stewart."

"And that Donna Reed," Nicholas said. "That is one low-maintenance woman."

"Like me," I said.

He smiled. "Just like you."

I MUST have been exhausted, because I don't remember falling asleep next to him. Actually, on him. I woke with my head on his shoulder. I jumped up.

"The pies?" I said. "I didn't hear the buzzer."

"I got them out. They look perfect."

He turned off the television, then walked me to my bedroom. I sat down on the edge of the bed, yawning. "Thank you."

"You're welcome. I'll see you tomorrow. I'll just let myself out."

"Nicholas," I said. "Are you glad you signed the contract?"

He smiled and kissed me on the forehead. "I'd do it again."

THANKSGIVING arrived with a heavy snowfall, and I woke to the sound of plows scraping the road. Around nine the snow stopped, and the roads were clear by the time Nicholas arrived at two. Traversing a slippery sidewalk, we carried the pies out to his car, laid them on lipped cookie sheets on his backseat, and drove off to Thanksgiving dinner.

"Tell me about the Hitesmans," I said as we drove.

"You'll like them. Good people. Scott is one of those small-town boys who made good. He grew up in Burley, Idaho, working the potato fields. Went to Yale for law. The firm picked him up out of college."

"What's his wife's name?"

"Sharon. You'll love her. She's one of those people who's always baking bread for the neighbors or visiting people in the hospital."

THE Hitesmans lived in a medium-size home in the northernmost section of the Avenues. Nicholas rang the doorbell, then opened the door before anyone could answer. We were engulfed by the warmth of the home, the smell of baking, and the sound of the Carpenters' Christmas music playing from another room.

A woman walked into the foyer to greet us. She looked to be about my age, pretty, with short, spiky auburn hair. Over a red knit shirt she wore a black apron.

"Nicholas," she said joyfully. "This must be Elise. I'm Sharon."

"Hello," I said. "Happy Thanksgiving."

"Happy Thanksgiving to you too." She looked down at the pies we carried. "Those look delicious; let me take that from you." She took the cookie sheet from my hands. "Boys, come here. Fast."

Two young boys, close in age, appeared at her side.

"Carry these into the kitchen and don't drop them."

"Okay," they said in unison.

"Now we can properly greet," she said, hugging me first, then hugging and kissing Nicholas. "It's so good to see you. You haven't been around much lately."

"Work," he said. "And more work."

"You lawyers work too much. But Scott says your absence might have something to do with your new friend," she said, looking at me. "Elise, we're so pleased you've joined us. Nicholas has told us so much about you."

"Good things, I hope."

"All good." Suddenly her brow fell. "Wait, have we met before?"

"I don't think so."

"You look familiar. I have a pretty good memory for faces. You aren't famous, are you?"

"No."

"You haven't been in the newspaper or on TV?"

I froze. "I . . ."

"Sharon," Nicholas said lightly, "stop interrogating her. She just has one of those faces."

Sharon smiled. "She definitely has a pretty one. Now come in. We're almost ready to eat. Make yourself at home. I need to check on the rolls, but let me take your coats."

I shrugged off my coat and handed it to her. As she turned away, a man, stocky and broad shouldered with blond hair, walked up behind her. "St. Nick," he said, extending his hands to Nicholas in greeting.

"Hey, buddy," Nicholas returned. They man-hugged and then Nicholas said to me, "This is Scott."

Scott reached his hand out to me. "So glad you could come."

I took his hand. "Thank you. I was glad to be invited."

"I guarantee you won't go away hungry," Scott said. He turned to Nicholas. "I hate to do this today, but can I ask you something about the Avalon case? I've got to get back to them by seven."

"No rest for the wicked," Nicholas said. He turned back to me. "Sorry, I'll be right back. Just . . . mingle."

As they slipped off to Scott's den, I walked into the living room and kitchen area. Adjoining the living room was the dining room, with a long table that was beautifully set with a copper-colored linen tablecloth, gold-trimmed china plates on gold chargers, and crystal stemware. There was a floral centerpiece in autumn colors.

The two boys were playing a video game in front of the fireplace. On the sofa was an elderly woman I guessed to be the grandmother. She looked like she was asleep. I drifted toward the kitchen, where Sharon was brushing butter over Parker House rolls.

"May I help?" I asked.

"Would you open that can of cranberry

sauce and put it on a plate?" she said. "The can opener is in that drawer right there."

I found the can opener, opened the can, and arranged the sauce.

"Your pies look divine," Sharon said.

"Thank you. I like making pies. Except mincemeat. We bought the mincemeat."

"I'm not a mincemeat fan either. It's really just for Grandma."

"That's what Nicholas said."

"He didn't bring it one year. Grandma let him know that she wasn't happy." We both looked over at the old woman. "It's a lot of work making pies. Especially the lattice tops," Sharon remarked.

"I enjoy making them," I said again. "And Nicholas helped."

She looked at me with surprise. "Nicholas helped you make pies? Wow. Things must be going well with you two."

I didn't know how to respond. Finally I said, "We're having fun."

"Fun is good." Sharon donned hot mitts, then opened the oven. She pulled a large roaster out and set it on the granite-topped island. She lifted the lid, exposing a large browned turkey.

At that moment, Nicholas walked in, trailed by Scott. "I see you put her to work," Nicholas said to Sharon.

"I did," Sharon said.

Nicholas said to me, "She comes across as nice, but she's really a heartless taskmaster. Last year she made Scott and me put together the boys' Christmas bikes before we could eat."

"Shhh!" she said. "Santa brought those bikes."

Nicholas grinned. "Sorry." He turned to me. "Did you meet Grandma?"

"Not yet," I said. "She's asleep."

"And don't wake her," Sharon said. "Let sleeping dogs lie."

"I heard that," Grandma shouted. "I'm not a dog. I'm old, not deaf."

I glanced furtively at Nicholas, who looked like he might burst out laughing.

"I want a Dr Pepper," she shouted. "No ice."

"Would you mind?" Sharon said to Nicholas. "There's one in the fridge. She likes it in a plastic cup, no ice."

"Sure," he said. He retrieved the soda, poured it into the cup, then took my hand

and led me over to the woman. "Here you go, Grandma," he said, offering her the drink.

She snatched it from him, took a long drink, burped, then handed the half-full cup back to him without thanks.

"Elise, this is Grandma Wilma," Nicholas said. "Grandma, this is Elise."

"Did you bring the mincemeat?" she said.

"Of course."

"One year he didn't bring it," she said to me.

"That must have been really awful," I said.

Nicholas stifled a laugh. Grandma looked at me. "Who are you?"

"I'm Elise."

"You his wife?"

"No. We're just friends."

"There's nothing wrong with marriage. No one gets married these days. Why would they buy the cow when the milk's free?"

"Grandma," Sharon said from the kitchen. "That's enough."

"It's nice to meet you," I said.

"It's time to eat?" she said back.

"She said *meet*," Nicholas clarified.

"We got a turkey," she said. "That's all the meat we need." She turned to Sharon. "When do we eat? I haven't got all day."

"Nick," Sharon said. "Will you carve the turkey? Then we can eat. Scott, take the rolls in. Boys, stop playing that stupid game."

Nicholas walked over to the bird. He pulled a knife from a wooden block and began carving while I helped Sharon carry the last of the food over to the table.

After we had all settled in at the table, Sharon and Scott held hands and Sharon said, "Nick, will you say a prayer over the food?"

"I'd be happy to." He took my hand, and we all bowed our heads.

"Dear Father in Heaven, we are grateful for this day to consider our blessings. We are grateful for the abundance of our lives. We are grateful to be together, safe and well. We ask a blessing to be upon this home and Scott and Sharon and their family. We are grateful that Elise has joined us this year and ask that she might feel as blessed as she makes others feel. Amen."

I looked over at him. "Thank you. That was sweet."

"He says the best prayers," Sharon said. "That's why we always ask him to pray."

SCOTT was right: There was no way we were leaving the table hungry. There was turkey, corn-bread stuffing, pecan-crusted candied yams, mashed potatoes and gravy, sweet corn, Parker House rolls, apple-pineapple salad, and green beans with bacon. By the time we were through eating, I was too full for pie. We all helped with the dishes. Then Nicholas said, "I think I need a walk."

"I'll join you," I said.

We retrieved our coats and went outside. The sun had fallen below the western mountains, and we walked out into the vacant, snow-packed street. Nicholas turned to me. "Having fun?"

"Yes. They're nice people. Grandma's a hoot."

"I know. Every year they say this is her last year, but it never is. I think she'll outlive all of us. When death comes for her, she'll slap his face and tell him to get her a Dr Pepper, no ice."

I laughed. "Why do you think old age does that to people?"

"I don't know. Old age seems to make some people meaner and some sweeter. Maybe it's just an amplifier." I slipped on a patch of ice, and Nicholas grabbed my arm. I noticed that he didn't let go. "So how does this compare to your normal Thanksgiving?"

"The food is better. The company is *much* better."

"I'm sure the harem isn't the same without you."

"Dan will survive."

"What is Dan like? Or have I crossed the line of addendum one?"

"We have pretty much obliterated addendum one," I said. "How do I describe Dan?" I thought a moment, then said, "His good side, he's not bad-looking and he's ambitious. He has big dreams."

"And the dark side?"

"He's got a nasty temper, and he's a narcissist. He's a womanizer. On our wedding day, he flirted with some of the guests. It's funny how different kids can be from their parents. Dan's father is the most humble man you'll ever meet. He adores his wife and treats her like a queen." I breathed the cold air in. "May I ask you a deep, probing question?"

"It's only fair," he said.

"Do you ever wish you were married and had children?"

He thought a moment. "Yes. To both."

"Then why don't you? It's not like that would be hard for you. Just in my office I know two women who would be more than happy to oblige you."

"I guess it's just taken me a little while to get to this place."

"So why the contract? Why not just date?"

"Training wheels," he replied.

"Training wheels," I repeated, smiling. "I like that." I slipped again. Again Nicholas caught me.

"It's the shoes," I said. "They don't do snow."

"I think *you* need training wheels. Let's go back and have some of that pie," he said.

"All right. Just don't let me fall."

BY THE time we returned from our walk, the boys had disappeared and Grandma Wilma had already eaten her sliver of mince-meat and retired to the guest room to nap.

Nicholas and I joined Scott and Sharon at the table for coffee and pie.

"Elise," Sharon said. "Your pies are divine. This pecan pie is amazing."

"Thank you," I said.

"You're definitely on our guest list next year."

"Or at least your pies are," Scott joked. "In case this doesn't work out."

I furtively glanced at Nicholas, who didn't respond.

We sat around and talked for nearly an hour. Eventually our conversation turned to the natural sleep agent properties of tryptophan in turkey, to which Nicholas yawned and said, "I need a nap." He looked at me as if seeking permission.

"Go for it," I said.

He went into the living room, leaving the three of us at the table.

"The food was really great," I said to Sharon. "Thank you for letting me join you."

"Thank you for coming," Sharon said. "You're good for him."

Scott nodded. "I've never seen Nick this happy."

Sharon nodded. "He's definitely in love."

The word paralyzed me. The L word. I suddenly wished that Nicholas had told them the truth about us.

"I think I'll check on Nicholas," I said. I went into the living room. The room was lit by the orange-yellow fire.

Nicholas was asleep on the sofa in front of the fireplace. I sat down next to the couch and looked at him, the flickering flames reflecting off his face. He was beautiful. *Do I really make him happy? Why does our relationship feel so real?* I took a deep breath. An inner voice said to me, *You're losing it, Elise. You know it's not real. You're going to get your heart broken.* Then another voice said, *I don't care.* I lay my head against him, closed my eyes, and pretended that we were the couple everyone thought we were.

Chapter Six

I woke the next morning to my phone ringing. It was still dark outside.

"Hello?" I said groggily.

"What are you doing?" Nicholas asked.

"I'm sleeping. What time is it?"

"Six. Almost."

"Why are you calling me so early?"

"It's Black Friday," he said. "I need to do some Christmas shopping. Want to come?"

"Is this on our schedule?"

"No, I'm completely ad-libbing here."

"Can I get ready first?"

"Of course. I'll be over in twenty minutes."

"I can't be ready in twenty minutes. Give me an hour."

"That's a lot of daylight," he said.

"I need an hour," I said firmly.

"All right. See you in an hour. Bye."

"Bye." I hung up, then climbed out of bed and took a shower to wake myself up. As usual, Nicholas was right on time.

"Where are we going?" I asked with my eyes closed, reclining the seat in his car.

"City Creek Center."

"It's going to be a zoo. Why aren't you tired?"

"It's a day off. Do you really want to sleep through it?"

"Yes," I said.

The shopping center was crowded, and

parking was at a premium. We passed two people trying to pull into the same slot in the parking garage, both unwilling to yield.

"Think we'll find a space?" I asked.

"I'd bet on it," he said. He pulled into a reserved spot with his name on it, and we took the elevator up to the ground level.

The shopping center was an upscale, open-air mall. It occupied six acres in downtown Salt Lake City.

We were walking out of Godiva, where we had stopped for chocolate-covered strawberries (which was probably the best breakfast I'd had in years), when Nicholas said, "I need to stop at the Coach store to pick up a bag for a partner. Do you mind?"

"Of course not." I followed him to the shop.

A professional-looking man, bald with a graying goatee, approached Nicholas. "May I help you, sir?"

"I'm looking for a leather carry-on bag."

"I've got just the thing," said the man. He led us over to a wall display of leather bags.

Nicholas lifted one to examine it more

closely. "How much is this bag?" he asked.

"It's four hundred and ninety-eight dollars."

That was almost my entire life savings.

"What colors does it come in?" Nicholas asked.

"Just what you see here, black and brass."

"I'll take the brass."

"Very good choice. Give me just a moment and I'll ring you up."

"Here's my card," Nicholas said, handing the man a black credit card. There was a long line of people making purchases.

"That's a nice bag," I said.

"It's for one of my partners," he said. "He likes luggage."

As we waited in line, I noticed that there was a Pandora shop across the way. Cathy was a Pandora fanatic, and she always loved getting new charms.

"Nicholas," I said, "I'm going to go over to the Pandora shop."

"No problem. I'll come over after."

I walked over to the store and browsed the display cases until I found a sterling silver clover with green enamel. It was perfect. Cathy was Irish and proud of it.

"May I help you?" a woman asked. I looked up. The woman was about my age, heavy with gold, permed hair.

"I'd like to purchase that charm," I said, pointing to the piece.

She lifted it from the display case. "Will that be cash or plastic?"

"Plastic," I said, handing her my Visa card. She ran my card, glanced at the name, then back up at me. "Do I know you?"

"I don't think so."

She glanced once more at my name on the credit card. "Elise Dutton. No, I think I do. What school did you go to?"

"I'm not from around here."

"Hmm," she said, handing me back my card. Then a look of recognition came to her eyes. "I know who you are. I read a story about you a few years back. You—" She stopped abruptly.

"Yes?" I said.

"I'm sorry," she said. "I'm mistaken."

She quickly packaged up my purchase and handed me the bag. "Thank you for shopping. Have a good day."

"Happy holidays," I said dully, then quickly left the store.

Nicholas met me as I was walking out. "Sorry that took so long," he said. "That guy was inept with a cash register." He looked at me closely. "Are you okay?"

"I'm not feeling well," I said. "Can we go?"

"Of course. Come on. It's too crowded here anyway."

THE next Monday was calmer than usual since we didn't have any tours that week. The holidays were our slow time of the year.

A little before noon, I looked up to see Dan standing in the doorway of my office. "Flowers. Where'd you get those?"

"What do you want?" I asked.

He stepped into my office. "You weren't at Thanksgiving dinner."

"I told your parents I wouldn't be there."

"You didn't tell me."

"What do you want, Dan?"

"I came to see what's up. Why you didn't come."

"I was busy."

"On Thanksgiving?"

"I had another invitation to dinner," I said, annoyed by his persistence.

"An invitation from who?"

"A friend."

"A friend," he said suspiciously. "Male or female?"

"I don't need to report to you."

"A man, huh?" He walked closer to my desk. "Tell you what—I'll take you to lunch, and you can tell me about this guy. I'll pay."

"I already have lunch plans," I said.

"Since when do you have lunch plans?"

"Where's Kayla?" I said. "Why don't you take her to lunch?"

"I need to talk to you about her. Who are you lunching with?"

"A friend," I said.

"The Thanksgiving guy?"

"That's none of your business."

"What's Thanksgiving guy's name?"

"Nicholas," Nicholas said, walking into my office.

Dan turned around. The look on his face was priceless, a mix of surprise and fear.

"Hi, Elise," Nicholas said. He kissed me on the cheek.

Dan glanced back and forth between us.

"This is Dan," I said. "My ex-husband."

Nicholas looked at him coolly. "Dan."

"Whassup," Dan said. I knew Dan well enough to know that he was intimidated. Subconsciously, he threw his chest out a little.

Nicholas turned back to me. "Are you ready?"

"Yes." I took his hand. "I'll talk to you later," I said to Dan.

Nicholas and I walked out of my office, leaving Dan standing there alone. I should have known that he'd never leave my new relationship alone.

DAN was waiting on the landing outside my apartment when I got home from work.

"Whassup?" he said. "I was just in the area, thought I'd stop by."

"What were you doing in the area?" I asked. I unlocked the door and walked in.

"I came to see you." He followed me inside, took off his coat, and threw it, then himself, on my couch. "So how was your date?"

"What date?"

"The one I caught you on. With what's-his-name."

"You didn't *catch* me," I said. "And you know his name."

"Whatever. The Nick-man. So he's like your boyfriend now?"

"Something like that. What's it to you?"

"Kayla's gone. She cheated on me. With some old rich guy."

"She's a cheater. What did you expect?"

"I expected she would be loyal."

"Like you?"

"I was loyal to *her*."

I breathed out in exasperation. "What do you want, Dan?"

"I want you. I want us to be like we were."

"That ship has sailed," I said.

"You didn't give me a chance. I stuck by you when you screwed up, but I slip up and you're gone."

"*You* didn't stick by me. You divorced *me*."

"Only because you were going to divorce me."

"I never said I was going to divorce you. You were cheating on me with my best friend while I was in the ICU clinging to life."

His voice softened. "We understand each other. We've been through the storms together. We should be together. You know it."

"I believed that once," I said. "I don't anymore."

"Why, because some rich lawyer comes knocking at your door? How long have you known him?"

"A few weeks."

"I don't trust him."

I groaned with exasperation. "I'm not having this conversation."

"Come on, 'Lise. We match. Just admit it. If we didn't, then why did you marry me?"

"I was desperate."

"No, you believed in us. And you were right. Drop the lawyer and I'll move in with you."

"It's not going to happen, Dan. Now you need to go."

He grabbed his coat and smiled. "You'll come around. Like a boomerang. You'll see the light. Who else knows everything about you? You know how people are when they learn about . . ."

"About what?"

"You know. Hannah."

"Get out," I said.

He remained undaunted. "See you later,

'Lise." He stepped across the threshold, then said, "Boomerang."

I shut the door after him. As much as I hated hearing it from him, Dan was right. Whenever people made the connection between me and the woman in the newspaper who killed her daughter, they just mysteriously disappeared. I leaned against the door and cried.

THE ICE Christmas party was a potluck affair that was held at my boss's home. He lived in a Tudor-style house decorated with plastic reindeer in the front yard.

Nicholas had picked me up along with my pomegranate-and-poppy-seed-dressed salad. I brought the same salad every year and took it home every year barely eaten, since most of the office avoided salad like a toxin. Still, Mark insisted that I bring it because his wife once remarked that she liked it. I had concluded that she was only being polite since she hadn't eaten it for two years.

Nicholas parked his BMW across the street from the house, and I carried my bowl up to the door.

"Shall I ring the bell?" Nicholas asked.

"No. They won't answer; just walk in."

He opened the door. As I anticipated, there was no one to greet us, and the only sounds came from the TV in the family room.

"I'll take your coat," Nicholas said.

I set my salad on the floor, then took off my coat and handed it to him. "They put them in the living room," I said.

Nicholas added our coats to a pile of outerwear already covering the crushed-velvet sofa. Then we walked into the kitchen. No one noticed (or cared) as I lay my salad on the counter.

My boss, Mark, was tightfisted, and the party's food was grocery-store platters of meat and cheese laid out next to plates of Ritz and saltine crackers dressed with cheese from a can. There were also jalapeño poppers and store-bought rolls to make sandwiches.

The one place Mark splurged was on beer. His refrigerator was stocked with Budweiser. I think he caught on that his guests rated the party by the level of intoxication they achieved, which was just one reason that I was always the first to leave.

Everyone else was already there. Mark and his wife, Shelley; Cathy, who brought Maureen, her sister. And Brent and Margaret, our two group escorts, whom we rarely saw because they were on the road more than two hundred days out of the year.

Closest to the kitchen were Zoey and her date. As usual, she had brought someone none of us had ever seen. Her boy du jour was tall and muscular, handsome but not especially bright-looking. He wore a sleeveless Utah Jazz jersey, which emphasized his biceps but seemed out of place considering the abundance of snow outside.

Everyone was sitting around the family room eating nachos and watching the Jazz play the Portland Trail Blazers. They had all gotten an early start on drinking, and empty beer cans littered the coffee table that three of them had their feet on. Cathy was the first to notice us. "Elise. Nicholas," she said. "You made it."

"Hi, everyone," I said.

Nicholas looked as unsure of himself as he had when he first approached me in the food court.

"Hey," Mark said. "Help yourself to a beer in the fridge."

"Thank you." Nicholas made no movement to act on the offer.

"Come watch the game," Zoey said.

"Go ahead, sit," I said to Nicholas. "I'll get us some food."

Nicholas sat down on a chair next to the others. Zoey was holding an open beer. She leaned toward Nicholas, drawn like steel to a magnet. I walked to the kitchen table and began making ham and cheese sandwiches.

"Thanks for all the gifts you've been sending," Zoey said to him. "Especially the cheesecake. It was *dreamy*."

"I'm glad you liked it," Nicholas said casually, looking back at the television. "What quarter are we in?" he asked.

"Just started the third," Mark said. "You ever watch the Jazz play?"

"Sometimes. We've got box seats," he said. "At the firm."

"And you're a partner, right?" Zoey asked rhetorically.

"Yes."

Zoey's date just stared ahead at the screen,

sucking on a beer, completely oblivious to her obvious interest in my date.

I walked back over with our food. "Here you go," I said, handing Nicholas a plate with some of my salad and a sandwich. I sat down between Nicholas and Zoey.

"Thank you," Nicholas said, turning all his attention to me. For the next hour we just watched the game, which the Jazz ended up losing by four points.

"Are you ready to go?" I asked Nicholas.

"Whatever you want," he said.

"I'm ready."

"Okay," he said. "I'll get the coats." He walked out of the room.

Zoey stood and walked out after him. I also stood up and walked out, stopping in the hall just outside the living room. I could hear Zoey talking. "So where did you and Elise meet?"

"We just bumped into each other. In the building."

"I'm in the building," she said. There was a short pause; then she added, "I'm sorry we never bumped into each other. I mean, before you two." There was another pause. "Is it serious? You and Elise."

"You mean, would I be interested in exploring other romantic possibilities?"

"You're so smart," she said. "Yes. I mean, hypo"—she struggled with the word—"hypo . . . hypothetically."

"That's a big word," Nicholas said.

"I'm not dumb," she said. "Maybe a little drunk."

"Hypothetically, I wouldn't. You better get back to your date."

"He's an idiot," she said.

"We'll just keep that to ourselves," Nicholas replied.

I wasn't surprised by Zoey's antics, but I was still angry. I walked into the room, glaring at her. "Let's get out of here," I said to Nicholas.

Zoey was either too drunk or too dumb to realize that I'd been listening. "Bye, Elise," she said.

I didn't answer her. I was fuming.

Nicholas took my arm. "Let's go home."

I DIDN'T say much on the way back to my apartment. Nicholas must have known how I was feeling because he didn't pry.

Outside my apartment door, Nicholas asked, "Are you okay?"

I blew up. "I can't believe she hit on you."

"Yes, you can," he said calmly. "She was drunk."

"She would have done it anyway."

"Maybe."

"Why are you defending her?"

"I'm not. But don't go too hard on her. If she was happy with her life, she wouldn't have come after me. *And* she'd been drinking."

I took a deep breath. "I don't have to like her."

"No. But you do have to work with her. So you might as well keep things civil."

"Civil," I said angrily. "I want to pluck her eyelashes."

Nicholas laughed. "Promise me you won't do that. Just let it go."

"But she's a—"

He put a finger to my lips. "Trust me. Promise me," he said.

Honestly, I liked that he was touching my lips. "All right." After a moment I said, "May I ask you something? If it wasn't for the contract, would you have hooked up with her?"

"No. She's not my type." He kissed me on the cheek. "Good night, Elise. I enjoyed being with you." He started to walk away, then stopped and turned back. "Oh, do you know what today is?"

"No."

"It's our midpoint. We're halfway through our contract." He turned and walked away.

I watched him walk out to his car. His final words hurt my heart even more than Zoey's betrayal.

In spite of my promise to Nicholas, the next day at work I treated Zoey coldly. I was still hurt and jealous. Even if Nicholas wasn't really mine, Zoey didn't know that. She had scores of men, and she went after mine. I'd never forgive her for being so cruel.

A little before noon, Zoey brought a package into my office. "Here's your present," she said softly.

I glanced up only for a second, then went back to my work. "Just put it on the chair."

"Okay," she said. She didn't leave my office. "Elise, I'm sorry."

"For what?" I asked innocently, forcing her confession.

"I had too much to drink last night, and I hit on Nicholas at the party. I feel really bad."

"Why would you do that to me?" I asked, unleashing my anger. "What have I ever done to you?"

"I'm so sorry." Her eyes began welling up with tears. She wiped at them. "I'm an idiot; I know it. And just so you know, Nick didn't go for it for a second. He's completely loyal to you."

I still wasn't in a mood to forgive her, so I didn't say anything. Zoey started crying. "When I got home, I was really mad at myself. I thought, *Why would I do that? Elise is such a good person.*" She grabbed a Kleenex from my desk. "The thing is, I'm really insecure. I have this need to prove myself. It's like . . ." She took a deep breath. "I'm sorry. I'm just really jealous of you. Because Nick is great and he loves you, and the guys I meet just love my body, and no one wants to keep me; they just want to use me. But Nick loves you inside and out. And you deserve that. You deserve a nice guy like him." I couldn't believe that Zoey was jealous of me. She said,

"I'll quit bothering you. But I'm sorry." She turned to go.

"Zoey," I said.

She slowly turned back, wiping her eyes.

"I understand."

"You do?"

"I didn't know you felt that way. I've judged you wrong. I'm sorry."

After a minute she said, "Can I give you a hug?"

"Yes."

I stood while Zoey came around my desk and put her arms around me. "I'll never do that again," she said. "I promise. If I can do anything to make it up to you, just ask."

I looked at her a moment before asking, "Do you mean that?"

She nodded.

"I have some parties coming up with Nicholas, and I don't have anything to wear."

"You want to borrow my clothes?"

"Right," I said. "I couldn't fit this body into anything you own. But I'm not good with fashion. I've been out of the game for too long. And everyone he works with is rich and cool."

She suddenly smiled. "You want me to dress you?"

"If you would."

"I'd love to."

"I don't have much money."

"We don't need money," she said. "I have friends. We'll knock Nicholas off his feet. When's your next party?"

"Saturday night."

"Okay. I hope your Saturday is open, because we've got some work to do."

Chapter Seven

DECEMBER first. Exactly one month since Nicholas had approached me in the food court. Zoey arrived at my apartment Saturday afternoon with a pile of dress bags, two large makeup boxes, a jewelry box, four shoe boxes, and a canvas bag filled with hair supplies. It took us three trips to get everything in from her car.

She had found me four dresses, all on "loan" from Nordstrom, where one of her ex-boyfriends was a manager. There were also several sets of matching jewelry for each dress.

All the dresses were stunning. I tried them all on. It took us an hour to settle on two. The one I would wear that night at the firm party was a black form-fitting crepe sheath with a sheer top.

The other dress was the most expensive of the four: a one-shoulder nude evening gown with beads. I decided to save it for the partners' party, because we guessed it would be the fanciest of Nicholas's events.

We looked through her boxes of shoes, and for the first dress I chose a simple but elegant pair of black patent leather pumps. For the partners' party I chose a glittery pair of peep-toed high heels. Then we chose earrings and necklaces for both dresses.

With the dresses and accessories selected, we discussed my general look, experimenting with different shades of makeup for almost an hour. As Zoey worked on my makeup, she taught me some new techniques.

"You *can* teach an old dog new tricks," I said.

Zoey stepped back to look at me. "You're not *old*, and you're not a *dog*. Never, ever call yourself that."

"I was just joking," I said.

"Especially joking," she said. "Your subconscious mind doesn't know the difference. You need to be your own best cheerleader."

I was impressed by her counsel. There was a lot more to Zoey than I'd given her credit for.

SITTING in my kitchen, Zoey wasn't the same girl I knew in the office. She was much more funny, relaxed, and vulnerable. She was also sweet. She kept telling me that with my natural beauty I didn't need a makeover, just a few enhancements. "You don't make over gorgeous," she said.

I hadn't had a girlfriend since Kayla had betrayed me, and it was wonderful to have female companionship again. I wondered if, in spite of the age difference, Zoey and I might be friends. Nicholas had brought me out of my cave, and I was going to need someone to do things with after our contract expired.

Zoey worked on my hair for over an hour and experimented with several shades of lipstick before finding the right one. Finally, she stepped back and scrutinized me like a sculptor examining her creation. She nodded, then said, "Oh my, Elise. Look at yourself."

I walked out to the hall mirror. I couldn't believe it. "I look pretty," I said.

"No, you look *hot*. He's in serious trouble."

ZOEY left just a few minutes before Nicholas arrived. He rang the doorbell at seven. "Come in," I shouted, wanting to present myself properly.

He let himself in. "Hi, it's me."

"I'll be out in just a minute."

"How was your day?"

"Good. Zoey came over."

"After the other night, I'm surprised that you two are talking."

"She apologized for coming on to you."

I took a good look at myself, then walked out into my front room. Nicholas was sitting on my couch. He immediately stood. "Wow."

"What?" I asked innocently.

"You look amazing."

I smiled. "Shall we go?"

NICHOLAS'S office party was held each year at La Caille, an expensive French restaurant tucked away on a twenty-acre reserve at the mouth of Little Cottonwood Canyon. I had been to the restaurant only once before, for a wedding of one of Dan's coworkers, and I had never forgotten it. Housed in a stucco, ivy-covered French château, it had its own three-acre vineyard. During the warmer months, peacocks roamed the yard amid statuary and topiaries, while black and white swans glided in the swan pool. Tonight, the grounds were covered in snow and were extravagantly lit with strings of white lights.

Nicholas pulled his car up the restaurant's tree-lined cobblestone drive to a roundabout near the front door. He handed his keys to the valet, then took my arm and led me inside. The lobby was exquisite, with a large antique chandelier and parquet-tile floor. Harpsichord music softly echoed through the tile and stucco interior.

The hostess who greeted us looked like a model. The waitresses wore low-cut gowns that were presumably all the rage in eighteenth-century France.

We walked up a circular stairway to the main dining room, which was crowded with several hundred of the firm's staff and guests. Everyone seemed pleased to see Nicholas.

"You're very popular," I said.

"Of course," he said. "I'm a partner. I help decide what they get paid. Would you like something to drink? They have remarkable eggnog."

"I would love an eggnog," I said.

"Coming up."

A few minutes later, Nicholas returned carrying two glasses. He handed me my drink. "One eggnog."

"Thank you," I said.

He took my arm. "Let me introduce you to some people here."

He introduced me to what seemed like a hundred strangers. Near the center of the room I was glad to see Scott and Sharon Hitesman. While Nicholas and Scott talked, Sharon sidled up to me.

"Elise, you look stunning."

"Thank you. And thank you again for letting me crash your Thanksgiving dinner."

"You have no idea how glad I was to finally see Nicholas with someone. He deserves someone like you."

"Someone like me?" I said.

She smiled at me. "Someone who makes him happy."

A minute later, Nicholas returned to my side to resume our tour of the floor. He was definitely well liked. And everyone was friendly.

"Hungry?" Nicholas asked.

"I'm starving."

"Me too. Enough of this obligatory socializing. Let's eat."

Like the surroundings, the fare was extravagant—the opposite of my office party. Instead of a refrigerator filled with Budweiser, there were silver ice buckets with expensive wines.

"It's not Café Rio," Nicholas said, "but it's edible."

"It may surprise you, but I actually eat more than Café Rio."

"Yes, I've seen you eat turkey. And steak. And Chinese food."

"And Thai," I added.

"I think I'm getting through to you," he said, setting some shrimp on his plate. "I love shrimp."

"I love shrimp too," I said.

"I'll get enough for both of us." He loaded

up his own plate, then pointed at other things for me to get. Salmon on rice, roast chicken, crab-stuffed mushrooms, Brie and pâté de foie gras with crackers, chocolate-dipped strawberries, and puff pastries shaped like swans.

We carried our plates up the stairs to a small dining room. Nicholas found us a quiet place tucked behind the servers' station.

"So what do you think of our party?"

"I feel a little out of place," I said. "Everything is so nice."

"You deserve nice," he said. "Thank you for coming with me. Usually I just put in my time, eat a few shrimp, and bolt. It's been really nice having you here."

"I think everyone's fooled. They really think we're a couple."

He ate a few more shrimp, then said, "You know what's sad is that we might be one of the most authentic couples here tonight."

"What do you mean?"

"Charles and Blake are having affairs. Phil and his paralegal Rachel have mysteriously disappeared at the same time every Thursday afternoon for the last three years, and Kurt is waiting for the optimum financial opportunity to divorce his wife. What we have might be more real than much of what we have seen here tonight."

"Are Scott and Sharon happy?"

"Yes. They're the real thing."

"They seem happy," I said.

Nicholas must have tired of the topic because he took a drink of eggnog and said, "I know I said it before, but you really do look beautiful tonight."

"It's the dress."

"That's like saying the *Mona Lisa* is beautiful because of its frame."

WE STOLE off from the party without saying good-bye. Nicholas took the long way back to my place. I didn't want the night to end. It was almost midnight when he pulled up in front of my apartment.

"I hope that wasn't too painful," he said.

"No. It was nice. Actually, I haven't been anywhere that nice for a long time. They treated me better than my own colleagues."

"You can accuse us lawyers of many things, but we are civil." He leaned over and kissed me on the cheek. "Good night, Elise."

"Good night." I reached for the door

handle, then looked back. "May I ask you something? Why are you so nice to me?"

He was quiet a moment, then said, "It makes me sad that you had to ask."

I didn't know what to say to that. "Good night, Nicholas. Thank you for a lovely evening."

"It was my pleasure."

That night as I lay alone in bed thinking about how nice the evening had been, a terrible thought crossed my mind. *Maybe I shouldn't have signed the contract after all.* Sometimes it's just better not to know what you're missing.

FOR the first time since I'd started working at ICE, I looked forward to Monday. More specifically, seeing Nicholas. And I loved anticipating his gifts. Monday I got a candle scented like Christmas sugar cookies, on Tuesday a DVD of *A Christmas Carol* (the George C. Scott version of course), and on Wednesday a CD of a Kenny G Christmas album.

On Thursday the sixth, something changed. There was no gift. And Nicholas was different. He was tense and withdrawn.

At lunch he barely ate. He barely spoke. He barely even looked at me. I wondered if I'd done something to upset him.

Finally, I asked, "Is something wrong at work?"

"No," he said darkly. "Same old tricks. People suing each other, divorcing each other, everyone looking out for themselves. As if there weren't already enough pain in this godforsaken world."

The tone of his voice frightened me. I asked, "Are you okay?"

He pushed his salad around a little, then looked up. "I'm fine."

"You're not yourself today."

"It's nothing," he said.

We sat quietly for a moment until I said, "If I did something . . ."

"It's nothing," he repeated sharply.

Emotion rose in my chest. "I'm sorry." I stood. "I better go."

He likewise stood, reaching for my arm. "No, please. I'm sorry. I didn't mean that." He hesitated for a moment. "I'm just under a lot of pressure. I'm really sorry I snapped. Please . . . forgive me."

I looked into his anxious eyes. There was

pain in them. "Okay." We both sat back down. After a moment I said, "It's not your fault. I kept pushing you. I was afraid that I'd done something wrong."

He looked at me for a moment, then said, "It's not you."

"If I can do anything to make you feel better . . ."

He reached across the table and took my hand. "If there were something anyone could do, you would be the one I'd go to. I'll be okay. I go through this every year around this time. It will pass."

I wondered what he'd meant by that, but I wasn't about to ask. We sat there for a few more minutes, eating in awkward silence. I wasn't really hungry anymore, and there didn't seem to be much more to say. "I guess I better let you go," I said.

He looked sad. "I'm sorry I wasn't better company." We both stood. "I'll see you on Monday." He turned to go.

"Nicholas," I said. I walked up to him and put my arms around him. "I don't know what's going on. But I care."

When I stepped back, I noticed that his eyes were slightly red. "Thank you," he said

softly. "That means more than you know."
He turned and walked away.

THE next day I didn't leave my office at
lunchtime, which everyone noticed.

"Where's Nick?" Zoey asked.

"He's out of town," I said, not really knowing where he was.

"Good. Then you can come to lunch with
us," Zoey said. "Cathy and I are going to get
sushi."

"Thanks," I said. "But I'm not hungry."

Zoey touched my arm. "Are you okay?"

"Nicholas is just acting a little different."

She nodded. "Sometimes men just need
some space."

I forced a smile. "I'm sure you're right."
Inside I wasn't sure.

I worried about Nicholas all weekend. I
wanted to call him, but never did. Maybe it
was just fear, but something told me not to.
Our time apart revealed to me just how much
I cared about him and needed him. I was
beginning to fear Christmas.

I WAS anxious from the moment I woke
on Monday. For the first time since I'd

signed the contract, I was nervous to see Nicholas. My anxiety grew as lunchtime neared.

About a half hour before noon, Mark walked into my office. "We've got a problem," he said. "The Marriott you booked in New York for our Dayton group has a gas leak and had to evacuate. We've got sixty kids on a bus and no place to stay for the night."

I groaned. "All right. I'll get on the phone." I pulled up my list of New York hotels and began calling. Nicholas called from the food court at a quarter after noon. I had been so involved in my crisis that I hadn't realized what time it was.

"You're standing me up?" he asked.

"I'm sorry, I didn't realize it was so late."

"Then I'll wait," he said.

"No, I can't come."

"Then you *are* standing me up?"

"It's just, I have a problem. One of my hotels shut down. I need to find a place for sixty kids to stay. This might take all afternoon."

He said, "Well, you have to eat. I'll bring something up."

"That would be great," I said.

"Pork salad?"

"Anything," I said.

Nicholas arrived about fifteen minutes later carrying a bag of food. As worried as I had been to see him, he looked fine. He set the bag on my desk. "Here you go," he said. "Change of cuisine. A Chick-fil-A sandwich. I figured you need something you can eat while you talk on the phone." He brought out the sandwich and a drink and laid them on my desk. "How's it going?"

"Not well. It's hard finding a block of that many rooms last minute."

"Can I help you call?"

"Really?"

"Why not?"

"How much time do you have?"

"Maybe forty-five minutes."

"That would help." I printed off a list of hotels, then tore it in half. "Just tell them it's an emergency and ask if they have a block of thirty-two rooms, double-occupancy, for tonight."

"What phone should I use?"

"There's one out in the reception area. Use line three."

"Line three," he said, walking out with

the paper I'd given him. Less than a half hour later, he walked back into my office. "I've got one on the line," he said. He laid the list down on my desk. "I circled it," he said. "The Liss Suites in Brooklyn."

He had doodled all over my phone list. There was a cartoon picture of a woman with her hair on fire.

"Is this supposed to be me?"

"No. Maybe."

In spite of my stress I laughed. "Okay, did they give you a rate?"

"The manager said they'd match your rate if it was reasonable."

"You're a doll," I said. I picked up the phone while Nicholas sat back and watched. The hotel worked out perfectly. It was actually nicer than the one I had originally reserved.

"Sounds like my work here is done," Nicholas said as I hung up.

"Thank you. Thank you."

"You're welcome."

"You're good at this. You might put me out of my job someday."

"I've been looking for something meaningful to do with my life."

"You saved sixty kids from sleeping on the streets of New York."

He stood. "Sorry to save the day and run, but I need to get back to my other job."

"I'll walk you to the elevator," I said.

In the hallway he asked, "How was your weekend?"

I looked him in the eyes. "Awful." We stopped in front of the elevator. "All I did was worry about you."

He was quiet a moment, then said, "Thank you for worrying." He pushed the UP button and said, "I told you I'd be okay."

"I know. You look much better."

"I am."

"So, I'll see you tomorrow?"

"I'm around all week. And we have the partners' party this Friday."

"When do you leave for New York?"

"Monday. Have you ever been to New York at Christmastime?"

"I've never been to New York at any time."

"That's a shame," he said. "There's no place like New York at Christmas. It's magical. Come with me next week."

"Yeah, right," I said.

He looked at me seriously. "You said we'd

see how things were going. I think they're going well, don't you?"

"Yes," I said.

"Then come with me. I'll have meetings during the day, but you can go sightseeing. Then at night, we'll go out on the town."

"I'd have to see if I can take the time off."

"How much vacation time do you have?"

"I don't know."

"When was the last time you took a vacation?"

"I don't know."

"Exactly. Time to cash some in. When are you going to get another offer for an all-expenses-paid trip to New York City?"

"I'll think about it," I said.

"All right. You think about it. But let me know soon so we can book your flight. The flights get pretty full this time of year."

"Okay," I said. "I'll let you know by tomorrow."

Just then the elevator bell rang. Zoey and Cathy stepped out.

"Hi, Nick," Zoey said. "Hi, Elise."

"Hello, ladies," Nicholas said. He kissed me on the cheek. "Think about it." He stepped into the elevator. "Have a good day."

After the door shut, Zoey said, "Think about what?"

"He wants me to go to New York with him," I said.

"At Christmas?" Zoey said. "New York is amazing at Christmas. What's there to think about?"

I thought for just a moment, then said, "You're right."

I called Nicholas just ten minutes later. "I want to go."

"Excellent," he said. "I'll have Sabrina book the flight."

"I'm so excited."

"Me too," he said. "You're going to love it."

NICHOLAS and I skipped lunch the next Friday because he had too much to do before leaving town. I spent my lunch break with Zoey, who fixed my hair for Nicholas's part-ners' party.

"You better take a lot of pictures tonight," she said. "I want to see you in that dress."

"I'm a little nervous," I said. "That first

party was so fancy, but I'm afraid this one is going to be more so."

"Just have fun. You're going to be great."

WHEN I got home from work, I took a quick shower, then put on *the dress*—the silk masterpiece Zoey and I had chosen for tonight. I had never worn anything so elegant. It hung from one shoulder, and the beads sewn into the fabric shimmered as I moved. Then I put on the jewelry that we had picked out. The earrings were larger than I was used to, but they matched the elegance of the dress. The heels I'd chosen were also taller than I usually wore, but they made a statement as well. I felt gorgeous.

Nicholas shook his head when he saw me. "Wow," he said. "Just wow."

THE party was held at the founder's home on Walker Lane. It was only twenty minutes from my apartment but a world away.

The house was a mansion. Or, more accurately, a villa, since it was Italian in design with rock and stucco exterior, a large, pillared portico, and beautiful wrought-iron front doors. Gas lights highlighted the brick-lined arched portals of the four-car garage. The yard was lit like a resort with lush landscaping and statuary.

Nicholas took my arm, and we walked up to the front door. A man standing in the lit portico opened the door for us. As we stepped inside the foyer, we were embraced by a rush of light, smells, and music. The floor was polished wood, covered in places with lush area rugs. A brass chandelier, at least eight feet in diameter, hung above us from the high, domed ceiling.

In the sitting room across from the front door, a young woman was playing a harp next to a group I assumed, from the instruments around them, were members of a string quartet taking a break. I had never been inside such a luxurious home. I felt even more out of place than I had at La Caille. As usual, Nicholas was in his element.

"I don't think they'll be serving jalapeño poppers and Budweiser," I said.

"And the party will be the worse for it," he replied.

"May I take your coat?" a young man asked.

"Yes, please," Nicholas said. He helped me off with the stole Zoey had also brought me and handed it to the man.

Just then a mature, silver-haired man wearing a beautiful burgundy suit walked up to us. He was accompanied by an elegant woman I guessed to be his wife. "Nicholas," he said. "You made it."

"And this time you brought someone," the woman said. "And she's lovely."

"Thank you," I said.

"Elise, this is Alan McKay, our senior partner, and his better half, Careen."

"Thank you for having us," I said. "Your home is beautiful."

"Thank you, dear. We enjoy it."

"Food and drink is that way," Alan said, pointing to a side room. "Please, enjoy yourselves."

"Thanks, Alan," Nicholas said. "Careen."

Our hosts flitted away like butterflies.

"They were nice," I said.

"They're good people," Nicholas said. "Alan is the firm's founder and senior partner. He's also the one who brought me over from the prosecutor's office."

The party was considerably smaller than

the one at La Caille, with maybe thirty guests in all. As we walked around, I recognized some of the lawyers from a couple weeks earlier.

"Will Scott and Sharon be here?" I asked.

"No. Scott's not a partner. At least not yet."

"How many partners are there?"

"Eleven."

"And how many lawyers does your firm have?"

"Ninety-seven."

There were two food tables in the dining room, one savory, one sweet. At the head of the savory table was a man in a white chef's coat and hat, carving roast beef. There were also bacon-wrapped scallops, crab puffs, jumbo prawns, caviar, carpaccio, and sushi.

The sweet table had three chocolate fountains with dark, white, and milk chocolates, the bases of the fountains surrounded by fruit. There were miniature key lime pies and cheesecakes, croissants, puff pastries, baklava, millefoglie, and dipped chocolates.

"This is amazing," I said. "I think I'm going to gain weight."

"I'll help," Nicholas said.

We filled up our plates and sat near the musicians. A few people came by to talk to Nicholas. They were very warm and welcoming.

When I had finished my plate, Nicholas said, "Would you like to see the house?"

"I'd love to. Will they mind?"

"No," Nicholas said. "Alan loves to show it off."

Nicholas led me up the circular stairs to a long hallway, both sides of which were lined with doors. The hallway led to another hall-way and ended at a loft and another set of stairs.

"I could get lost in here," I said.

"Lots of people do," he said. "Come look at this." We walked into a spacious room lined with bookshelves, many filled with leather books. It had a fireplace with an antique model of a ship on its mantel, and in the center of the room was a beautiful antique desk.

"This is Alan's den," Nicholas said.

"It's beautiful. Are Alan and Careen happy?"

"They've been married almost forty years, so I hope so. Alan's not an especially affectionate man, so their relationship is very partner-like, which isn't necessarily a bad thing."

"But he's not cheating on her."

"Oh no. He's a man of strong ethics and a very conservative Catholic. He once told one of the lawyers, 'If you're going through a midlife crisis, don't cheat. Buy yourself a Ferrari instead. It's cheaper.'" Nicholas smiled. "Want to see something cool?"

"Yes."

He pushed on one of the shelves, and it opened into a room. I clapped. "That's like in the movies."

"Every man wants a bookshelf that opens into a secret room. Come inside," he said.

We stepped into the room. Like the outer room, it had bookshelves, though the books weren't legal tomes but novels and personal reading. There were also several framed photographs of Alan with famous people, including President Bill Clinton, Bob Hope, and Maureen O'Hara.

"Actually, it's a safe room," Nicholas said. "In case terrorists or someone crazy breaks into his house. They can hide in here until the police arrive."

"Sometimes I'd like a safe room to hide in," I said.

"To hide from what?" Nicholas asked.

"Life."

Nicholas nodded as if he understood. "My father served in Vietnam. When I was young, he told me that everyone needs an emotional foxhole. A place to hide when life's storms hit."

"Do you?"

"Of course," he said. "There's a quote widely misattributed to Plato that says, 'Be kind, for everyone you meet is fighting a hard battle.' It's true. Everyone has struggles. Everyone has suffered more than you know. That includes you and me."

I didn't know what to say, so I just nodded.

We walked back downstairs. The string quartet had resumed playing. We went back and sat down next to the musicians.

As I looked around the ornately furnished room, I wondered what Nicholas's house must be like. "Where do *you* live?" I asked.

"Not far from here, actually." He suddenly smiled. "Would you like to see my house?"

"Yes."

His smile turned to a conspicuous grin.
"What?" I asked.

"When I first offered the contract, you asked if this ended up back at my place. I bet you didn't think you'd be asking me to go."

I grinned back. "A lot has changed since then," I said.

NICHOLAS lived less than ten minutes away. His home was new, a Cape Cod–style house with shutters and a large front porch. He pulled his car into the garage. The door from the garage opened into the kitchen, where he flipped on the lights. The room was bright and immaculate, with not even a dish in the sink.

"This is really cute," I said.

"Wasn't really going for *cute*," he replied.

"It's big," I said.

"For one person it is."

"It's big for a lot of people," I said.

"Hopefully I won't always be living here alone," he replied.

There were pictures on the wall. "Is this your family?" I asked.

He nodded.

"This is you with the long hair?"

"I'm afraid so."

"How old were you?"

He leaned forward for a closer look. "I think I was fifteen." In none of the pictures was Nicholas older than fifteen or sixteen.

"You know, you might be the cleanest bachelor in the country. You must have a cleaner."

"Rosa," he said. "She comes once a week. But actually, I'm pretty OCD. I don't like a messy house."

"I would drive you crazy."

I looked over a row of porcelain figurines he had displayed on a shelf. He had three female nudes with angel wings and a glossy figurine of Don Quixote sitting in a chair holding an open book on his lap and a sword in his hand. "Tell me about these," I said.

"I collect Lladró. I just think they're beautiful. There's one piece I'm coveting, but I haven't gotten up the nerve to buy it yet. It's Cinderella in her pumpkin carriage with her horses and groomsmen. It's more than thirty thousand dollars."

"Wow," I said. "I can't imagine spending that much on art. Do you think you'll buy it?"

"I'll buy it someday," he said.

"I hope you let me see it when you do."

"Of course." He changed the subject. "So are you ready for New York?"

"I haven't finished packing, but I'm very excited." I looked at him. "May I ask you a delicate question?"

"Of course."

"Are we sharing a room in New York?"

For a moment he just looked at me, and I had no idea how he was taking the question. Had I embarrassed him by implying that I didn't want to be with him, or had I embarrassed myself by presuming that he would? "I'm sorry," I said. "I didn't know."

"No, we're not," he said. "I booked you a separate room. It's in the contract." The moment settled into silence. Then he said, "It's late. I better get you home."

We were mostly quiet on the drive back to my apartment. He pulled up front and walked me to my door.

"Thank you for coming with me tonight," he said. "I've never enjoyed the partners' party more."

"Best partners' party I've ever been to," I said, smiling.

We stood looking at each other. I suppose I was still afraid I had offended him with my question about rooms in New York. But even greater than my fear was my desire that he would kiss me—not on the cheek as he did in public, but really kiss me, passionately. Finally he leaned forward and kissed me on the cheek. "Good night, Elise."

"Good night, Nicholas," I said softly, hiding my disappointment.

He turned and walked away. I walked alone into my dark apartment. *The night had been magical. Why didn't he kiss me?*

Chapter Eight

MONDAY morning, Nicholas arrived at my apartment a little after eight thirty. I came to the door dragging my suitcase, which he looked at in wonder. "Did I tell you we'd be gone for five days or five weeks?"

"A woman needs more things."

"Playing the gender card," he said, smiling. "Let me get that." He lugged my massive bag down the stairs, opened his car trunk, and dropped it inside while I climbed into the passenger seat.

He turned to me and said, "Ready for an adventure?"

"I'm always ready for an adventure," I said.

On the way to the airport, Nicholas asked, "When was the last time you flew?"

"About eleven years ago. It was my honeymoon."

"Where did you go?"

"We went to Disneyland."

The airport was thick with travelers.

"Is it always this crowded?" I said.

"It's the season. The airports are always crazy during the holidays." He looked at me. "Are you afraid of flying?"

"No," I said, shaking my head. "I'm afraid of . . . *not* flying."

"What do you mean?"

"As long as you're in the air, there's no problem, right? It's coming back to earth that's the problem."

He grinned. "I think you just said something profound about life."

OUR flight was direct from Salt Lake to JFK. Nicholas had booked two first-class tickets. I had never flown first-class before.

We boarded before the throng of passengers surrounding the gate.

"So this is how the other half lives," I said, sitting back in the wide, padded seat.

"When you fly as much as I do, it's more of a necessity than a luxury."

"It's still luxury," I said.

I must have looked a little nervous as the plane took off because he reached over and took my hand. Or maybe he just wanted to hold my hand. I hoped for the latter.

"Is our hotel in the city?" I asked.

"We're staying at the Parker Meridien on Fifty-Sixth. It's a nice hotel. French. It's only six blocks from Rockefeller Center."

"That's where the big Christmas tree is," I said.

He nodded. "And we're only one block from Fifth Avenue."

The flight was just a little over four hours. Nicholas fell asleep shortly after they served us lunch. As hard as he worked, I wasn't surprised. Even though I hadn't slept well the night before, I couldn't sleep on the plane. I was too excited. Nicholas didn't wake until we began our descent. He rubbed his eyes,

The Mistletoe Promise   171

then checked his watch. "I slept for two hours. Why didn't you wake me?"

"You needed the sleep," I said.

After we had disembarked, I followed Nicholas through the labyrinth of JFK to get our luggage. Next to the baggage carousel was a man in a black suit holding a sign with my name on it.

"Is that for me?" I asked, which I realized was a foolish question.

"Of course," Nicholas said.

"I've never had someone holding a sign for me."

The man took our bags, and we followed him out into the cold to a black Lincoln Town Car. The ride took us across the Triborough Bridge into Manhattan, which gave us a clear view of the city's famous skyline. "Is that the Empire State Building?" I asked, pointing at a tall building lit red and green.

Nicholas nodded. "They light it for the season."

The Parker Meridien was just off Sixth Avenue. The lobby was spacious with a modern European design and a wry sense of humor. The elevators had televisions that played old Charlie Chaplin movies or *Tom and Jerry* cartoons, and the room's DO NOT DISTURB sign was a long hanger that read FUGGETABOUTIT.

After Nicholas checked us in, a bellman brought our bags to our rooms on the eleventh floor, just two doors from each other.

For dinner we ate Thai food at a tiny restaurant near the hotel. We said good night to each other outside my hotel room.

"I need to do some prep work for tomorrow," Nicholas said. "So I'll see you in the morning. My meetings begin at nine. If you'd like to have breakfast together, there's Norma's on the main floor. Or you can sleep in and order room service. Whatever you want."

"I want to be with you," I said.

He looked pleased with my reply. "I'll knock on your door at seven forty-five." He kissed me on the cheek. "Sleep tight."

I shut my door and lay down on top of the bed thinking about how happy I was. I had never had so much fun.

There was only one week left on our contract.

I DIDN'T FALL ASLEEP until after two, so I was tired when Nicholas knocked on my door at a quarter to eight. He looked sharp in his suit and tie.

"You look nice," I said. "Very professional." I didn't. I had just pulled on some jeans and a sweater.

"Shall we go?"

Norma's was a hip restaurant located in the hotel's lobby. I looked over the menu. "So many choices. Everything looks good."

"They're famous for their breakfasts."

"Oh my," I said, laughing. "Look at this. The Zillion-Dollar Lobster Frittata. It's a thousand dollars."

"That's with ten ounces of sevruga caviar," he said. "Read what it says underneath the price."

"Norma dares you to expense this." I looked up. "What would you do if I ordered that?"

"Cancel tonight's dinner."

"I'll get something else," I said quickly. "Who are you meeting with this morning?"

"It's a software company called Revelar. They're buying up a competitor, and I'm here to make sure that they cross their *t*'s and dot their *i*'s. What are you going to do today?"

"I'm not sure yet. I thought I'd walk around and see the sights."

"You could take a tour of the Empire State Building. Also, you're not far from Fifth Avenue, where all the good shopping is—Saks, Tiffany's, Prada. I'll be done a little after four. I made reservations for six at Keens Steakhouse. Then I thought we'd take in a show."

"What are we going to see?"

"That's a surprise." He looked at his watch. "I better go." He downed his coffee, then stood. "I'll see you this afternoon." He stopped and turned back. "I almost forgot." He handed me his credit card. "Have fun."

I just looked at it. "What am I supposed to do with it?"

"Use it."

I watched him walk out. Then I put the card in my pocket and ordered another cup of hot chocolate.

I WENT back to my room to finish getting ready; then I took a taxi to the Empire State

Building and rode the elevator one hundred two floors to the top observation deck. It was amazing to look out over the entire city. Afterward I walked a few blocks to Macy's, joining the throngs of sightseers gathered in front of the store to see the famous animated holiday windows. The theme was the Magic of Christmas, which seemed appropriate for me this year.

I got into a taxi to go back to the hotel but, on a whim, asked the driver for a recommendation for a good place to eat lunch. He was from São Paulo, and he took me to a café in Little Brazil just a block off Sixth Avenue. The stew my waiter recommended was different but good. To drink I had a sugarcane juice mixed with pineapple juice. I walked the ten blocks back to the hotel, undressed, and took a nap. I woke to my room phone ringing.

"I'm sorry I'm late," Nicholas said. "Our meetings went long."

"What time is it?" I asked, sitting up.

"Did I wake you?"

"Yes."

"It's almost five. We should leave for dinner in a half hour."

"I'll be ready." I got out of bed, splashed water on my face, and dressed in a nicer outfit. I was putting on makeup when he knocked. I opened the door. He was wearing his suit but with a fresh shirt and his collar open. He looked handsome. He always looked handsome.

KEENS Steakhouse was in the Garment District between Fifth and Sixth avenues, though, at the time of its founding in 1885, the area was considered the Theater District.

The restaurant was crowded, and the inside was paneled in dark mahogany, covered with framed black-and-white pictures, creating the ambience of a nineteenth-century gentlemen's club. The tables were close together, skirted with white linen cloths.

Nicholas ordered a half-dozen oysters on the shell, which I tried but didn't care for. Then I had tomatoes and onions with blue Stilton cheese, and we shared a Chateaubriand steak for two. The food was incredible.

"What's that on the ceiling?" I asked.

He looked up. "Clay smoking pipes. Every

one is numbered. In the old days you would request your pipe, and they would find it by its number and bring it to your table. I'm not sure how many pipes are still up there, but I've heard more than eighty thousand. They belonged to people like Teddy Roosevelt, Babe Ruth, Albert Einstein, Buffalo Bill Cody, pretty much everybody who was famous came here. Except the women. It used to be that women weren't allowed inside. It took a lawsuit from King Edward the Seventh's paramour to open it to women."

Our conversation was interrupted by my cell phone ringing. "Sorry, I forgot to turn it off," I said. I glanced at the screen, then quickly pressed the power button.

"Was it important?"

"No. It was Dan."

"Does he call you often?"

"No. More lately since his wife left him."

"His wife," Nicholas said. "The one that was your friend?"

I nodded. "Kayla."

"And he wants a shoulder to cry on?"

"He wants more than a shoulder. He wants to get back together."

"He told you that?"

"After he reminded me that it was my fault he divorced me."

"Your fault?"

I nodded. "Because of—" I caught myself. "It doesn't matter," I said. "There's no way I would ever go back to him."

Nicholas nodded. "Good," he said. "You deserve better than him. So what did you do today?"

"I went to the top of the Empire State Building. Then I walked to Macy's and looked at their windows; then I went to a café in Little Brazil for lunch and had this interesting stew. I don't remember what it's called, but the waiter said it's the Brazilian national dish."

"It's called *feijoada*," Nicholas said.

I looked at him in amazement. "Is there anything you don't know?"

He shook his head. "I don't know."

I laughed. "You are the smartest person I know."

"Then you must not know many people," he replied.

After we finished dessert, he glanced down at his watch. "We better get going."

"Where are we going?"

"Radio City Music Hall."

THE cab dropped us off a half block away from Radio City. The sign on the marquee read:

The Radio City Christmas Spectacular
Featuring the Rockettes

We picked up our tickets and found our seats in the fifth row of the middle section. The room buzzed with excitement. Nicholas leaned into me. "I think you'll like this."

"Have you seen it before?"

"No. But I've heard good things about it. Everyone needs to see the Rockettes at least once in their lifetime."

"When I think of the Rockettes, I just think of legs," I said.

He laughed. "Well, that's what they're famous for. And dancing."

There were fourteen musical numbers, concluding with a living nativity, the Wise Men arriving at the manger on a caravan of real camels. The showstopper was the fifth act, "The Parade of the Wooden Soldiers," when, in the finale, a cannon shot knocked the dancers over like a line of dominoes. As the curtain fell, the crowd joined in singing "Joy to the World."

The temperature outside had dropped to well below freezing, and Nicholas pulled me in close as we walked back to our hotel. I only wished that it was farther away.

I SLEPT in the next morning. Nicholas had a breakfast meeting with his client, so he left without waking me. He had left a note under my door asking if I would do him a favor and pick up something for him at Tiffany on Fifth Avenue. I had already planned on shopping. I wanted to get something for Nicholas.

I ordered room service, which was another first for me, then sat in a robe near the window looking out over the city while I ate my oatmeal brûlée. I felt a long way from Montezuma Creek.

After breakfast, I took a cab to the Metropolitan Museum. Since I had started working at ICE, I had purchased more than a thousand tickets for the museum, but I had never been there. I went into the sales office and met my sales representative, Justin, who was demonstrably excited to meet me after all these years. He was flamboyant, chubby, and bald and looked nothing like I expected.

He insisted on taking me on a personal tour of the museum's highlights. The breadth of the collection was stunning. I was amazed to see actual Picassos and Rembrandts and van Goghs.

Around two o'clock, I thanked Justin and took a cab to the Montblanc store on Madison Avenue. As I looked over a display of pens, one of the sales personnel approached me. "May I help you?"

"Hi," I said. "I need to buy a gift for a friend. A pen."

"Male or female?" he asked.

"Male. And he's a lawyer."

He smiled a little at my description. "I can find you something that will impress him. How much were you thinking of spending?"

I swallowed. Many of the pens were in excess of a thousand dollars. I lightly grimaced. "About five hundred dollars."

The man just nodded. "We'll find him a pen he'll never forget."

Even though the price of the pen was just a fraction of what Nicholas had spent on me, it was nearly all my savings. But it was something I wanted to do for him. It wasn't the amount of money he'd spent on me as much as it was the way he'd done it. Lovingly. He had shown me more love than my own husband and my own father ever had. In our pretend affair, he had opened my eyes to what a real relationship could and should be.

"I recommend this one," the man said, delicately presenting me a pen. "We just got it in. This is our Bohème Marron pen. The rollerball is a bit more practical than the fountain pen, and better priced."

"It's pretty," I said. "Is that a gem?"

"Yes. It's a brown topaz."

"How much is it?"

"It's five hundred and twenty-five dollars, plus tax."

"Okay," I said. "I read that you can engrave something on it."

"Yes, ma'am."

"How long does that take?"

"It usually takes a day or two."

"Is it possible to do it any sooner? I was hoping to give it to him this evening."

He smiled at me. "If you can come back in an hour, I'll walk it over to the engraver myself. What would you like engraved on it?"

I thought for a moment, then said, "Love, Elise."

"Let me get an order form." He wrote down my words, then showed it to me for approval and a signature. I gave him my credit card. "Very well, Ms. Elise, I will have this for you in one hour."

"Thank you."

I left Montblanc and walked a block to the famous Tiffany store. I went up to the first sales counter I saw. "I'm here to pick something up that a friend of mine has purchased."

"What name would that be under?" she said.

"Nicholas Derr," I said.

"Just a moment." She typed something into her computer, then walked away from the counter, returning about five minutes later. "Mr. Derr requested that the gift remained wrapped," she said. "I will need to see some ID."

"Of course." I brought out my wallet. "There's my license."

She looked at it. "Elise Dutton." She looked at the receipt on the box. "Very good." She handed me back my license, then the box. "Let me get you a bag for that." She lifted the famous robin's egg blue bag and set the box inside. "Thank you for visiting us."

I walked back to Montblanc, picked up the pen, then walked the four blocks to the hotel. My phone rang on the way. I was excited to talk to Nicholas but disappointed when I saw it was Dan calling.

"What do you want, Dan?"

"We need to talk, Elise. I've discovered some things about your new *friend*. So open your door."

"I'm not home. I'm in New York."

He paused. "What are you doing in New York?"

"Living," I said. I hung up on him. He

called back, but I didn't answer. Then he texted me.

> We need to talk about your lawyer "friend." Crucial

I shook my head. There wasn't a thing he could tell me that I would consider crucial. Still, his text made me curious. What could Dan possibly know about Nicholas? Then my phone rang again. I was going to tell Dan to stop calling when I saw it was Nicholas.

"Hi," I said.

"Hi. Are you at the hotel?"

"Not yet. I'm just walking back."

"Good. We have dinner reservations at six. We should leave a half hour before."

"I'll be ready," I said. "What are we having for dinner?"

"How does Italian sound?"

"I love Italian."

"You'll love this place," he said. "See you in a few minutes."

NICHOLAS knocked on my door at five thirty. He smiled when I opened. "Hi."

"How was your day?" I asked.

"Challenging. But let's not talk about it."

"Let me grab my coat," I said. "Just a minute."

"Did you get a chance to run by Tiffany's?" he asked.

"Yes. Let me grab that for you." I put on my coat, secretly put the Montblanc box in my purse, then brought over the Tiffany bag.

"Thanks for picking that up for me."

"No problem."

"I better leave it in my room," he said. "I'll be right back." He walked to his room, then returned empty-handed. "Shall we go?"

We had to wait awhile for a cab, and we arrived a few minutes late for our dinner reservation. The restaurant Nicholas had decided on was called Babbo, and it had a famous chef, Mario Batali. The atmosphere was elegant with, incongruently, loud rock music.

Everything was exquisite. I ordered a Calabrian wine called Cirò with my meal. Nicholas ordered sparkling water. After the waiter left, I asked, "Do you drink?"

He shook his head and said, "No," but nothing more.

The evening passed quietly between us. Nicholas seemed a little lost in thought, something I attributed to his "challenging" day.

As we were finishing our meals, Nicholas said, "Did you recognize who's sitting behind me?"

I looked over his shoulder. "Is that really Kevin Bacon?"

He nodded. "And his wife, Kyra Sedgwick. That's one thing about New York. It's a cultural mecca. Now you can say you've been one degree from Kevin Bacon. Did you enjoy your meal?"

"Immensely. I don't think I'll ever be able to eat store-bought spaghetti sauce again. What was that last dish you had?"

"Lamb's brain Francobolli."

I just looked at him. "I can't tell if you're kidding me or not."

He smiled. "I'm not. They're famous for some interesting fare. But there was a reason I chose this place besides the food."

"And what was that?"

"Just a moment," he said. He stood up

and left the table. He returned a couple minutes later and sat down. "I have something for you." He brought from his pocket the Tiffany box I had picked up earlier and set it in front of me.

"That was for me?"

"Of course."

I took the beautiful blue box, untied its ribbon, and lifted the lid. Inside was a velvet jewelry box. "What did you do?" I asked.

"Keep going," he said.

I pried open the box's lid. Inside was an exquisite, conical rose gold pendant, about an inch long, with elegant spiraled lines. I gasped.

"Do you like it?"

I looked up at him. "It's beautiful."

"It's from Paloma Picasso's collection," he said. "It was inspired by the hanging lanterns of Venice. That's why I thought it was appropriate we had Italian for dinner."

"This is too much."

"I know," he said. "Try it on."

I lifted the pendant from the box. "Would you help me put it on?"

"I'd love to," he said. He stood and walked around the table. I lifted the back of my hair as he draped the chain around my neck. The pendant fell to the top of my cleavage.

"I've never had anything so nice before," I said.

"Then it's about time," he said.

I stood up and hugged him. "Thank you."

"I'm glad you like it."

"I don't like it—I love it."

We finished our desserts, olive oil and rosemary cake with a pistachio gelato; then we took a cab to Rockefeller Center to see the tree. Even though it was cold enough to see our breath, I left my coat open to reveal my new necklace.

The eighty-foot tree was brilliantly lit, and the plaza was crowded with tourists. Beneath the statue of Prometheus, skaters glided gracefully, and some not so gracefully, across the rink.

We had been there for a while when I said, "I have something for you too."

Nicholas looked at me in surprise. "You do?"

"Remember when we signed the contract, I asked you if you had a pen? You said, 'I'm a lawyer. That's like asking me if I have a lung.'"

He grinned. "And you made a snarky remark about me not having a heart."

"I was wrong," I said. "You're all heart." I took the pen from my purse and handed it to him.

"What's this?"

"It's a present."

He unwrapped the box. "You bought me a Montblanc pen." He looked up at me. "Elise, this is way too expensive."

"It's nothing compared to what you've spent on me."

"You can't . . ."

I touched his lips. "Remember when you got mad at me for complaining you spend too much? Now I'm telling you the same thing. I know it's not much in your world, but it's all I have. Please let me enjoy this."

He just stood there quietly as the world noisily swirled around us. He looked deeply affected. "Thank you."

"I just wanted to give you something that you would use. And maybe when you saw it, you would think of me. And remember this time that we had together."

"I don't need a pen for that," he said softly. "Thank you for bringing me to New York.

Thank you for everything you've done this season. I don't know why you've done all this, but thank you."

"You still don't know why?"

I dared not say what I hoped, that he felt about me the way I did about him. That he loved me. We gazed into each other's eyes, then he put his hand behind my head and gently pulled me into him and we kissed. Then we kissed and kissed. It was the first time I'd kissed anyone in years, but I'd never kissed anyone like that in my entire life. I had never felt more swept away, more lost in someone else. When we parted, I said breathlessly, "So much for the platonic clause."

"Men can't have platonic relationships."

We kissed again. In spite of my best efforts, I'd done exactly what I knew I shouldn't. I'd fallen deeply in love with a man who was going to leave me.

WE WALKED back to the hotel holding hands. We stopped outside my room and kissed again.

"Do you want to come inside?" I asked.

"Desperately." He breathed out slowly. "But I better not."

We kissed some more, and then I reluctantly pulled back a little, just until our lips were apart, our noses still touching.

"Thank you for tonight. For everything. I love my necklace."

"I love *you*," he said.

The words shocked me. I pulled back and looked at him. As much as I had wanted to hear those words, I hadn't expected to. Emotion welled up inside me. Of course I loved him, but he couldn't love me.

"What's wrong?" he said.

I couldn't speak. I quickly ducked inside my room, leaving him standing in the hallway. I fell on my bed and cried. I felt confused, torn by two equally powerful emotions, joy for being loved and fear of being loved, horrified by the truth that he'd fallen in love with someone he didn't really know and wouldn't love once he did.

Chapter Nine

I woke the next morning crying. I had had a terrible nightmare. Nicholas and I had gotten married. I was in an elegant ivory wedding dress; he was in tails with a wing-tip shirt and red band tie. We ran from the church to a car decorated by our guests, climbed inside, and drove off. Nicholas looked in the mirror. "What's that?"

"What's what, dear?" I asked.

"In the backseat. There's a box or some-thing." We both turned around. In the back-seat was my daughter's coffin.

I LOOKED in the mirror at my necklace. It was the most beautiful piece of jewelry I had ever owned. Even my wedding ring paled in comparison. But I couldn't keep it. Just like I couldn't keep him.

Nicholas called my room three times the next morning. I didn't answer. I was too afraid. Finally he knocked on my door. "Elise," he asked through the door. "Are you all right?"

I should have answered the phone, I thought. Now he was going to see me, puffy eyes and all.

"Elise, are you all right?"

I opened the door just enough to see him. "I'm okay," I said.

He looked at me anxiously. "What's wrong?"

"It's nothing," I said. "We can talk later after your meetings."

He said, "I meant what I said last night. I do love you."

My eyes welled up. "I know."

"I'll be back soon. We'll talk. Everything will be all right."

"Okay," I said.

He walked off down the hall. I dressed and went out. I wandered around Central Park. I tried to calm myself, but the fear didn't leave. It had been with me for so long it didn't take eviction lightly.

After all the attacks and abandonment I'd endured since Hannah's death, my heart wasn't about to believe that someone might be different, even someone as beautiful as Nicholas.

Nicholas came back to the hotel at four, and we went to dinner at a restaurant close by, the Redeye Grill. We started with small talk. He waited until we had eaten before asking, "Elise, what's wrong?"

I didn't answer. I was afraid to answer.

"Was it because I told you that I love you?"

I slowly nodded.

He frowned deeply. "And you don't love me."

"I'm madly in love with you," I said.

His look of sadness gave way to a smile. "Then what's the problem?"

"You can't really love me," I said. "You don't know me."

"I know you," he said. "I know that in spite of a harsh childhood you're kind and giving. I know that you give more than you take. I know that you're grateful for the smallest acts of kindness. And I know that I can't live without you. What more do I need to know?"

My eyes welled up with pain. "There's something you don't know about me. Something I've done. Something horrible."

He looked at me, then said, "Does it have to do with Hannah?"

EVERY part of me froze. When I could speak, I asked, "How do you know about Hannah?"

He didn't answer. I felt as if my skin had been flayed, my innermost parts exposed to the world. "How long have you known this?" I asked. "Did you know before the contract?"

He gazed at me anxiously, then said softly, "I knew long before the contract."

"How?"

He looked down for a moment, then said, "We've met before."

"I've never met you before."

"Yes, we have," he said. "But in the state you were in, I doubt you would remember. I wouldn't have." After a pause he said, "Do you remember that I told you I worked for the prosecutor's office?" He paused again. "I had been there about a year when we got a call from the Salt Lake County Sheriff's Office saying a child had been left in a car and died of hyperthermia. They weren't sure whether to arrest the mother. I was sent out to assess the situation."

Suddenly I knew who he was. Tears welled up in my eyes. "You're the man who interviewed me."

He nodded. "I knew it was an accident the moment I saw you. And that no punishment the justice system could dish out would be as bad as what you were already experiencing. I went back and convinced them not to prosecute."

His words rushed through me, freezing me like ice. No, broken ice. I felt shattered and pierced. "You knew the whole time."

He warily gazed into my eyes, then slowly nodded.

"Have you been stalking me for all these years?"

"Of course not. A couple of months ago, I saw you in the elevator. I knew I recognized you; I just didn't remember from where. After I got out I remembered."

For several minutes I was speechless. "Why did you lie to me?"

"I didn't lie to you."

"You withheld the truth. That's the same as a lie."

"It wasn't important."

I stared at him incredulously. "It wasn't important? It was to me. How could you be so cruel?"

He looked stunned. "Elise . . ."

"I need to go," I said.

"Elise, please."

"I need to go," I repeated. "Now."

"All right. We'll go."

"Alone," I said.

He looked at me for a moment, then nodded. "All right."

I retrieved my coat from the coat check and walked alone back to the hotel.

THE night passed in a strange delirium. Nothing was what I thought it was. My Nicholas, my beautiful, safe fantasy man, was an intricate part of my worst nightmare. He was part of my past, and whether he had intended to or not, he had reengulfed me in it.

The next morning, Nicholas called me several times, but I didn't answer. The fourth time he left a message. "Elise, your flight to Salt Lake leaves at two ten. It's an hour ride to the airport, so you better leave by noon. I booked a car. It will be downstairs waiting for you at twelve. It will have a sign in the window with your name. Don't worry about checking out; I'll take care of everything.

"I won't be going with you. I'm going to stay here for an extra day so you can have time to think. I'm sorry for hurting you. I didn't mean to. I would never intentionally hurt you. I hope you can forgive me." Then he said something I didn't understand. "Please have faith in me. I understand your pain better than you know."

Hearing his voice intensified my emotion. I sat on the floor of the shower crying for nearly an hour, the water pouring over me, mixing with my tears and carrying them to the drain.

Part of me wanted to run to Nicholas for comfort. To be held and loved and protected by him. The other half wanted to deny ever knowing him and everything that had happened since the contract.

I packed my bag. A few minutes before twelve, I dragged my bag out of the room. I stole a glance at Nicholas's door. I hoped he would be watching for me, but he wasn't.

The elevator door opened into the lobby, and I walked out to the street. A black town car was waiting at the curb with a sign that read DUTTON. The bellman put my bag in the trunk, and I cried as the car pulled away from the hotel.

"Are you okay, ma'am?" the driver asked.

I shook my head. "No."

He didn't say anything more.

My flight landed in Salt Lake a few minutes before five. I retrieved my bag, then took a cab back to my apartment. I poured myself a glass of wine and drank it. Then another. It had been a long time since I'd drunk to get drunk, but that's exactly what I was doing. Then I lay down on my bed and cried myself to sleep.

The next day was Saturday. I lay in bed until almost one in the afternoon. My head ached. I wondered if Nicholas had made it back to Salt Lake. I missed him as much as I feared him. I hoped he would call, but he never did.

MY DOORBELL rang twice on Christmas Eve. Both times filled me with anticipation. The first time was the UPS man delivering a package from New York. It was from Nicholas. I supposed it was my last gift. I couldn't bring myself to open it.

The second time the doorbell rang was later that afternoon. I was sure it was Nicholas. I took a deep breath before looking through my door's peephole. Dan was standing outside.

I pulled open the door. "What do you want?"

"Glad you finally decided to come home," he said.

"What do you want?" I repeated.

"I told you what I want. I want us again. The way it should be."

"And I told you I wasn't interested."

"Why? Because you think you're in love?"

"No," I said. "It's over."

"So things didn't work out with the lawyer in New York."

I didn't answer.

"Well, it's for the better. With a past like his, you didn't want to get mixed up with that guy anyway."

"What are you talking about?" I said.

"Will you let me in? It's freezing out here."

I stepped back from the door, and he walked in. He sat on my sofa. "Your lawyer is not who you think he is."

"No one ever is," I said.

"That's where you're wrong," Dan said. "I am. With me, what you see is what you get."

"You mean a narcissistic cheater," I said.

He grinned. "Looks like you've finally grown some attitude. So let me tell you about your *friend*. He's a first-class loser."

Hearing this made me angry. "No, he's nothing like you."

"Then you won't mind me telling you that he's a drunk."

I shook my head. "He doesn't even drink."

"Then maybe he stopped after he killed the family."

I looked at him. "What are you talking about?"

"Your friend was driving drunk when he crashed his car into a family crossing a crosswalk. Two parents and two children. He killed three of them."

"You're a liar."

"I brought proof. I printed it off the Internet."

He unfolded a piece of paper from his coat pocket and handed it to me.

For Three Deaths Teen Gets Two Years

Nicholas Derr, a 16-year-old Highland High School student, was sentenced to juvenile detention for up to two years after admitting Monday that he killed three and injured one in a DUI accident.

There were shouts of protest in 3rd District Juvenile Court when Judge Anders handed down the sentence.

"He kills three people and he's out in just two years?" said Mark Buhler, a friend of the deceased family. "Where's the justice? Is that all their lives are worth?"

Derr had a blood-alcohol level of 0.10 percent; the Utah legal limit is 0.08. Derr and a friend (name withheld) were driving down 2100 south from a Parley's Canyon party where alcohol was being served when his vehicle struck the Hayes family in a crosswalk just north of Sugar House Park at 8:41 p.m. on December 7.

Vance Hayes (28), Michelle Hayes (27), and their two daughters, Olivia (3) and Victoria (1), were leaving the park when witnesses say that Derr ran a red light and struck the family. The children were in a double stroller. Derr's car was estimated to be traveling nearly twice the speed limit of the 30 mph zone. The father and one-year-old were killed instantly. The mother was DOA at University of Utah Hospital. Only the three-year-old survived. She sustained multiple broken bones and internal injuries, but doctors believe she will recover. Derr and his friend were uninjured.

Derr, who had just received his driver's license two weeks before the accident, pleaded guilty to three counts of second-degree felony automobile homicide and one count of negligent injury. Derr has no previous DUIs.

"He's a good kid," a neighbor said of Derr. "He mows the lawn of a widow on our street and shovels her walk in the winter. One time some bullies were picking on my son and Nick protected him. I don't know what happened with this accident. He made some bad choices, like any kid could."

Earlier this month, Judge Anders decided against ordering Derr to stand trial in adult court, where the teen would have faced up to 30 years at Utah State Prison. Derr will be eligible for parole in as few as twenty-four months.

I looked at the picture of an upside-down car and an area cordoned off with police tape. Then I looked up at Dan. His dark eyes brimmed with satisfaction. "Looks like the two of you have more in common than you thought."

"Get out of here," I said.

"Don't kill the messenger, honey."

"Get out of here!" I screamed.

He looked at me for a moment, then stood. "I should've figured. Two killers, no jail time. You're perfect for each other."

I slapped him so hard my hand stung. "Don't you ever call me that again!" I shouted. "Do you hear me? Never call me that again!"

Dan was stunned. The imprint of my hand was fresh on his cheek. "I've paid a thousand times over for my mistake. I have suffered for something that I would give my life to have prevented. I would have traded my life for hers, but I can't. But you will not hold this over my head anymore. Do you understand?"

He didn't answer.

"Do you understand me?"

"Yes, 'Lise."

"Now get out of here."

He slowly turned his back on me. He had just walked out the door when I shouted after him, "And you're right. Nicholas and I *are* perfect for each other." I slammed the door shut after him.

For the first time since the day Hannah died, I felt free. And I fully understood why Nicholas had been so good to me. He understood. He had weathered the same fierce storm.

I grabbed the package he'd sent and tore back the paper to reveal a satin box marked WATERFORD CRYSTAL. I lifted the lid. Inside the red-velvet-lined box was a crystal Christmas ornament. A star. Next to the star was a scrolled parchment note tied with ribbon. I untied the ribbon and unrolled the note. It was written in Nicholas's hand.

My dear Elise,

It's been said that the Magi, wise men, gazed up into the night skies, following a star. But they were not looking for a star.

They were looking for hope. Light is not found in dark places, and hope is not found looking down or looking back. May you always look up. It has been my great joy spending this holiday season with you. And though things did not end between us as I hoped, I will always hope the best for you and be forever grateful for your love. I will always love you.

Nick

When I arrived at Nicholas's home, I knocked on his door, then rang his doorbell, but he didn't answer. I guessed he had gone somewhere. I sat on the cold concrete porch to wait. The temperature dropped with the sun until it was well below freezing. I shivered with cold, but I wasn't going to leave.

It was after dark when Nicholas's car turned in to his driveway. His garage door opened, but he saw me and stopped before pulling in. He got out and walked up to me. "What are you doing here?"

My chin quivered with the cold. "We had a date. Remember?"

He said, "That was before you said I was cruel and ran away."

My words pierced me. "I came to apologize."

For a moment he seemed unsure of what to say. "How long have you been waiting here?"

"Three hours."

"You must be freezing."

I nodded, my body involuntarily shuddering with the suggestion.

He put out his hand. "Come in and get warm."

He unlocked the front door, and we stepped into the foyer. His home was warm and dark, illuminated only by the colorful blinking strands of his Christmas tree. He led me to a den, told me to sit on the sofa, and then left the room. I could hear him moving around in the kitchen. He returned carrying a mug. "Drink this. It's hot cider."

"Thank you," I said, taking the cup from him with both hands. I sipped the hot drink while he sat down backward on the piano bench. The warm drink spread through my body.

I didn't know what to say, and I'm not sure he did either because the silence was interminable. Finally I took a deep breath and said, "Dan came by to see me this afternoon. He's still trying to get me back. He thought he could scare me away from you with this." I set the newspaper article on the table between us.

Nicholas barely glanced at it. "And he didn't even need it. I scared you away without it." He took a deep breath. "And you think I owe you an explanation?"

"You don't owe me anything," I said.

"Then why are you here?"

The question stung, filling my eyes with tears. I bowed my head, afraid to show my eyes, afraid to look into his. "After reading the article, I realized that you really did understand me. And that you might be the only one in the world who could really love me."

He was silent for a moment, then said, "I'd like to explain what happened. I was sixteen years old, a sophomore in high school. My girlfriend had broken up with me. I was depressed and had pretty much taken to my bed, listening to music all night. A friend came over to cheer me up. He talked me into going to a party.

"They had a keg. Everyone was drunk or getting there. I resisted, at first. My parents were Mormon. I had never even drunk alcohol before. But between the peer pressure, my depression, and my friend nagging, I gave in. It was the worst mistake of my life. It didn't take much to get me drunk. I had maybe three beers. My friend was completely wasted, so I took his keys and drove us home."

I could see the pain grow in his eyes.

"We were coming down Parley's Canyon onto Twenty-First south. I was driving fast, close to sixty miles per hour, when I reached Sugar House Park. There was a family in the crosswalk. A mom, dad, a three- and a one-year-old in a double stroller. It was dark, and I was driving so fast I don't know if I would have seen them, but I hit them. The father was killed instantly. I hit him and his wife and clipped the stroller, then rolled the car into a telephone pole.

"The mother was thrown more than eighty feet, but somehow she was still alive when the ambulance arrived. I climbed out of the car and walked around the scene like I was in a nightmare, listening to the mother scream for her children. When I have night-mares, that's what I hear, that mother's screams." He looked into my eyes. "The three-year-old lived. Her name is Olivia. She's seventeen now."

I let the story settle over me. I asked, "Have you met her?"

"A year ago," he said softly. "I've taken flowers to the grave every year on the anni-versary of their deaths."

"December seventh," I said. "That's where you were."

He nodded. "Last year I was in the cem-etery, just kneeling there, praying for for-giveness, like I always do. When I stood, there was a teenage girl behind me. I hadn't heard her come up. She just looked at me for a moment, and then she said, 'It's you, isn't it?'

"I said, 'I'm so sorry.' She looked at me; then she said, 'I forgive you.'" Nicholas's eyes welled up. "The power of those words. I fell back to my knees and wept. Olivia was almost the same age I was when I took her parents and sister from her. I don't know how she did it. But she knelt next to me and held me. She said, 'You were just a kid, like me. Sometimes we do dumb things. Sometimes there are consequences.' I don't know how she found the strength to say that to the man who had killed her parents."

"What happened after the accident?" I asked.

"I was arrested. I was put in youth corrections for nineteen months—until my eighteenth birthday. It would have been longer—much longer—but because I was underage and it was my first offense, the judge ruled that I would be tried as an adolescent. A lot of people wanted me tried as an adult. Some of those people were waiting outside the juvie center with placards when I got out. They stood there and jeered at me. One called me a murderer."

"I understand," I said.

"I know you do. You also understand that even though the law was done with me, my punishment had just begun. I carried the weight of what I'd done every day of my life. My relationship with my parents changed. My trial had just about bankrupted them.

"My mother was severely depressed. She was very religious, and she blamed herself for what had happened. She felt like God was punishing her for being a bad mother. She became addicted to prescription medications. My dad tried to keep things together, but eventually it was too much for him too. My parents divorced. My brother and sister blamed me for destroying the family. Since then I've been alone. None of them will talk to me. My mother died of an overdose six years ago. It's been a long road. It seemed like anytime I started to feel happiness, the memory of the Hayeses' deaths or my mother's death would rise up to smack me back down.

"I don't know why I decided to go into law, maybe it was all the time I'd spent in court and working with lawyers, but I had an aptitude for it. I got the second highest LSAT score in the state of Utah. I focused all my energy on my career. I worked hard, not just to succeed, but because there was nothing else in my life.

"But no amount of success in my career could fill that hole inside me. It was always there. I never felt free to find joy until I met Olivia. That's when I decided I would find someone to spend my life with. I dated some, but I suppose I felt like you did. I didn't think they could comprehend or love the real me.

"When I saw you in that elevator, I was speechless. I knew you didn't recognize me, but I recognized you. I felt like, in some way, we were kindred spirits. I wanted to know you better."

"That's why you came up with the contract," I said.

"It seemed like a safe way to get close without hurting anyone. But then I fell in love." He looked into my eyes. "It wasn't hard. You're very lovable."

I looked at him gratefully but didn't speak.

"I wanted to protect you," he said. "From the world and from your past. But I'm part of that past, so that meant protecting you from me as well. I know I should have told you, but the stronger my feelings grew, the more afraid I was of losing you. I was fighting the same demon you were—I wondered whether you would reject me too if you knew the real me."

"I'm sorry I left you. You've had enough abandonment from those you loved." My voice fell with shame. "You didn't need it from me." I looked down as the emotion of the moment filled me. Then I looked back up into his eyes. "Could you still love me?"

It seemed an eternity that we gazed into each other's eyes, and then Nicholas came over to me and we embraced. Then we kissed. Passionately. Honestly. For the first time, we kissed without masks. When our lips parted, I whispered, "I want to renew the contract."

He said, "It's got to be a different contract." He leaned back to look into my eyes. "We need to change the expiration date."

"To what?" I asked.

"In perpetuity."

I laughed. "You sound like such a lawyer."

"I am," he replied. "And no more platonic clause. It's definitely not going to be platonic."

A wide smile crossed my lips. "No," I said. "It's definitely not going to be platonic." I looked deep into his eyes. "In perpetuity?"

He nodded. "This time you really are signing your soul away."

I looked at him and said, "All right, Mr. Lawyer. Got a pen?"

Epilogue

NICHOLAS and I were married the next spring in a small Italian village called Greve, nineteen miles south of Florence, in the Chianti wine district. It was a very small wedding. My sister, Cosette, and her husband, Ron, came. From the law firm there were Alan and Careen McKay and Scott and Sharon Hitesman. From ICE, Zoey was there.

The biggest surprise of our wedding day was the arrival of Nicholas's sister, Sheridan. She came without telling him. And she came to forgive. I don't think his joy could have been more full. To this day, it's one of the few times I've seen Nicholas cry. We still have hopes that his brother might someday forgive him as well.

After our wedding, we honeymooned in Rome and Sorrento and on Capri and the Amalfi coast. When we got back to our home in Utah, there was a special wedding gift waiting for me—a Lladró of Cinderella and her pumpkin carriage. It was perfect.

I no longer work at ICE. I quit two months after I found out I was pregnant. I'm due next February, coincidentally the same month my Hannah was born.

Life is good. I'd be lying if I said that I had stopped being haunted by ghosts or trying myself in the court of regret. But things are different. The judge and jury are more merciful. After all these years, they are willing to listen to reason. And in court I'm no longer arguing my case alone. I found myself a pretty good lawyer.

VAUGHAN'S amnesia prevents
him from remembering anything
about the wife he is divorcing. So
he falls for her all over again.

Chapter 1

I REMEMBER when I was a child I used to watch a television program called *Mr. & Mrs.* We all did; it seemed like the only option available, so everyone just put up with it. We all watched the procession of unglamorous couples go through the embarrassment of revealing all the little things that they didn't know about each other. Or worse still, that there weren't any.

If they had wanted to increase the ratings, perhaps they should have done more research about the big stuff the partners didn't know. "So, Geoff, do you think that Julie's favorite way to spend a Saturday night is: (a) Watching television? (b) Going to the cinema? Or (c) Secretly meeting her illicit lover Gerald?"

But the subtext of *Mr. & Mrs.* was that all there was to marriage was knowing each other very well. Like two lifers sharing a prison cell, you spent so much time in each other's company that there shouldn't be anything that might surprise either of you.

My marriage was not like that.

Lots of husbands forget things. They forget that their wives had an important meeting that morning, or they forget to pick up the dry cleaning, or they forget to buy their wife a birthday present until the night before. It drives their partners mad that men can be so self-obsessed as to overlook a major event in the life of their other half.

I didn't suffer from this careless absent-mindedness. I just completely forgot who my wife was. Her name, her face, our history together was all wiped, leaving me with no knowledge that she even existed. In my defense, it wasn't just my wife I forgot; it was everything else as well. During the dark ages of my amnesia I had no idea who i was either. I had no memory of friends, family, personal experience, or identity; I didn't even know what my name was.

My BIZARRE reawakening occurred on a London underground train at some point after it had emerged into the daylight. It was a drizzly afternoon in the autumn. There was no blinding flash, just a creeping confusion about where I was. Not only did I not know where I was going, but I couldn't remember where I had come from. Am I going to work? What is my work? I don't know. The panic was rising inside me. I'm not well; I need to go home and go to bed. Where is home? I don't know where I live. Think! Think—it will come back to me!

"Come on—" I said out loud, intending to address myself by my own name. But the end of the sentence wasn't there. I searched for a wallet, a diary, a mobile phone, anything that might make it all fall back into place. My pockets were empty—just a train ticket and a bit of money. There was a small red stain on my jeans. I wondered how that got there. My brain had rebooted, but all the old files had been wiped.

I felt as lost and lonely as it is possible to be.

HALF an hour later, as the only person standing still in a teeming railway terminal, I scanned the boards for some route back to my previous life. Ceaseless information scrolled across screens, and distorted announcements filled my ears. I ventured into a public toilet just to stare into a mirror and was shocked by the age of the bearded stranger I saw frowning back at me. I guessed I was around forty, graying at the temples and thinning on top. I'd presumed I was somewhere in my early twenties.

Passersby just ignored my requests for help; eye contact was avoided, wired-up ears were deaf to my pleas. Trapped as I was in some suspended state, I think I learned the most basic human need of all—the reassurance that you are alive and will be acknowledged by other human beings.

My mental vacuum had physical symptoms; I was shaking and short of breath. I watched a rushing commuter aim an empty coffee cup at the trolley of a litter collector but then continue on her way when it fell to the floor. I picked it up and added it to the other rubbish that was being collected by the elderly Asian man.

"Thank you," he said.

"Um, excuse me, I think I've had some sort of stroke or something . . ." I said as I began to explain my predicament.

"You need the hospital. King Edward's is up the road," he said, pointing in the general direction. "I would take you there, but . . . I'd lose my job."

It was the first compassion anyone had shown me, and suddenly I felt like crying. Of course—medical help, I thought. That's what I need.

"Thank you! Thank you!" I gushed. I strode up to the busy main road like an alien from another planet, trying to take it all in, some of it strangely familiar, some of it completely bizarre. And then the towering concrete block ahead turned into the hospital and I felt my pace quicken, as if the people in there might somehow immediately make everything better.

"EXCUSE me—I really need to see a doctor," I gabbled at the front desk of Accident and Emergency. "I think I've had a sort of brain freeze or something. I can't remember who I am."

"Right. Could I take your name, please?"

There was a split second when I actually went to answer this question in the casual manner in which it had been posed.

"That's what I'm saying—I can't even remember my own name! It's like all personal information has suddenly been erased . . ."

"I see. Well, could I take your address then, please?"

"Um—sorry—I can't remember a single thing about myself."

The receptionist managed to look harassed and bored at the same time. "Right. Who's your doctor?"

"Well, *I don't know*, obviously. I can't remember where I live, where I work, or what my name is."

"I'm sorry, but we're not allowed to process you without asking these questions. Could you please provide the name and contact details for your spouse or next of kin?"

That's when I first noticed it. The indented ring of white flesh on my fourth finger. The ghostly scar where a wedding ring had been.

"Yes, next of kin! I have a wife maybe?" I said excitedly. Perhaps I had been robbed and concussed, and maybe my dear wife was looking for me right now. "Maybe my wife is calling all the hospitals, trying to find me," I said.

A week later I was still in the hospital waiting for her call.

I HAD A LABEL ON my wrist that said "unknown white male," though the hospital porters had dubbed me "Jason" after the fictional amnesiac in *The Bourne Identity*. However, it turned out that knowing nothing about yourself was not quite as exciting as it appeared in Hollywood blockbusters. My status seemed to have evolved from emergency inpatient to layabout lodger at King Edward's Hospital in West London.

I had no illness as such. I had been examined on the first day, but there was no logical explanation for why on Tuesday, October 22, my brain had suddenly decided to restore factory settings. I had been seen by a regular stream of doctors, neurologists, and attendant students, for whom I was paraded as something of a novelty. None of them had the faintest idea what had happened to me.

It only compounded my depression to realize that, at the moment, my best friend in the whole world was Annoying Bernard in the next bed. Bernard meant well; he wasn't unpleasant—in fact, he was unremittingly jolly. I just found it a bit wearing to have to spend twenty-four hours a day with someone who seemed to think that my neurological disorder could be overcome if I was just upbeat about the whole "bloomin' business."

"I tell you what, there's a few embarrassing things in my past that I wouldn't mind forgetting, I can tell you!" he chuckled.

Eventually one doctor seemed to take the lead on my case. Dr. Anne Lewington was a slightly mad-looking consultant neurologist in her fifties who made a point of seeing me every day. Under her supervision I had a brain scan, I had wires attached to my head, I had audiovisual stimuli tests; but in every case the activity in my brain was apparently "completely normal." It took me a day or two to work out that Dr. Lewington's excitement at my results bore no relation to understanding what had happened to me.

"Oooh, that's interesting! Both hippocampi are normal, the volumes of both entorhinal cortices and temporal lobes are normal."

"Right—so does that explain anything?"

"Nothing at all. That's what's so interesting! It would appear that your extra-personal memories have been consolidated in the neocortex independently of the medial temporal lobe."

"Is that good or bad?"

"Well, there's no discernible logic or pattern to any of it," she said, clapping her hands together in delight. "That's what makes it so utterly compelling!"

It was quite a few days before Dr. Lewington sat by my bed to explain what she thought had happened. She talked so quietly that Bernard was forced to turn off his radio on the other side of the curtain.

"From cases similar to your own, it seems that you have experienced a 'psychogenic fugue,' literally a 'flight' from your previous life, possibly triggered by extreme stress."

"A fugue?"

"Yes. This only happens to a handful of people every year. The loss of personal items was probably deliberate as you slipped into the 'fugue state,' and it's usual to have no recall of consciously abandoning all traces of your former life. Clearly, you have not forgotten everything, but typically with 'retrograde amnesia' the patient would know, say, who Princess Diana was, but might not know that she had died."

"Paris. 1998," I said, showing off a little.

"1997!" came Bernard's voice from the other side of the curtain.

"Your recall of these *extra-personal* memories suggests you stand a good chance of getting your *personal* memories back."

"But when exactly?"

"Thirty-first of August," said Bernard. "She was pronounced dead around four a.m."

Dr. Lewington had to concede that there was no guarantee that I would definitely recover. And so I was left wondering if I would ever make contact with my previous life again.

"Maybe you're a serial killer?" said Bernard's nonchalant voice.

"Sorry, Bernard, are you talking to me?"

"Well, she said it might have been caused by a need to shut out your past; perhaps you couldn't stand the torment of being an undetected murderer."

I dismissed Bernard's speculation as ridiculous, and then later that afternoon felt a flush of fear and guilt as I was informed that there were two policemen waiting for me in the ward sister's office. It turned out that they had come with a large file of "Missing Persons," which they now went through very slowly, staring carefully at each photo before looking studiously at me.

"Well, that one's clearly not me," I found myself interjecting, desperate to see if I was on any of the later pages.

"We have to give due consideration to every single file, sir."

"Yes, but I'm not that fat. Or black. Or a woman."

They reluctantly turned the page.

"Hmmm, what do you think?" said the officer, looking between my face and the photo of a wizened old pensioner.

"He's about eighty!" I objected.

"How long have you had that beard?"

"I don't know! My mind is a blank about everything prior to last Tuesday."

They shook their heads in exasperation then continued looking.

The fact that no one had reported me missing seemed to tell a story of its own. Had I been this lonely before my fugue? I wondered; had that been the stress that provoked my mental Etch A Sketch into shaking the screen clear to start again?

"Could we get something in the news-paper?" I kept suggesting to the ward sister. "A sort of 'Do you know this man?' feature next to my photo?" She eventually agreed that this might be a good idea, and I sat in her office while she rang the news desk at the *London Evening Standard*. I only heard her side of the conversation.

"They want to know if you are brilliant at the piano or anything like that?"

"Well—I can't remember."

The paper said they might run the story if we sent over all the details with an up-to-date photo. The next day there was a huge double spread headed "Who's the Mystery Man?" Beneath it was a picture of a well-groomed young man standing beside Pippa Middleton at a charity polo match. There was nothing about me. It transpired that they had been intending to run my story, but the editor had ruled that they couldn't have two "mystery man" stories in the same edition. The journalist who had taken our call was now on holiday, so the potential story was now assigned to another reporter.

"Tell me," she asked, "are you, like, really brilliant at the piano or anything?"

"LOOK, I GOT A BOOK for you from the newsagent's in the lobby," declared Bernard. He had decided that one way to trigger a memory of my own identity might be to read out every single male name in *Name Your Baby*.

During the course of that long afternoon it became clear why *Name Your Baby* has never been a huge hit as an audiobook. Sure, there are lots of characters, but none of them is ever developed. "Aaron," for example, has a walk-on part right at the beginning, but then we never hear from him again.

"I'm not sure you should lie down like that," said Bernard. "You're still really concentrating, aren't you?"

"I'm just closing my eyes so I can be sure there's nothing to distract me . . ."

I EVENTUALLY woke up to "Francis? Frank? Franklin?" Bernard was still declaring every name with extraordinary gusto and optimism. I had just had the same dream I'd experienced a couple of times now: a snapshot of a moment sharing laughter with a woman. I couldn't remember a face or a name, but she seemed to love me as I loved her. The sensation was pure happiness, and I was crushed when I awoke to the huge void that was my life right now.

"Garth? Garvin? Gary?"

And then something extraordinary happened. On hearing the word "Gary," I heard myself mumble "Zero-seven-seven-zero-zero."

"What was that?" said Bernard.

"I don't know," I said, sitting up. "It just came out when you said 'Gary.'"

"Is that it? Is that you? Are you *Gary?*"

"I don't think so. Say it again."

"Gary!"

"Zero-seven-seven-zero-zero . . ." There was more. "Nine-zero-zero . . . nine-zero-three." It just felt natural that those numbers followed that name.

"That's a telephone number!" said Bernard excitedly, writing it down.

We had discovered a fragment of DNA from my past life. Bernard had successfully shown the way to my hinterland. I might have congratulated him if I hadn't noticed him reach for his mobile phone and start dialing.

"What are you doing?" I screamed.

"Ringing Gary."

"No, don't! I'm not ready! We should talk to the doctor!"

"It's ringing!" and he threw the handset over to me.

Slowly I raised it to my ear.

"Hello?" said a male voice on a weak, distorted signal.

"Um . . . hello? Is that . . . er, Gary, by any chance?" I stammered.

"Vaughan! Is that you? Where the hell have you been?"

In a panic I dropped the call and threw the handset back to Bernard.

"Did you recognize his voice?"

"Er, no. No, I . . . It's probably just some random bloke," I stammered. But the stranger was ringing straight back. And soon they were having quite an animated chat about me.

"Not anymore," said Bernard. "I think *I'm* his best friend now."

GARY hugged me meaningfully while I just stood there, enduring the physical contact like some teenage boy cuddled by his aunt at Christmas.

"Vaughan! I was so worried about you. I love you, man!"

"You love me?" I stammered. "Are we, like, *homosexuals?*"

The meaningful embrace ended very suddenly. "No, I don't love you like *that*. I mean we're like brothers, you and me. Gazoody-baby!"

"What?"

"That's what we used to say, isn't it? Gazoooooooody-baby! Remember?" and he gave me a little playful punch on the arm.

The doctor had warned him on the phone that I might react nervously if he was over-familiar. The sudden friendliness of this stranger felt inappropriate. "Look, I know this is going to sound a bit rude, but I really don't know who you are. Until you called me 'Vaughan,' I didn't even know that was my Christian name."

"Actually, it's your surname. That's just what everybody calls you."

"I didn't know that! I don't know anything. Do I have a mother?"

The man paused and placed his hand on my shoulder. "I'm sorry, mate. Your old mum kicked the bucket about five years ago."

"Oh, okay." I shrugged. "Well, I don't remember her anyway."

And he laughed as if I were making a joke. "Do you want to go and get a pint or two?"

"He's not allowed to leave the hospital!" interjected Bernard, looking put out by this interloper's arrival.

I might have hesitated had Bernard not explicitly forbidden me to leave the ward.

WALKING out of the hospital with Gary felt both exhilarating and terrifying. I had almost forgotten what fresh air smelled like, and here was someone who knew all the secrets of my past life. Gary was a tall, spindly man about my age who dressed in the clothes of someone twenty years younger. He wore a leather jacket and exuded an air of confidence and a reek of nicotine. It was refreshing to be talked to as if I were normal. It made me like him—this was my friend "Gary." I had a friend, and we were off to the pub together.

"So we might as well get this out of the way . . ." he said as we got to the street corner, "but you do remember you owe me two grand?"

"Do I? Sorry, I don't have any money . . .
I . . . if you could just hang on a bit?" and
then I caught the glint in his eye.

"It's all right!" He burst out laughing.
"Can you not remember anything?"

"I have no idea what I've been doing for
the past forty years."

"Yeah, well, I know how you feel."

It turned out I was thirty-nine, and according to Gary, my fugue state was just "a
typical midlife crisis."

The pub was filling up with lunchtime
customers, so we grabbed the last booth. I
chose a pint of Guinness because Gary told
me that's what I usually had. Now that I had
free rein to ask him whatever I wanted, the
infinite possibilities felt overwhelming. I resolved to ask the questions in chronological
order.

"So. Have I got any brothers and sisters?"

"Nope. You're an only child."

"Where am I from?"

"Nowhere really. Your dad was in the
forces, so you lived in West Germany, Cy-
prus, Malaysia, er . . . Yorkshire. I remember
you saying that you were never in the same
school for more than a year."

"So I'm the son of a soldier?"

"Air force. He was quite high ranking, though he only did the accounts or something. Poor bloke had a heart attack soon after your mum died."

"Oh."

"But I remember your parents from when we were younger. A lovely couple, God bless them. Very powerful homemade wine."

I learned that Gary and I had shared a student house in North Wales, that I had been on a college football team with Gary, and that I had gotten the same degree as Gary. Frankly, it was fascinating to find out so much about myself.

He walked over to the bar and came back with another pint and a graying pickled egg. The whole time he'd been at the bar I had found myself staring down at the white shadow where the ring had been. I was almost too nervous to broach the subject. If there was a wife out there, I wanted to know who I was when I got married.

"So you don't remember this pub at all?" said Gary, sitting down. "You used to sell crack in here before all that trouble with the Russian mafia kicked off—"

"Oh, yeah, of course, the Russian mafia."
I nodded. "It's weird. I don't know who I
am, but I know I wasn't a crack dealer."

"No, drugs were never your scene. You
fret about whether it's acceptable to give your
kids an aspirin."

That was how I discovered I was a father.

"Yeah, you've got two nippers," said Gary
when I pressed him for more information.
"Boy and a girl, Jamie who's about fifteen or
twelve, and then there's Dillie who's younger,
like ten maybe. Actually, she must be eleven,
'cause they're both at secondary school.
Though not at your school."

"What do you mean 'my school'?"

"Your school where you teach."

"So I'm a teacher? Look, just slow down a
minute, will you? See, this is why I wanted
to do everything chronologically. Tell me
about my children first."

"Well, they're just kids, you know. They're
cute. I'm actually godfather to Jamie. Or is it
Dillie? I can't remember. But, yeah, great
kids. You can be really proud of them."

"Mind if we sit here?" interjected a woman
carrying shopping bags, and without waiting for an answer, she slumped into one of

the two spare places at our table. "Over here, Meg!"

I was a parent to two strangers. But these children would know me; hopefully, they would love me.

"Get a menu!" shouted the lady to her companion.

"So what are my kids like?"

The woman did a poor job of pretending not to listen.

"Well, Jamie looks just like you, actually. He doesn't say a great deal, but that's probably just his age. He's getting quite tall now, trendy, into music."

"What about my daughter—Dillie? Is that her real name or is it short for something?"

"Could be Dilys," said the woman at our table.

"Sorry?"

"Your daughter's name? Dillie could be short for Dilys. Or 'Dillwyn' is a name. Welsh, I think. You're not Welsh, are you?"

"I dunno. Am I Welsh?"

"Nah, don't think so."

The detail of my own parenthood suddenly recast everything in an even more serious light. Now my mental breakdown was something that had happened not just to me, but to a whole family.

"Been in prison, have you?" inquired the woman nonchalantly.

"Er, something like that." I smiled.

"So what other news can I tell you?" Gary said. "The Tories are back in power. And everyone has mobile phones and home computers—"

"I know all that stuff. I just can't remember anyone's name or anything about them."

"Ha! That's just being a bloke, isn't it?" said the woman with a sigh.

After that we talked in hushed mumbles. Now that we seemed to have abandoned any idea of doing my life in chronological order, I jumped to the question that had been gnawing away at me.

"So I'm father to two children. Tell me about their mother."

There was a pause.

"Er—she's cool, yeah. Actually, this egg is disgusting. I might get something else—"

"No, no—hang on. What's her name?"

"Her name? Madeleine. Maddy."

"My wife is called Madeleine!" I rolled the name about in my head. This would surely be the foundation stone on which my life would be rebuilt. "So where did I meet her?"

"You hooked up in your first term at university, didn't you? You were, like, so totally into one another, it was actually quite annoying for the rest of us. After college you both spent a few years doing nothing. And 'cause you didn't have the faintest idea what to do, you decided to be a teacher."

"Wow! That's a vocation! A teacher . . ." I stroked my beard as I pictured myself as Robin Williams in *Dead Poets' Society*. "What do I teach? Tell me it's not metalwork . . ."

"You teach history—and sometimes 'citizenship,' whatever that is."

"A history teacher? Ha! The historian with no history of his own."

"I suppose that is ironic. You don't know anything about the past, but then neither do any of your pupils."

"But hang on, we need to tell Madeleine and the kids I'm okay, don't we? I've been missing for over a week. Were they worried about me?"

"I dunno, mate. I haven't spoken to her."

"I was missing for a week, and she didn't call you?"

"Well, it wasn't really like that . . ."

"Wasn't like what? Is Madeleine away or ill or something?"

"You and Maddy have been through a bit of a tough time recently. When I spoke to your doctor on the phone, she asked if you'd experienced any stress prior to your memory wipe, and I said, 'Yeah, he's just split up with his wife.'"

I tried to digest the crippling news that the wife I had just learned about had split up with me. It must have been the shortest marriage in history.

I FOUND myself squinting at the bright sunshine as we stepped out of the dingy pub. Gary lit a cigarette and offered me one.

"No, thanks."

"No? You normally smoke like a beagle."

"Really?" So far Gary had told me that I was a chain-smoking teacher whose marriage was on the rocks. Normally one would discover this about oneself over a period of decades.

"Are you all right, mate? You look kinda weird."

"Can I just go back to the hospital, please?"

"You know, you can always shack up at my place. You stayed for a while when things started to go a bit wrong on the marriage front."

"When things started to go a bit wrong?"

"Yeah," he chuckled. "You turned up at my place with this blood-soaked bandage on your hand, saying the marriage was over."

Then the penny dropped. "Oh, I get it! This is another of your stupid jokes, isn't it? Maddy and I aren't separated at all, are we?"

Gary winced. "No joke, mate. You and Maddy can't stand each other no more. Oh, and that's the other reason you can't stay in the hospital. You're divorcing her on Thursday. Oh, hang on, no, I've got that wrong. When's the first of November? That's Friday, isn't it? You're divorcing her on Friday."

Chapter 2

GOOGLE Images had revealed that there was more than one person in the world called "Madeleine Vaughan." It was just a question of scrolling through every picture on the Internet tagged with any version of her name and seeing if any of them looked remotely likely.

That night I had gone upstairs to spend some time on the hospital computer terminal. Researching details about myself had been no easier. I couldn't believe I hadn't asked Gary what my first name actually was. I found a secondary school in the location Gary had described, and on a list of staff members at "Wandle Academy" was "Jack Vaughan—History." There were a couple of references to "Jack Vaughan" at an education conference in Kettering at which I'd spoken a year earlier. On the school website I scanned photographs and finally spotted myself on the edge of a staff group shot. I felt as if some identity thief had been walking around pretending to be me: teaching history, talking at conferences, alienating my wife.

It was nearly dawn by the time I forced myself to stop. I spent the following morning trying to catch up on my sleep, attempting to ignore Bernard. Suddenly the curtain around my bed was pulled back, and there stood Gary with a smartly dressed blond woman who looked younger than us.

"Ta da!" exclaimed Gary. "Vaughan— meet the missus!"

The woman beside him gave me a nervous smile and attempted a rather girlie wave. "Hello, Vaughan. Remember me?"

"Erm . . . no, I don't, sorry. Are you Maddy?"

"Not *your* missus, *my* missus! This is Linda!" Gary turned to her. "See, I told you, didn't I? He's forgotten everything. So he won't remember that embarrassing affair the two of you had in Lanzarote."

She giggled and gave him a playful slap. "Honestly, Gary! Don't worry, Vaughan— we didn't. Gary's explained what happened, and we're going to take you back home and look after you, aren't we?"

Linda had rung the ward to make her offer earlier that morning. It had been a big decision. Various medics had given their professional opinions on my fragile psychological state and whether a change of location might impede my progress. Then they balanced that against how much the hospital needed my bed and said, "How quickly can he leave?"

Dr. Lewington formally presented me

with a leaving present. "There is no guarantee that your memory will not wipe itself all over again, leaving you lost as before. So I want you to wear this identity tag round your neck at all times; it has emergency contact details for this hospital."

"Do pop over and say hello when you're back for your checkups," said Bernard a little forlornly.

"Of course, Bernard. If you're not out of here by then."

"Have you got the same thing as Mr. Memory Man here?" Gary asked.

"No. I've got a brain tumor," Bernard said brightly.

"Oh," said Linda. "I'm very sorry to hear that."

"I don't let it get me down. I say anything that rhymes with 'humor' can't be all that bad."

"Right . . ." reflected Gary.

Linda was not the spouse I would have cast for Gary. I would have expected some spiky-haired punk chick. Linda was not only conventional but surprisingly posh, and she glowed with vigorous good health. "Actually, we do have some rather big news since we last saw you," she said, standing by the lift and smiling at her husband. "You know we've been trying for a baby?"

"No?"

"No, of course not. Well, the wonderful thing is—it's happened! We're going to be a proper family."

She said this as if it was the cue for me to scream in excitement, and when I merely gave my polite congratulations, she looked a little put out. As we traveled down in the lift, she began to provide anecdotes and accounts of past episodes as if to prove that I did know them very well. Apparently I had been Gary's best man at their recent wedding; I had played football with Gary every Tuesday night for years; I had even been on holiday with them.

"I'm sorry, I don't remember any of it," I mumbled. "It's like I was the best man at your wedding, but now I don't even know what Gary and I have in common. I mean, what did we used to talk about?"

"I don't think you ever had an actual conversation," said Linda. "You just compared apps on your iPhones."

It was a sunny, windy day as we drove out

of the hospital car park. I had presumed that we would be going straight back to Gary and Linda's flat, but they clearly had other plans.

"Okay, groovy people, we are welcoming you aboard Gary and Linda's famous Magicking Mystery Tour!" announced my driver, doing his best impression of a German tour guide. "On this evening's super-hip sightsee trip, we will point out some of most famous landmarks of Vaughan's life." Linda was laughing.

Gary pointed out a pub we popped into about ten years ago. He had given up on the foreign accent, though the concept of the tour guide was still clinging on.

"If you look out of the left-hand window, you can see a branch of McDonald's, which is where your parents hoped you might work if you realized your full potential. Tragically, you became a history teacher instead."

We crossed the river, and Gary pointed out a couple more pubs we had frequented. I recognized some roads and not others; it seemed that a generic knowledge of London's main streets and bridges had survived. We pulled up outside a modern school building.

"This is where I teach?"

"Wow, you remember it!"

"No—you just said my school was in Wandsworth, and so I found Wandle Academy on the Internet."

"Oh. Well, anyway, not exactly Hogwarts, is it?"

The concrete edifice did look a bit shabby and foreboding. The entrance was litter-strewn, and a couple of silver birch saplings had been snapped off.

"So am I just a classroom teacher or a head of year or anything?"

Linda explained that during my decade at the school I had been promoted to "Head of Humans, or something."

"Humanities?"

"Yeah, that sounds right."

I felt a twinge of worry that there were classes of children wondering what had happened to Mr. Vaughan.

"But my own kids don't come here?"

"Don't be ridiculous! Maddy knows what the teachers are like!"

"They go to a school closer to where you live," explained Linda. "Dillie's only just left that primary."

"So what do you two do for a living?"

"Well," said Linda, "I'm in recruitment, and Gary is in computers—Internet and all that."

"Right." I nodded neutrally. "Not data recovery by any chance?"

"Ha! No, I work for myself, designing websites, developing new ideas for the Net."

"Wow! What sort of ideas?"

"Okay, well, I might as well tell you about our big project then."

"*Our* big project?"

"Yeah, you and me have been developing a site that will revolutionize how we consume news." I noticed a sudden degree of self-belief in Gary. "See, currently all news is top down. Some fascist corporation decides the most important story, then serves up all the lies to the trusting public."

Linda was nodding supportively.

"The Internet allows you to turn that model on its head. Imagine millions of readers writing up whatever they might have just witnessed around the globe, uploading their own photos, video footage, and text. Hey presto! The story with the most hits becomes the main item of news on the world's most democratic and unbiased news outlet! YouNews is the future; you said so yourself. You can search by region, subject, protest movement, whatever."

"So no reporters or editors?" I observed.

"Exactly! No hacks filing their expenses from around the world, and no press barons protecting their political allies or paymasters."

I thought about this for a moment. "But how do you know it's true?"

"True?"

"Yes, a story that some member of the public has uploaded. How do you know they haven't just made it up?"

"Well, if they've made it up," explained Gary, "then you always said that other members of the public will say so in the comment thread and it will lose credibility. Or they can reedit it themselves—it's like Wikipedia, but for current affairs. You're really into it, believe me."

Eventually we reached the address where I had been living right up until my fugue. I learned that after moving out of my family home I had sofa-surfed between a number of temporary addresses, most recently house-sitting for a rich family who were in New York for three months. When I had disappeared, I had left my clothes and my belongings there, which were now in boxes at Gary and Linda's.

"Wow! What an amazing house. And I had it all to myself?"

"Yeah—but you didn't like it. It made you, like, really tense being responsible for all the fancy furniture and that."

The family were apparently now back home, so this private mansion was no longer an option for me.

"And you don't recognize that either? That is really amazing! So is there anything you can remember?"

"Actually, I have this vague memory of really laughing with a girl when I was younger. And we're sheltering under a canopy or something but still getting wet, but we don't mind. But I can't remember who she was. I just remember being really, really happy."

We turned into a residential street. Rows of midsize Victorian houses were interspersed with a few ugly 1950s blocks. On the corner was number 27, which looked like the best house on the street, with dormer windows at the top and a little turret that gazed out over the London skyline.

"Recognize this?"

"Don't tell me—it's where I was born?"

At that moment the front door opened and a striking redhead stepped out into the autumn sunshine and dropped a bag into the garbage bin.

"Wow! Who is that?" I whispered. "She is gorgeous! Was she living there when I was? Should we go and say hello?"

"Blimey, Vaughan, you've gone bright red," said Linda. "Gary, we probably shouldn't hang about. We don't want her to see us here."

He was already putting the car in gear and pulling away.

"Hang on. Where are we? Who is that beautiful woman?"

"That, Vaughan, was the house you lived in for twenty years," said my tour guide. "And that was Madeleine, the woman you're about to divorce."

As YOU came in the front door, the first thing you saw was a baby gate across the foot of the stairs and a brand-new stroller folded up by the coat hooks. In the lounge was a big Thomas the Tank Engine rug.

"Sorry, are you expecting *another* baby, or will this one be your first?"

"No, it's just the two of us at the moment," confirmed Gary. "It's just that Linda likes buying all the stuff, you know."

"I always loved your home, Vaughan," enthused Linda, "brimming with children's toys and everything."

She proudly showed me into the room where I would be staying. In the corner was a brand-new crib surrounded by mobiles. Teddy-bear wallpaper was softly lit by the light from a Disney lampshade. The extended sofa bed that had been made up for me rather spoiled the nursery atmosphere.

In a wardrobe hung a range of men's clothes, the jeans, shirts, and sweaters that belonged to me before my fugue. There were a few frayed-looking suits, presumably my teaching uniform, and some uninspiring ties.

Linda had kindly prepared everything for my stay, and there was even a new toothbrush still in its packet. "This is the bathroom, Vaughan—I thought you might fancy a bath."

"Do you think she looked sad?"

"Who?"

"Maddy? I thought she looked a little sad . . ."

"Er, no, she looked pretty much how she usually looks to me . . . Dirty laundry goes in there, and I'll show you how to use the washing machine."

A few minutes later I was taking off my clothes in the private space of virtual strangers. I felt like the intruder in a family bathroom. I still wanted to ask them so much more. When did things go wrong with Maddy? Did I move out? Did she kick me out? Did one of us have an affair?

The bath was foamy and scented, and I submerged my aching head under the suds, letting my senses deaden to the outside world. I slowly came up for air. This was the most relaxed I could remember feeling. My head felt completely empty. And then it happened. From nowhere, I recovered my first memory—the whole episode fell into my head all at once.

MADDY and I are walking up a grassy hill hand in hand, nimbly hopping over cowpats and rabbit holes, until we stand at the summit and feel the wind and sun on our faces. We continue to the next hill, backpacks and camping gear doing little to slow us down as we march optimistically across the Irish countryside. This is our first holiday together—it is sunny, we have a brand-new tent—what can possibly go wrong?

"Oh, no! I don't believe it!" exclaims Maddy, sounding genuinely alarmed.

"What is it?"

"I forgot to send off that postcard to Great-Auntie Brenda. Again!"

The postcard to Great-Auntie Brenda features a smiling cartoon leprechaun drinking a pint of Guinness and bears the caption "Top o' the mornin' to yers!" I suggest that it might be of questionable taste, but Maddy stands firmly by her selection for her elderly great-aunt.

"I thought she'd like it. She has gnomes in her garden."

The leprechaun is not looking any less cheerful for having been stuffed into the side pocket of Madeleine's rucksack for three days. Maddy has already written a message on the back, completed the address, and affixed a stamp. Just that last detail of putting the card in a postbox keeps eluding her. And when Maddy gets back to England and unpacks her bag, there is the leprechaun, still wishing her the top o' the mornin'. She gives it to me to post when I am going out that evening, and I place it carefully in my inside jacket pocket. It is several months later that I find it there.

Maddy and I have hitched and walked through West Cork and now gaze down on a huge stretch of sand known as Barleycove. Hills on either side lead down to a perfect beach with steep, grassy dunes behind. The hazy horizon is punctured by the tiny outline of the Fastnet lighthouse.

"Why don't we camp for the night?" I suggest. "We could swim and make a fire out of driftwood and barbecue those sausages."

"But the lady in the pub said there was going to be a storm, remember? We could go back. That pub had a few rooms upstairs."

"Come on—it's blazing sunshine. This is the perfect spot. This is what it's all about!" and I am already taking off my backpack.

Six hours later we are awoken by the tent's top sheet coming loose in the gale. Now the rain drums even more noisily against the canvas sound box in which we're supposed to be sleeping as water trickles down the tent pole. Despite the foolhardy decision to ignore the local prophet, the nighttime storm has actually made us even cozier inside.

"I told you to take no notice of that woman in the pub."

"You were right. Everyone knows it never rains in Ireland."

Another violent gust of wind makes the tent shudder, and then the guy ropes break free on one side and the roof collapses on top of us. I swear loudly, which prompts shrieks of laughter from Maddy, who is still enjoying the effects of a bottle of white wine. I attempt to right the tent poles from inside, but the gale pulls the tent flat again as a stream of water flows onto our things. Maddy sticks her head out of the tent to see what she can see.

"Maybe you should go out and try to fix it from the outside?" she suggests.

"But I'm completely naked!"

"Yeah—well, there's not going to be anyone out there on a night like this, is there?" she points out.

And so my pale, naked frame steps out into the night to do battle against the wind and rain. From inside the tent Maddy hears an elderly-sounding

Irishman nonchalantly ask me if I am "all right there."

"Oh, hello, er, yes, thank you very much. Our tent blew over . . ."

"Ah, well, I saw that you'd camped down here," the old man muses from the shelter of a golfing umbrella, "so I thought I'd better check you hadn't blown away, like."

I can just hear Maddy giggling inside the tent—she had obviously seen him coming and had deliberately set me up.

"There's a barn up the lane. You could move up there if you want."

"Thank you, that's very kind."

"But you don't want to be prancing about in this weather stark-naked. You'll catch your death of cold."

"Good advice. I'll get back inside right now. Thanks for checking on us."

The guy ropes are never reset, and the tent stays collapsed on us all night, but it doesn't matter that we barely sleep and have to dry out our things tomorrow, because right now all we want to do is laugh and laugh. Maddy doesn't mind that I ignored her advice and was proved wrong; nothing is going to be allowed to spoil our happiness. We are young and can doze with

canvas on our faces and arms half wrapped
around one another; we are immunized against
discomfort by the euphoria of just being
together.

"I'VE had a memory!" I exclaimed.

We sat around their kitchen table, and they assured me that this was only the beginning, that other memories would surely start to flow back. But while I wanted to find out more about my marriage, Gary felt I needed to focus on the ending of it. I was reminded that I was due in court on Friday for the final stage of what they earnestly assured me had been a long, painful, and expensive business. I was going to have to go to a court of law and pretend to a judge that nothing had happened to me in order to terminate a marriage I knew nothing about.

"But what if they ask a question I don't know the answer to?"

"Your lawyer will tell you what to say," Gary assured me.

"And he'll know about my condition?"

"Er, probably not," said Gary. "We could risk telling them, but what will they do?

Postpone the case and charge you another ten grand."

"Maddy and the kids are geared up to it happening on Friday. They need closure," said Linda.

Gary was insistent that I would deeply regret not having gone through with the divorce if my memory suddenly returned and I awoke to discover that I had lost the chance to break free from an unhappy marriage.

"Yes, you *say* it was an unhappy marriage . . ." I ventured.

"Well, you *are* getting divorced," pointed out Gary.

On digging deeper I learned that it was not until the actual divorce process was under way that things had turned nasty. It was only after Maddy and I learned of the provocative claims being made by the other side's lawyers that personal hostilities spiraled out of control. "You compared the divorce process to war," recalled Gary.

However persuasive they were that we'd be better off apart, I couldn't agree there and then to take this momentous step in the dark. I announced that I'd like to go out for a walk, to have a bit of a think, and somewhere be-tween Linda's nervous concern and Gary's total indifference, we reached a compromise that it would be fine as long as I took their address and phone number and twenty pounds in cash.

As soon as their front door was closed be-hind me, I began retracing my steps the mile or so to where we had seen Maddy. I was go-ing to meet my wife. I had resolved that she had to know about my condition; the event had major consequences for her own life, our children, the court case. I owed it to her to tell her face-to-face what had happened. It should be done before the children were home from school and with time to postpone the court hearing, and that meant I had to do it right now.

In any case, I told myself, before I divorce my wife, I'd like to get to know her a bit.

I STOOD before the family home once again, a place with so many memories, but none of them currently mine. My intention had been to march right up and ring the doorbell, but my finger was shaking as I reached for the button. I left it hovering there uncertainly. What if one of my children was off from school and rushed down to say hello? I imagined my daughter emerging with a friend and me not knowing to which girl I was father. It was not just my own mental health that was at issue here.

But it had to be done. I pressed the buzzer. To my surprise this prompted the sound of loud barking from the other side of the door. There was a dog! This was the furious bark of a guard dog in the house on his own—an angry warning that was not mollified by any owner calling him away from the door. Maddy was out. I peered through the letter box, calling an optimistic "Hello?" and instantly the dog's demeanor changed. Suddenly he was howling with excitement as he recognized me. He was a big golden retriever, licking the hand that held open the letter box, then breaking off to howl his emotional hellos. I hadn't thought about whether I liked dogs or not, but I instinctively felt affection for this one.

I crossed the road to get a better view of the house. I was struck by what a beautiful home we'd created. It was brimming with character, with brightly painted shutters and blooming window boxes. Dormer windows peeked out from the slate-tiled roof, and the middle floor had a balcony. From the side I spotted a faded sun canopy, which over-looked the back garden, where a chaotic Virginia creeper was in its final blush of copper.

I tried to imagine myself sitting out on the balcony with Maddy, sharing a bottle of white wine on a summer's night, as the kids played in the garden. So lost was I in speculation that I didn't notice a car drawing up a few spaces away. I felt terror-stricken and thrilled all at once when I realized who it was, and dived behind a parked van. I watched in the van's mirror as Maddy reversed into the tightest of spaces, rather expertly, I thought. She stepped out, wearing a funky orange coat that flared out below the waist. Her hair was up, and she wore small earrings.

Seeing her again, I couldn't help but feel as if some enormous administrative mistake must have occurred and the authorities were proceeding with the wrong divorce. Why would I want to stop being married to such a beautiful woman? Well, now was my chance to introduce myself to my wife.

But just as I stepped out from behind the van, the passenger door of Maddy's car opened, and now I slipped out of view again as I spied a man getting out. The two of them set about taking large frames out of the back of the car and began carrying them up to the front door. The man was younger than me, and too snappily dressed to be a delivery man. Was Maddy a painter? An art dealer? Crouched down on the pavement out of view, I was transfixed as I scanned the situation for clues. There was nothing to suggest that these two were in any sort of relationship. My guess was that Maddy had bought the frames off him and now he was helping to deliver them. But that was a more personal service than you'd expect from a picture framer. I wanted to see if this man followed her into the house.

Maddy unlocked the front door and patted the excited dog, who circled her, wagging his backside. The dog sniffed the air as she went inside, but instead of following her, he started down the steps. Maddy called his name, but the dog had gotten the scent of something, and then I saw the panic in her face as he headed toward the road. The dog looked unstoppable.

That was the moment I realized that the scent the dog had picked up was mine and he was running across the road to where I was hiding. Maddy was following and would find me lurking here, and my first encounter with her since my breakdown would be as some creepy stalker. Behind me was a passageway that led down the side of the house opposite ours. I ran down there and dived around the back of a wooden shed. Almost immediately the dog caught up with me, excitedly jumping up to lick my face.

"Woody! Woody!" Maddy was desperately calling, getting closer.

"Woody, you bad dog!" I scolded in hushed desperation. "Go home now!" and amazingly, a rather disappointed Woody scampered back in the direction he had come from. I heard her say, "There you are, you naughty dog!"

I was safe. She wouldn't come down here. I closed my eyes and let out a huge sigh of relief.

"What are you doing in my garden?" said

an indignant upper-class voice. I turned round to see a rotund figure in his early sixties. "Oh, Vaughan, it's you! How are you? Haven't seen you for ages."

"Oh, er—hello!"

"I think I know why you're here." My mind was racing. Had he seen me spying on my own wife? "You want your thingamajig back, don't you?"

"My thingamajig?"

"I meant to bring it back ages ago—very remiss of me. Anyway, help yourself—it's in the shed."

I obediently opened the shed door and stared at the chaotic arrangement of garden furniture, abandoned lawn mowers, rusting barbecues, and plant pots piled up before me.

"How's Madeleine?" he inquired as I scanned the space in front of me.

"She's, er, fine," I blurted.

"Well, you two must come round for dinner soon."

"Thank you. That's very nice of you."

"Really?"

I seemed to have given a reply that surprised him. In that moment I understood that previous offers must have always been rebuffed.

"Great, well, what about this weekend? Arabella was just saying we hadn't seen much of you, and we're not doing anything on Saturday."

Without even knowing him or his wife, I could already sense that the bitterness of my marital breakup would not be ameliorated by committing Maddy and myself to a dinner party with these neighbors. "Er, it's a bit difficult, actually. Maddy and I are having a trial separation."

"A trial separation?"

"Yeah, you know . . . a trial divorce. Just to see how that goes for a while."

This embarrassing news cut the conversation short. The neighbor came into the shed himself, where it turned out the thing I had come round to collect was right under my nose. "Silly me!" I tutted.

Ten minutes later I was standing on a busy underground train, noticing that people were giving me more space than might usually be expected. Perhaps it was the three-foot-long serrated blade of the electric hedge trimmer I was clutching.

Chapter 3

I FELT as if I had stared at my bedroom clock for an entire night. Lying there, in the half-light of the nursery, everything was quiet and still except for the manic pendulum on the wall opposite. It featured a happy clown clinging onto a rainbow, swinging back and forth, forever. His situation still seemed to make more sense than my own. By about half past three it became clear that the clown was not going to take a rest, and so I got up and tiptoed into the kitchen for a glass of water.

When dawn came, it would be the day of my court case. I sat at the pine table for a while, listening to the rhythmical dripping of the tap. I spotted Gary and Linda's address book and started to flick through the pages. "Vaughan and Maddy" was filed under "V." There was my family's telephone number glaring at me from the yellowing paper, a series of digits that I must have effortlessly recited a thousand times. I could just dial that number right now and talk to Maddy. Although ringing up my ex-wife at half past three in the morning might not be the best way to reassure her of my sanity.

My personal effects had been rediscovered in a jacket pocket, and now, seated at the kitchen table, I carefully dealt out the cards from my wallet: That's the Blockbuster video card, a sign that you might enjoy renting movies. Combined with a library card and a Clapham Picturehouse membership, this suggests you are quite a cultured person. In terms of wealth, there is only one basic credit card. On the plus side, your Caffè Nero loyalty card shows that you are only two stamps away from a free cappuccino . . .

I took a pen and attempted to copy the signature on my bank card. I could produce nothing even vaguely similar. My phone was out of battery, which had been something of a relief. I had been frightened that names would flash on the screen expecting to pick up where they had left off with me and I would know nothing at all about them. But now, under cover of darkness, I plugged it in and watched the screen come back to life. I had forty-seven missed calls and seventeen messages.

I didn't recognize the first caller. "Vaughan, hi, it's me, there's a curriculum problem I need you to sort out. If you could check the schedule for Day Six—" And then I stopped it and just pressed "Delete All."

I rested my forehead on the kitchen table for a while and thought about the ordeal of the day ahead. The court case had not been postponed, because I had never been assertive enough to insist that Maddy or my lawyer be informed about my condition. Gary had maintained that we were definitely doing the right thing and that my life could begin again once this "last little formality" was out of the way. I was to learn the hard way about the wisdom of taking legal advice from a man with an earring.

I WAS woken by the sound of crockery being placed on the kitchen table beside my head.

"Sorry to wake you there, Vaughan, mate. I'm just doing breakfast. Do you want any prawn balls?"

"What?"

"With sweet-and-sour sauce. And some special fried rice, though it's a bit less special than it was a couple of days ago." The microwave gave out a beep.

"Er—no, thanks. What time is it?"

"It's getting on a bit, actually. You're supposed to be in court in an hour."

"VAUGHAN! There you are!" said a posh young man with a voice even louder than his tie. "I thought you wanted to meet a bit earlier?"

"Are you Vaughan's lawyer?" said Gary. "We spoke on the phone."

"Yes, hello. So, Vaughan, according to your friend here, you wanted to go through the questions likely to come up in court *again*," he said pointedly.

"Again?" I asked without checking myself.

"That's exactly what we did last time I saw you."

"Er, Vaughan said that was incredibly useful," interjected Gary, "but when I was just doing a final rehearsal with him, it turned out that he was a little confused about one or two minor aspects."

"I see," said the lawyer. "Which particular areas?"

"Well," I said, "the whole thing, really. Getting divorced?" I found it difficult to concentrate when I was looking over his shoulder to see if I could spot Maddy coming in.

"Mrs. Vaughan is being incredibly unreasonable," commented the lawyer.

"There are two sides to everything," I interjected. "I mean, her lawyer probably thinks I'm being incredibly unreasonable too."

He seemed to be pulled up short by this comment. "Well, Mr. Vaughan, I must say you seem to have mellowed somewhat."

Gary was anxious that my attitude not arouse suspicions. "I think with the divorce so close, you're preparing for the next stage, aren't you, mate? Forgiveness, reconciliation, cooperation. It's all in *Divorce for Dummies*."

"I haven't read that one," said the lawyer. He had never actually told us his name. "So you're completely clear about the CETV?"

"What?" I stuttered. "Will the judge ask me what that stands for?"

"No! The cash equivalent transfer value is the valuation technique both parties have agreed to pursue with regard to the pension. The difficulty being that Maddy is demanding half."

"Sounds reasonable," I commented cheerfully.

His stunned silence went on for so long I was worried the extra time would be added on to my bill. "I'm sorry, Mr. Vaughan, but we have been absolutely adamant on this point up till now."

"See, mate, you paid nearly all of the contributions into the pension," interjected Gary, "so you didn't see why she should receive half of it."

"But if she was looking after the kids, how could she pay any money in? She was making, like, a noncash contribution, wasn't she?"

"That is the point that *her* lawyer will be making. But we have consistently agreed that she could have worked but that she chose not to."

"Ah, well, that's a difficult one, isn't it?" I mused philosophically. "I mean, if I was working so hard at my job, perhaps that closed off the possibility of her resuming any meaningful career after we had children? I just think we are pursuing a rather hard-line stance."

The lawyer pressed his fingers to his temples as if he had suddenly developed a powerful headache. "This is the divorce court, Mr. Vaughan, not Disneyland. You either fight your corner or you get utterly destroyed."

He insisted that there was no alternative but to proceed on the basis already agreed. But I was alarmed at some of the stands adopted by my former self. To solve the practical problems of my demand that I have custody of the children, my lawyer had suggested that the kids move to the school where I was a teacher. It seemed wrong to cause further disruption to the children's lives; I couldn't understand the thinking of the Vaughan who had gone along with this. Finding out about myself was like peeling an onion. And the more I peeled, the more I felt like crying.

"Shall we go in?" suggested the lawyer. I discovered that Gary would not be allowed in the courtroom, and so I alone was solemnly escorted to the chamber where marriages went to die.

THE COURTROOM ITSELF was smaller and more modern than I had anticipated. We were joined by a barrister pupil and then a solicitor and trainee, and eventually Maddy and her team bustled in and placed themselves at the parallel bench. I leaned over and attempted a smile, but Maddy had clearly decided that our divorce hearing was not the occasion for friendly little waves. Her lawyer mumbled at her for several minutes, and she listened in intense concentration, only glancing up once, accidentally making eye contact with me and then quickly looking away. I was troubled by how little Maddy seemed able to smile. Of course I understood that this was not a happy occasion, but I still found myself wanting to make her feel better. As it turned out, my performance was to have the opposite effect.

There followed some procedural overtures before the hearing began in earnest. I gradually understood that the judge and the two lawyers were establishing the stages of the divorce process so far, during which I found my eye wandering back to the other half that I hadn't known I'd had. She was looking straight ahead, just enduring the ordeal.

The previous night I had worked hard to think of every possible question that might be thrown at me. My trainer Gary had said I should go into court feeling confident. "I'm sure you'll pick it up once you're in there."

I was wishing that he see how very wrong he had been. Right at the beginning they caught me out with a trick question.

"Could you state your full name, please?"

"Ooh, erm . . . let me see . . . Well, I'm Jack Vaughan, though everyone calls me Vaughan, but my full, complete, legal name with the middle name . . . or names, well, that would be . . . Sorry, I've gone blank."

The whole room was now staring at me.

"Bit nervous, sorry."

My lawyer gazed at me perplexed. "Your full name is, er, well, it will be on the original submission . . ."

"It's Jack Joseph Neil Vaughan," recited Maddy in a tone suggesting years of exasperation with the uselessness of the man she was divorcing.

I leaned across and mouthed "Thank

you," and her look back seemed to say, "What the hell are you doing?"

"My name is Jack Joseph Neal Vaughan," I declared with confidence.

"Is that Neil with an 'i' or with an 'a'?" interjected the clerk.

"It's with an 'a'!" I declared confidently.

"It's with an 'i,'" came the voice from the other side of the court.

The judge stared at me silently for a moment; he seemed to be lamenting the long-lost power of the judiciary to impose the death penalty at will.

The next section was manageable if a little uncomfortable. I swore an oath on the Holy Bible that everything that I would say would be the truth. I learned that I was the petitioner (amazingly, I was the one who had initiated divorce proceedings), and I confirmed my date of birth as the one I had seen printed on the forms.

"And your occupation?"

"Teacher!" I snapped back like a smug contestant in a TV quiz show.

Eventually we came to the part of the proceedings when I was to be cross-examined by my wife's lawyer.

"Mr. Vaughan, I want you to cast your mind back to 1998. You and your wife first employed the service of a financial advisor in that year, did you not?"

"I have no reason to disbelieve Madeleine if she says that we did."

"And did you not make a decision at that meeting on February seventeenth, 1998, that, in addition to your teacher's pension, you would also make voluntary contributions in your name only, because, as the only taxpayer at that point, you could then benefit from more tax relief than if they had been in Madeleine's name?"

I would have struggled to follow these financial details even with my brain in normal working order. "Er, it sounds quite possible. If there is a record of the payments after that date, then obviously I did take out an additional pension in my name."

"The existence of this pension plan is not the issue, Mr. Vaughan. The point is that you verbally assured your wife that this personal pension was intended for your joint benefit, but that it was only taken out in your name to save tax. Is this not the case?"

I felt a duty to be as honest as possible. "I

really can't remember," I declared. Maddy's lawyer looked stumped.

"Brilliant!" whispered my own counsel.

"How convenient for you . . ." scorned the opposing barrister.

"It was a long time ago, and I just can't recall."

The judge intervened. "Can we move on?"

"You don't remember any subsequent assurances to your wife, do you, Mr. Vaughan?" improvised her lawyer, now sounding a little desperate.

"Er, no. No, I don't."

Maddy shook her head in contempt. "It's not enough that you have all the money," she spat. "You have to come and take the hedge trimmer as well. You don't even have a garden anymore."

"I don't want the hedge trimmer. You can have it back . . ."

"Quiet, please!" insisted the judge, and the memory test now moved on to the years of our marriage and how they reflected the respective investment made by both parties.

"Mr. Vaughan, while you were at work, would you attempt to claim you were also doing fifty percent of the child care?"

"Er, I doubt it. It sounds like I was always still at work when they came home from school for a start."

"Quite," he commented meaningfully. "Would you even attempt to put a figure on the proportion of the child care you did?" He theatrically pretended to imagine the sort of tasks this might involve. "Picking them up from school? Helping with homework? Cooking their tea?"

"It's hard to say *exactly*," I said truthfully. "Much less than Madeleine, I'm sure." I glanced nervously at my lawyer.

"Would it be fair to say that if Madeleine had not done so much of the domestic work, then you would not have been able to work the long hours that both parties accept you put into your career?"

"I guess you're right . . ."

I noticed Maddy look up.

"So would you not agree that seventy/thirty represents an unfair reflection of the paid *and unpaid* work done by the two of you?"

"Yes, it is unfair. I think a fifty/fifty split would be fairer." And I stared directly at my wife. She looked astonished.

There was a moment of confused silence. It was as if Maddy's lawyer was only programmed to disagree and contradict; he tried to reach for words, but none would come. Now my own representative stood up.

"Your honor, the respondent's counsel is putting words into my client's mouth. Surely it is for the court to make a ruling after we have put our own case for a seventy/thirty split." And he urgently gestured for me to shut up.

"It appears, Mr. Cottington, that you and your client have come to court without agreeing in advance on the apportionment you are seeking."

Mr. *Cottington,* I thought. So that's my lawyer's name.

The judge entered into a whispered exchange with the clerk while I was left standing there. Although I felt certain I had done the right thing, I could feel my legs shaking. Then I suddenly got my first negative memory. Maddy was angrily berating me, and I was shouting back. I even felt a twinge of resentment rise up in me as I recalled how over the top she had been. The argument had arisen because I had apparently "endangered the family" by taking the battery out of a smoke alarm to put in my bike light.

"WHY the hell didn't you replace the battery?" she is shouting.

"I forgot, okay? Don't you ever forget things?"

"Not where the safety of our children is concerned."

"Well, this was for the safety of your husband on the dark road!"

"You could have bought a replacement battery—you just forgot about us but remembered you."

LOOKING at Madeleine, I couldn't believe that she was capable of so much anger about something as trivial as one AA battery.

The court had come to consider the key point in the settlement, the decision on the Property Adjustment Order. With no agreement on the house, it would have to be sold, but negotiations had broken down over a fair split of the money. The more I listened to the arguments from both sides, the clearer it became that neither Maddy nor I would be able to afford a house in the same area that would accommodate two children and an excitable golden retriever. It would mean moving the kids far away from their school; it would mean no garden and the children having tiny bedrooms and no space for friends to come and stay. One blindingly obvious solution to all this was not being suggested by anyone in the courtroom, and I felt a duty to point it out.

"Excuse me, your honor—is it possible to . . . change my mind?"

"You want a different arrangement regarding the property assets?"

"No, no—about the whole divorce thing," I heard myself say. "I wonder if we ought to try and give the marriage another go?"

"Vaughan, stop it!" said Maddy. "This is not a game."

"Vaughan, what are you doing?" pleaded my lawyer.

"If I'm the petitioner—can't I, like, withdraw the petition?"

It seemed like a reasonable question. But the judge's patience had now been exhausted, and he seemed at a loss over what to say. Deep down I had been hoping for him to declare, "This is most irregular, but given the circumstances, this court instructs

Vaughan and Madeleine to jet off to the Caribbean for a second honeymoon and for Mrs. Vaughan to fall in love with her husband all over again."

Instead, he declared that this case was "a disaster" and said he was faced with no alternative but an adjournment. Inside I felt a rush of elation, which lasted for just a split second as I watched Maddy burst into tears and then dash outside.

Mr. Cottington looked utterly shell-shocked. He chose to say nothing at all to me; he just left, followed by his trainees. The judge had already departed, and so I sat there in silence for a moment, trying to take in what it was I'd just done.

"Well, I've been in this job over twenty years, and I've never seen anything like that before," said the clerk.

I attempted a brave smile. "I just think we should be really sure," I ventured. "You know, before we finally cut the knot."

"Right." The clerk was straightening the chairs. "As I say, people are usually pretty sure by the time they get here."

I felt embarrassed and a little bit foolish. Part of me had wanted to rush after Maddy, but I didn't want to experience the angry side of her that I had just remembered. I sat staring straight ahead.

The clerk had finished gathering her things. "That was the last case before lunch, but I'm afraid I can't leave you in here on your own."

"No, of course," I said.

"Good luck sorting out your marriage— or we'll see you back here in a couple of months . . ."

MADDY and I are on a train. We have not been out of university that long and don't view this space as a train so much as a moving pub. I find the perfect double seat in the smoking compartment and buy enough drinks for the whole journey; an hour or so later Maddy goes off to buy the food I neglected to get. But she is taking much longer than I had. There is still no sign of her when a message comes over the loudspeaker.

"This is a passenger announcement . . ." For a split second I think, A female train guard— you don't hear that very often.

"British Rail would like to apologize for the man serving in the buffet car. British Rail now

accepts that none of the female passengers on this train wish to be asked for their phone number by a middle-aged man wearing a wedding ring and a name badge saying 'Jeff.'" Maddy has the monotone delivery to perfection. People in the seats around me are looking at each other with widening grins. "They would also appreciate it if Jeff could attempt to maintain eye contact while serving the All-Day Breakfast instead of staring at the breasts of the female on the other side of the counter."*

There is a spontaneous round of applause from all the women customers in our carriage. A couple of them even cheer.

I can't wait for Maddy to come back. I am so fantastically proud of her; she has made total strangers on a train start laughing and talking to one another. The hubbub is still going as she saunters through the door with a completely straight face. "There's our rogue announcer!" I boast loudly. It is probably a mistake to tell the whole carriage, but we don't particularly mind being turfed off the train at Didcot Parkway.

THE defining characteristic of this memory was the powerful sensations of love and pride it conjured up. And yet it was deeply frustrating to have so little else of our past lives in which to place it. My life map was incredibly detailed on everything I remembered since October 22, and then there were just a few aerial snapshots of the uncharted continent beyond.

I resolved that I was going to talk to Maddy alone. I felt I owed it to her to tell her, one to one, what had happened to me. If she was not at home, I had the address of "the studio" where she worked. I had learned that Madeleine was not a painter, but an artist nonetheless, selling huge framed photos she had taken of London landmarks, which funded her more experimental photographic works. Maddy was a photographer, and a classy one by the sound of it. It made me that little bit more proud of her.

"WHAT the hell are you doing here?" said Maddy, opening her front door.

"I wanted to meet—I mean, *talk* to you. Properly."

"You've got a nerve."

In my fantasy reunion I had imagined her being more pleased to see me. "I thought I owed you an explanation. Are you alone?"

The dog was barking from the back garden.

"What business is it of yours?"

"It's just—well, it's complicated, and if the kids are in, then . . ."

"No, they're at school, obviously." I hovered there for a decade or so. "All right, well, you'd better come in," and she headed inside.

The dog came bounding down the hallway and nearly knocked me over with his enthusiasm. I tried to give him some attention as I gazed around in wonder. I could feel myself shaking as we entered the kitchen. I didn't know quite where to start. A battered iPod was plugged into some speakers, and I recognized the song.

"Hey, you like Coldplay. I love Coldplay," I said.

"No, you don't. You hate Coldplay. You always made me turn it off."

"Oh. Well, I like it now . . ."

"So what's going on, Vaughan? You ignore all my emails and texts, and then you turn up to the court and pull a stunt like that." Her brow went all creased when she looked concerned.

"Erm, well, the thing is, that a couple of weeks ago—October twenty-second to be precise—at some point in the late afternoon I was sort of . . . reborn."

She looked at me with suspicion. "What are you talking about?"

"I was in hospital for a week or so, following a psychogenic fugue."

"A what?"

"It means that my mind completely wiped itself of personal memories. I lost all knowledge of my own name, identity, family, friends. I've been told I've known you for twenty years. But standing here right now, it's like I'm talking to you for the first time."

She regarded me suspiciously. "I don't know what your scam is, but you're not getting this house."

"Yeah, Gary told me that we were getting a divorce, although I don't remember why. The doctor said the stress I experienced from the marriage breakup might be what triggered the fugue."

"You weren't ever here to experience any stress; you were staying late at work or going round to Gary's to fart around on computers."

"It's a lovely kitchen. Really homey."

"Why are you being so weird, Vaughan? And why are you patting the dog like that; you know he doesn't like it—"

"No, *I don't know!* For most of last week I had a hospital label on my wrist saying 'unknown white male.' Look, I've still got it. And see this metal tag around my neck? It has my name and contact numbers on it in case my brain wipes all over again and I am left wandering the streets."

She plunked a mug of tea in front of me.

"Do you have any sugar?" I asked.

"You don't take sugar."

"That's what Gary said. He reckoned I used to smoke as well."

She leaned closer and smelled me. "That's what's different. You don't stink of stale nicotine. I can't believe you finally gave up."

"I didn't give up. It was wiped along with everything else."

She was leaning against the sink with her arms folded and seemed perplexed as to why I should make up such an extraordinary story. Then she pulled out her mobile phone, and I heard one end of a conversation with Linda. She was looking at me as she talked, her eyes widening and her face draining of color. When she had finished, she slumped down on a chair.

"That is so typical of you! All that crap I'm dealing with, and then you just wipe the slate clean and forget all about it . . ."

"Oh. Sorry." Part of me wanted to comfort her, but her body language did not suggest I should move in for a hug.

"How are the kids going to take this? It's bad enough that we've split up, but now their own father doesn't even know them! They'll be home from school in a few hours. You can't be here—they'll be scarred for life."

"Whatever you say. You know what's best for them—I don't."

"Yeah, well, no change there." She glanced up and then softened slightly. "I thought you were being odd in court. All that trying to catch my eye."

"It's just that normally you get to meet your wife *before* you divorce her."

"So . . . you literally cannot remember us? Or any of this?"

"Not really."

"Not really?"

"All right—not at all. Although a couple
of moments have come back. I remember the
tent collapsing in Ireland and you using the
loudspeaker on some long rail journey?"

"Oh, yeah, we got kicked off the train for
that."

"But that's all so far. Except the other
night I had a powerful dream about someone nicknamed Bambi."

Maddy blushed slightly but said nothing.

"What? You know, don't you? Who's
Bambi?"

"Bambi is what you used to call me when
we were at university. You said I had the
same eyes. Can't believe I fell for that." She
mimed putting her fingers down her throat.

"Well—if it's not too forward of me—you
have got very nice eyes."

Maddy sipped her tea. "You really have
forgotten everything, haven't you? I have
'nice eyes'? Where the hell does that come
from? You said I was a selfish cow; you said
I was ruining your life."

"Did I? I'm sorry if I said that. But I just
don't remember."

"Yeah, well, how nice for you."

"It's not very nice, really," I said slowly,

staring at the floor. "It was incredibly distressing to start with."

"So—like, you didn't know your own name or anything?"

"Not for the whole week I was in hospital. All I could think about was who I might have been before my amnesia. I began to worry whether my life had been a good one, whether I had been a good person, you know? Now I discover my marriage failed and I've been sleeping on people's sofas and have spent all my money on divorce lawyers."

She didn't know what to say to that. Instead, her eyes welled up, and then she began quietly crying. I so wanted to kiss her at that point; just to put my arms around my wife would have been wonderful. I finally leaned across and gently rubbed her arm.

"What are you doing?"

"Er—comforting you?"

"Well, don't!"

Then I spotted a photo on the fridge. "Are these our children? Is this what they look like?" The girl had a big, open-hearted smile for the camera, while the boy was doing his best to look cool. Dillie looked just like her mother, and Jamie looked just like me. "Wow! They're beautiful," I said.

"Dillie's a bit taller than that now. Jamie hates having his photo taken."

It was a surreal moment. The mother couldn't help but be proud of her children as she showed their father what they looked like. Maddy put her tongue out slightly as she straightened the photo, and in that moment all the emptiness I had felt since October 22 was filled with an overwhelming certainty. Just that sweet movement of her mouth made me feel whole.

"Beautiful," I said again. "Really beautiful."

ON THE walk home the whole world seemed different. I wanted to tell passing strangers that I had just met this wonderful girl. I was still elated when I found Gary in his kitchen with the insides of a laptop spread across the table.

"Gary! Something incredible has happened! I think I've fallen in love!"

"Wow! That's great news, man! What's her name?"

"Maddy. I've just met my wife, and she is

something else, isn't she? Her eyes are this beautiful hazel brown—"

Gary groaned. "Yeah, she is *something else*, Vaughan—she is your ex-wife. Listen, mate, this must be related to your condition. This is like an emotional memory coming back. It'll soon fade."

"No, it's not going to fade, Gary. This is forever. It feels as if all my life I've been waiting for that special someone, and I've finally met Miss Right."

"Okay. Except that all your adult life you've been married to her and finally decided she was Miss Wrong."

"I know we're getting divorced and that. But every relationship has to overcome a few obstacles—look at Romeo and Juliet."

"Yeah, they both die. You don't love her, Vaughan. You're delirious." Gary sat me down at the kitchen table. "If you are looking for someone who might be interested in making a future with you, I'd say the very last woman you should go after is the woman married to you for fifteen years who can't stand the sight of you."

"It's not like that. You don't know Maddy like I do—"

"No—I know her *better*. It's not going to happen, Vaughan. You've got to move on. Listen, I've had a brilliant idea for how you can find out more about your past . . ."

DEAR ALL,

As you may be aware, I recently experienced a form of amnesia that has wiped all my personal memories. This means that I cannot recall anything before October 22 this year. However, with your help I am hoping I can reconstruct my personal history from the fragments that you yourselves can remember.

It would be greatly appreciated if you could look at this Wikipedia page, which I have begun, and then add any details you remember. For example, if you were there with me at the University of Bangor, you might add the names of tutors I had or clubs I joined. My hope is that this online document will grow to become a complete account of my life before my amnesia.

Many thanks,
Vaughan

With his zealous belief in the power of user-generated content, Gary had come up with an initiative to establish a detailed account of my life to date. My appeal went out via email, Facebook, and, for what it was worth, the features pages of YouNews. I was going to have my own memoir collaboratively written online. I wondered how this perspective might affect the reader's sympathies. It would be like the United States having its history rewritten from scratch by Britain, Mexico, Japan, the Native Americans, and Iraq.

"IT's an interesting idea," said Dr. Lewington as I proudly told her how my personal memories were going to be compiled by others. It was now three weeks since I had had the fugue, and this was my first appointment back at the hospital. "Though you should continue to keep a separate record of your own memories. Are you writing them down?"

"Yes. I have a little notepad by my bed. With lots of blank pages."

"And how are you feeling in yourself? I

can refer you to a psychiatrist or a counselor if you feel that would be at all helpful."

"No, I'm fine, really. I think I've fallen in love."

"That's wonderful. I remember you were getting divorced."

"Yup, that's her. She still wants to get divorced, but I was hoping she might marry me again after that."

"Right. As I say, the offer of a psychiatrist is always there . . ."

At the end of our session Dr. Lewington asked to see my online biography, and I found myself feeling a little nervous as she clicked on the link. But in those first twenty-four hours no one had written a single word about me.

Over the next day or so I kept returning to the document. I could tell from checking the article history that a few people had opened the page, but no one had taken the trouble to write anything.

Not even Maddy had responded, and I worried about how she was dealing with the bombshell that her husband had forgotten their entire marriage. But then Linda took a phone call from Maddy; apparently she wanted to meet up with me "and have a serious talk."

"Ha, that's almost like a date, isn't it?" I suggested optimistically.

"Um, I don't think so, Vaughan."

A few minutes later I came out of my room to ask Linda's advice. "What do you think— is this shirt too bright? Would this one be better?"

"They're both fine. It doesn't matter what you wear. Just be yourself."

"Just be myself. So, er, what is 'myself,' exactly?"

I WAS ridiculously early to the café in Covent Garden and chose a seat outside so I'd be able to see her coming. Finally Madeleine approached, and I stood up. I went to give her a peck on the cheek, but she didn't move toward me. I was forced to pretend I was leaning over to pull out her chair.

"Hi! Great to see you! You look nice . . ."

"Shall we get on with it?" she said, playing it rather cool, I thought.

Today she was wearing her hair down, and I decided that she wasn't so much a redhead as a strawberry blonde. I asked her what sort of coffee she wanted; she requested a double espresso and insisted on handing over the exact amount in loose change.

"Hey, double espresso! Same as me!" I said with enthusiasm, wondering what that might taste like.

"No, you always have a cappuccino."

With her already knowing me so well, there was less of the exploratory trivia that I would have liked to warm up with.

"Anyway, listen, I talked to my lawyer, and I think it's actually good that the final hearing got postponed."

"Oh, great!" I said, trying not to wince at the strength of my black coffee.

"Yes—he said that if the hearing had gone ahead and it was then discovered that you were not in a fit state, then the whole divorce might have been invalidated. Better to get divorced when we know it would be cast-iron."

"Oh." I sighed. "I see."

"He says you have to get medical attestation that you have the mental capacity to give instruction. So you need to see a psychiatrist as soon as possible so that we can finalize the divorce."

"I'm not mad. Why does everyone think I need a psychiatrist?"

"You and me giving the marriage another go was pretty mad, you must admit."

If she could only get to know me, she would surely forget all that negative stuff she'd heard about me from her divorce lawyer and would be convinced that here, finally, was the man for her.

"How are the kids?"

"I've tried to give them an inkling of what's happened to you, but Dillie was quite upset by it all. We're going to have to handle it very carefully."

Privately I was frightened of being introduced to my own children. I was desperate to make the right first impression on two people who had known me all their lives.

"Okay, I'll follow your lead. But tell them I can't wait to meet them."

"No, I won't say that."

"I mean see them. *Again*."

I ripped open the top of a sugar sachet and shared the contents between my coffee cup and the surface of the table.

"Still taking sugar, then?"

"For as long as I can remember . . ."

"But you're not smoking? All those years I begged you to give up and you said it was impossible. And then you give up just like that!"

"That's all it takes, a bit of willpower. And a psychogenic fugue. Are you sure I can't get you a blueberry muffin or anything?"

"When have I ever eaten blueberry muffins?"

"I don't know, do I?"

"So just how much can you remember now? If you can remember the camping holiday and the time you got us kicked off the train . . . Is it all starting to come back?"

I thought about her shouting at me about the smoke alarm. "No, there's not much else yet."

"Well, maybe that's a blessing."

"I don't remember why we split up. I was serious about what I said in the courtroom. About us giving it another go."

"Come off it, Vaughan—our marriage was over a long time ago." And then her demeanor changed. "God, when I think of what I put up with!"

"There is something else I remember," I said triumphantly. "I remember you being too cross about trivial things. Going ballistic because I forgot to replace the battery in the smoke alarm—"

"Trivial?"

"I don't see why it was such a big deal."

She looked at me as if I was stupid. "Because there was a fire. That's why I was cross. There was a fire in our kitchen while we were all asleep, and the smoke alarm failed to go off because you had taken the battery out."

This is why it is best to be in full command of the facts when you get into an argument. "I . . . I don't remember that bit . . ." I mumbled.

"But you remember me being cross about it?"

"Vaguely . . . Were we outside?"

"Er, yes, because our house was on fire. The whole family was standing in the back garden in our pajamas while the fire brigade chucked all the smoldering kitchen units out onto the patio."

The scene was still lost to me. "Blimey. So who raised the alarm?"

"You nudged me and asked if I could smell smoke."

"Oh, well, so that sort of cancels out removing the battery."

"No, it does not—we could all have been killed!"

"I might have smelled smoke quicker than the alarm would have detected it."

"Okay—you were the hero of the hour. Wow, that is quite a rewriting of history there. Silly me—I must have remembered it all wrong."

I couldn't help thinking that this was our first argument, but thought it best not to mention it.

"A rose for the lady?" said a flower seller in a powerful Eastern European accent. The scent of roses was slightly lost in the fug of tobacco smoke from the wet cigarette hanging from his lip.

"Er, no. No, thank you."

"Hey, lady—you want him buy you romantic flower?"

"No, thank you very much."

The vendor wandered off, but his appearance had punctured the increasingly dangerous atmosphere.

"You can't just wipe the slate clean. You're attracted to this romantic idea of Vaughan and his happy wife, but your past wasn't all drunken giggling in a tent."

"Look, people change," I pleaded. "I'm really sorry about all the things that hurt you when our marriage went wrong. I can't imagine why I would have done them, but I clearly found it all so traumatic that my brain completely wiped any memory of it. And now the only thing I can remember about you is how passionately I felt when we first met."

"Well, you wait till you get the rest of your memory back. You don't love me, Vaughan. Your mind is still playing tricks on you."

The flower seller had started on the next café along from us.

"Excuse me!" I called across to him. "How much are the roses?"

"Vaughan—do *not* buy me a rose."

But the nicotine-stained fingers were already pulling out one cellophane-wrapped instant love token.

"I'll give you fifty pounds for the whole lot."

"Vaughan—you're wasting your money."

The man gave an impassive nod and quickly exchanged the notes in my hand for a huge bunch of skinny red roses.

"He love you very much."

"Actually, we were just finalizing our divorce," she explained.

"Your wife—funny lady!" laughed the flower seller. But neither of us joined in. My dramatic gesture had only irritated Maddy further.

Desperately I made one last pitch to her. "My memory loss might be the best thing that ever happened to us."

"For God's sake, Vaughan, one of the things that used to drive me mad about you was that you forgot everything I told you. If it was anything about *your* life, then you remembered it all right, but if it was something I was doing, then it wasn't important enough to register. You forgot I existed years ago. This isn't a mental illness. This is just who you are. It's over, Vaughan! We are getting a divorce. End of story. End of us."

And she got up and walked away, leaving fifty red roses on the table in front of me.

Chapter 4

"VAUGHAN. I've got some bad news, mate." It was exactly a month since my fugue, and I had come in to find Gary seated in the kitchen. "It's your father. He's had another heart attack."

"*My father?* My father is alive? Why didn't you say so?"

"You never specifically asked." Gary raised his hands defensively.

"But you talked about my parents in the *past tense*."

"Well—the past is like, when I knew them. So, anyway, that's good news then, if you thought he was dead. He's not—he's alive. Just. Although you might not want to leave it too long, mate . . ."

Questions I wished I had asked long before were fired at Gary. "How old is he?" "When was his last heart attack?" and "What do I call him?"

"I dunno. 'Dad,' I think."

All Gary knew was that Madeleine had called Linda to say that she was going to the hospital with the kids to see their grandfather.

He was out of intensive care and could be visited for a short period.

"Maybe I should call her. You know—to find out what time she's going to be there and how it works and everything."

"You could do. Except she said don't call her."

I had not felt ready to meet my own children yet. But with my father, events now forced me to arrange an immediate introduction. I had to get to know him so that I could be properly upset if he died.

THERE was a moment as I entered the hospital when I wondered if I ought to buy my dad something from the gift shop. But of course I had no knowledge of my father's tastes or interests. "Dad" was currently an amalgam of all the paternal role models that had survived my amnesia. Baron von Trapp and King Lear were mixed up with Homer Simpson.

On the fourth floor I was directed toward my father's room. Lying in the hospital bed, surrounded by purring machines, was a skeletal old man.

"Is that you, son?" he said through his oxygen mask.

"Yes. Yes, it's me."

"You are very good. To come and see me." His voice was weak.

"That's okay. How are you feeling?"

"Ooh, you know. Just pleased to be here."

"Is there anything I can get you?"

"Large whisky. No ice."

I smiled. I realized I already liked my dad. He managed to be humorous even though he was at death's door.

"Maddy and the kids. Were here . . . Wonderful children."

"They are. And they've coped so well with it all."

The old man processed what I'd just said. "Coped with what?"

Instantly it hit me that he knew nothing about our marriage breakup. Of course—my father had a heart condition; why would we have added the stress of telling him that his only child's marriage had failed? And by the same token, he clearly hadn't been told that I was suffering from amnesia.

"I mean, they've coped well with their grandfather having a heart attack."

I tried to imagine this man holding my infant hand and leading me across the road; I visualized us kicking a leather football together in some imaginary back garden. But none of it came into focus.

"Do you remember us playing football when I was little?" I asked.

"How could I forget? You were always . . ."—he paused for a moment as he searched for the right words—". . . so *useless!*"

I attempted to move on. "Well, football was never really my thing. Gary was reminding me how I used to sing in a band."

"Oh, yes. What a voice! Like a strangled cat."

I realized it was wonderful that my father was still able to tease me like this from his hospital bed. This was clearly Dad's way of showing his affection.

"But none of that matters, because the big thing in life . . . you got right." His voice was growing increasingly strained now.

"What—my job?"

"No. *Your wife.* You married the right girl." I struggled to hear the whispered sentences under his mask. "You two. Are perfect together."

Any sentence can seem apt and profound

if it's uttered on your deathbed. But for my own father to spare the breath to tell me that Madeleine and I were perfect together—it was the first time anyone had had anything positive to say about my marriage.

Then suddenly my time was up. "Bit tired now, son. Can't talk anymore."

"Okay." And then I forced myself to say it. "Okay, *Dad.*"

The noise of his breathing changed gear as he sank almost instantly into a deep sleep. I sat there, trying to spot myself in those weathered features. I had worried that seeing an unrecognizable parent would make me want to cry, but actually I found myself feeling uplifted. His instinct about Madeleine was the same as mine. "Perfect together" is what he had said.

I WAS disappointed to find Gary and Linda's flat empty when I got back. I had so wanted to tell them all about my father. Maybe I could call Maddy now and talk to her about him. What could be more natural, the two of us catching up about our respective visits to the hospital? I pressed the buttons on the phone. I was shocked that it was answered almost immediately.

"Hello?" said a girl's voice. "Hello, who is it, please?" she said after a pause. "Mum, they're not saying anything, but I think there's someone there." Then the line was cut off. That was the first time I had heard my daughter's voice.

I had used my own mobile phone but had withheld the caller ID. Looking at the phone, I suddenly noticed the camera icon on the menu. I excitedly scrolled across to find another icon labeled "Photos." Just one click and I uncovered a whole gallery of pictures of Jamie with the dog or Maddy with the dog or myself with the dog. Then there were images of Dillie as well, giving a big smile to the photographer. I scrolled through them all slowly and then nearly ran down the battery staring at pictures of Maddy, trying to discern her feelings in every photo. No rational thought could counter the overwhelming gravitational pull I felt toward the woman my father had said was perfect for me.

An hour later I stood in front of the bathroom mirror and raised the blade to my throat. Soon big gray-streaked tufts of beard were falling into the basin. Bit by bit I saw the shape of my face emerge from hiding. I tried to persuade myself I looked rather square-jawed and handsome, like James Bond—an effect only slightly spoiled by the specks of blood that needed immediate patching. The clean-shaven figure was still wearing the shabby old clothes I'd found in Gary and Linda's bedroom cupboard, but now I set about part two of my action plan.

Gary had said to me that my fugue was just some sort of midlife crisis. His words came back to me as I strode into the menswear section of a large department store.

The makers of the suits I liked best had spent money where no one else would see it; there were flowered linings and little extra pockets on the inside. I felt myself standing an inch taller in front of the mirror; I looked sharp and in control. I bought three designer suits, three shirts, and two pairs of shoes. I kept one of the suits on; my old clothes were placed inside shopping bags, even though I could never imagine wearing them again.

One month after my fugue I was self-consciously launching Vaughan 2.0. Yes, there had been teething problems with the operating system, and the memory was limited, but this model would look cleaner and sleeker; it would have a more user-friendly interface; it would not emit smoke or cause battery problems. My hope was that it would be exactly the sort of hardware that someone like Maddy, for example, might find desirable.

"There you are, sir!" said the shop assistant, passing over the suits in big, expensive-looking bags. "Special occasion, is it?"

"Sort of. I've just met my wife."

"Congratulations! When are you getting married?"

"Let's not get too hasty," I said. "I've got to divorce her first . . ."

WHEN I came back, Linda was in the kitchen stirring a saucepan. She let out a startled scream, then fought off this approaching stranger by striking me with a spoon covered in leek-and-potato soup.

"Linda! It's me!"

"Bloody hell, Vaughan—you look completely different."

"You've got gunge all over my new suit!"

"Sorry, I didn't recognize you. You look so smart! Well, you *did* anyway . . ." She took my jacket and was wiping it clean as Gary wandered in.

"Well?" she said to her husband expectantly.

"Er—new frock?"

"Not me—what about Vaughan?"

"What?"

"He's shaved his beard off!"

"Oh, that's what's different. I thought he'd just washed or something."

"And the suit?"

"Oh, yeah! Of course, it's the big day on Monday, isn't it? First day back at work . . ."

I had indeed resolved to return to my former workplace. Sitting around Gary and Linda's flat all day was not doing anything for my fragile sanity.

"HELLO, Vaughan, great to have you back," said the receptionist at my old school as I walked into the building. Helpfully, Jane Marshall wore a card round her neck that told you her name.

I knew the principal's name, but now I didn't know whether to call him "Peter" or

"Mr. Scott." He had personally undertaken the job of welcoming me back and talking to me about my "reintegration into the school community." The two of us were walking around the corridors, giving me a chance to meet staff and "refamiliarize" myself with the building. Everyone was behaving so normally, they'd obviously had a serious talk about behaving normally. Each of them smiled and proffered a warm hello as I passed, and then got back to gossiping about whether I was faking the whole thing.

I had been paid in full for all the time I had been off on leave, and today there would be a meeting at which we'd discuss what work I might realistically be able to undertake. "I've been rereading the syllabus—I'm keen to start teaching as soon as possible," I declared. "I owe it to the students to get back to work ASAP."

"Goodness. You really have forgotten everything, haven't you?"

Two pupils disappearing round a corner shouted, "Oi, Boggy Vaughan! Where's your bog brush?" and then ran away laughing.

"Boggy Vaughan?"

"It's just a minority of students who call

you that. You're known for many other things apart from the time you cleaned all the toilets."

"Why did I clean all the toilets?"

"To set an example to the students about 'declining lavatory standards.' I wouldn't have held up a toilet brush in assembly myself, but you got their attention, I suppose."

"Boggy Vaughan's back!" came a voice from the atrium as we passed.

"Oh, well, I'm sure it'll blow over . . ."

"Maybe. To be frank, Vaughan, I know you were having problems at home, but you stopped loving your job as well. Kids can always tell."

Perhaps I wasn't quite ready to face the students just yet. So we agreed that I might start with a little administration in the school office. But I was starting work again! This was my place of work.

SLOWLY I was groping my way toward some sort of purpose. I still didn't have a past, but like everything else in the modern world, you simply had to look it up on the Internet. That evening I logged on to see that my online memoir had changed completely. Now my life story was filling out. Although not everyone had entered into the exercise with the serious academic rigor that I had hoped for.

Jack Joseph Neil Vaughan, commonly known as "Vaughan," was born on May 6, 1971. With his father posted overseas with the Royal Air Force, Vaughan spent his childhood in many different parts of the world. He attended Bangor University, where he and his friend Gary Barnett played football together, although Vaughan became a substitute while Gary became the top scorer for two seasons in a row. In his first year at Bangor he met his future wife, Madeleine. Maddy is hot.

In 2001 Mr. Vaughan began teaching history at Wandle Academy. His nickname is "Boggy Vaughan" because he loves cleaning the bog. He is the Bogmeister General, Bogimus Maximus, the Boginator; Boggy! Boggy! Boggy! Oi! Oi! Oi!

Vaughan was a speaker at the "Lessons Worth Behaving For" Conference at Kettering and was very boring. Vaughan plays five-a-side football every Tuesday night and has all the grace and skill of an ostrich. Hello, Vaughan, long time no see, mate! Cheers! Karl.

I went to bed telling myself that the past was past and there was nothing I could do to change it. Apart from deleting how boring I was at Kettering—I could change that bit. And the references to how bad at football I was—it didn't need those.

It is the early 1990s, and Madeleine and I have been a couple for less than a year. Maddy has gone to Brussels with a friend. When she checks in at the hotel, the concierge says there is a letter waiting for her. She opens the envelope to find the battered postcard of the leprechaun still raising a pint of Guinness. She never mentions it to me.

Months after that I receive a huge parcel in the post. Inside is another cardboard box. Inside that is some packing material protecting a posh presentation case. After a dozen layers I finally get through to a small embossed envelope, and although I now realize that someone is playing an elaborate joke, it still has not oc-curred to me that I am about to get back the postcard I was supposed to have sent to Great-Auntie Brenda.

AND so the iconic symbol was passed back and forth down the years, with neither of us ever mentioning the game to the other. I would simply smile to myself at the ingenu-ity of my partner and bide my time as I plot-ted an even more elaborate way of placing it back into Maddy's custody. Receipt of the card meant that it was now that person's responsibility to post this bloody thing to Great-Auntie Brenda, even though she had long since died and the address on the card was now occupied by a family from Bangladesh.

One day when Maddy turned on her new computer, the screen was filled with a digital photo of the leprechaun. When she suggested I order a pizza from my usual home-delivery service, I opened the box to find that she had arranged to deliver me Great-Auntie Brenda's card instead. When Maddy had put tasteful framed black-and-white photographs of the children up the stairs, she came home one day to notice that every frame contained a photocopy of a grinning leprechaun saying "Top o' the mornin' to yers!"

The memory of all this came back to me in one split second, sitting in front of a computer during my first day back at work. I wanted to tell everyone seated around me, but the school admin team seemed uncomfortable enough with having one of the teachers parked in their office without me drawing attention to my strange mental illness.

My first day in my new job felt empowering. I was making a contribution; I had a reason to get up in the morning. My task for the day was entering data on the pupils, whether they were on free school meals or had English as an additional language. But I couldn't prevent my mind from returning to two children in particular.

I had agreed to go to the house at six o'clock that evening to take my son and daughter to the Winter Wonderland funfair on the Common. Then we would meet Maddy for a pizza, and by the end of the evening I would, I hoped, feel like a father again. They had been told about my neurological condition, though I was not confident they would understand the extent of my amnesia.

I ARRIVED at the house twenty minutes early. I walked up and down on the frosty pavement for a while until Madeleine opened the front door and shouted over to me. "So are you going to ring the buzzer or what?" She was wearing a red spotty dress that had an almost humorous edge to it, but standing at the open door, she folded her arms against the cold as I approached. "Kids!" she called out. "Your dad's here!"

An avalanche of enthusiasm came thundering down the stairs, knocking me off balance as both children threw their arms around me and hugged me tightly. They smelled of washing powder and hair conditioner—my children were all fresh and new. The dog, circling this melee, barked in enthusiasm. My heart definitely remembered what my head had forgotten: I felt like I had regained a couple of limbs that I had not realized had been amputated. I would need months of practice to be able to love them properly, but it was still a miracle—Maddy and I had made these beautiful human beings.

I asked them what they'd been up to and listened to funny stories from school, and I could sense Maddy watching me interact with them and noticed her smile a couple of times. They were confident and chatty—when Dillie was excited, she talked faster than I had imagined was humanly possible, segueing wildly from one subject to the next in mid-sentence. "Oh-my-god-it-was-so-funny-Miss-Kerrins-told-Nadim-in-science-not-to-bring-in-his-rat-yeah-'cause-like-it-always-gets-out-oh-I-like-your-suit-is-that-new-anyway-he-put-it-in-her-handbag-on-her-desk-oh-I-got-an-A-in-Math-by-the-way-so-she-is-like-totally-phobic-about-rats-so-she-screamed-and-ran-out-of-the-classroom-can-we-record-Friends-before-we-go?"

It seemed her brother had the skill to extricate the important points. "Yeah, why are you wearing a suit, Dad? And why did you shave your beard off? Are you having a midlife crisis?"

"Oh, fresh start and all that. Is it too much?"

"No," said Maddy. "It looks very nice."

"Dad, you're blushing. Why are you blushing?"

The kids were impatient to go to the Winter Wonderland funfair. "Are you sure you don't want to come?"

"No," said Maddy with a half smile. "You've got too much catching up to do to have me in the way."

"Well, I have a lot of catching up to do with you as well."

Maddy raised her eyebrows as if to suggest that I was close to crossing the line. "See you at the pizza place at half past seven." And the door was closed.

INSIDE the Hall of Mirrors I saw my distorted face smiling at the kids laughing and waving at our bizarre reflections.

"Of course, this might be what we actually look like," I ventured.

"No, because then our eyes would have to be wrong as well," pointed out Jamie, whose intelligent point was rather undermined by his forehead being longer than his legs.

"Depends what our brain does with the info it receives. Maybe we just see everything the way we want to see it."

"Dad?" Dillie asked. "Did you really completely forget me and Jamie?"

"Erm—well—it's all still in there," I said. "At the moment I don't remember lots of facts about you, but I haven't forgotten how I feel about you. I haven't forgotten . . . how much I love you."

"Aaaah," she said, while in the mirror I could see Jamie miming putting his fingers down his throat.

Jamie and Dillie dashed about, jumping forward and backward. I stopped looking at my own distorted image and watched my new son and daughter instead. They made me feel as if my lost past wasn't important; it was right here, right now that really mattered.

"Urgh—look what's happened to my body!" shrieked Jamie.

"That's what I say to the mirror every morning."

"Ahh, no, Dad," said Dillie. "You're in quite good shape. You know, for someone who's, like, really old."

I actually felt ten years younger today. The children's energy and optimism was infectious, and I felt a cocktail of pleasure, anxiety, responsibility, and delight that I realized was how it must feel to be a parent.

MADDY was already seated in Pizza Express when we arrived. She laughed when she saw her two kids with cotton candy stuck to their hair and faces. This response was surely a signal of approval, I thought. A woman who was 100 percent set on divorce would have interpreted this as evidence of my incompetence or irresponsibility.

The comfortable atmosphere prompted Dillie to ask if I was going to come and stay for Christmas, but Maddy took this opportunity to go to the ladies' room. Not a good sign.

"So kids, let's go out again soon. Or if your mum is busy one day, I could come round to the house and look after you."

"Hey, yeah!" said Dillie. "Or when Mum goes away after Christmas, you could come and stay instead of Granny."

"Oh, that would be wonderful. I'd love that. So where's Mum going?"

"She's going to Venice with Ralph," said Dillie as Jamie shot her a look.

"Ralph? Who's Ralph?"

"Durr! Ralph is Mum's boyfriend."

And Maddy returned to the table. "Everything all right?"

Chapter 5

"OH, VAUGHAN *is* marvelous!" said Maddy's mother, Jean, as I placed a couple of dirty plates near the dishwasher. "Isn't he marvelous, Madeleine?"

"It's only a couple of plates, Mum. It was *me* who bought the food, made the stuffing, set the table, and carved the turkey."

"Well, I think it's wonderful when a man helps around the kitchen. Look at that! He's scraping the plates into the bin. He *is* good."

I couldn't resist stirring things a little more by offering to make coffee.

"Oh, you are a dear. No, you sit down; you've done enough already. I'll make the coffee. Madeleine, can you give me a hand, dear?"

Christmas dinner had been easier than I had expected. Maddy's mother had showed no hostility to her estranged son-in-law; on the contrary, I found my apparently abundant qualities constantly highlighted, usually when Jean's own husband was in earshot. It might have been more honest for Jean to hold up large cards explaining the sledge-hammer subtext every time she spoke. "Your father never helped around the house, Madeleine. You must be finding it harder now, without Vaughan here to help?" telegraphed the message: *"My husband was much worse than yours, but I stuck with it."*

Maddy's father, Ron, might have felt offended by the stream of unsubtle reminders of his apparent failings as a father and husband, but long ago he had developed the skill of tuning out his wife, reacting only to occasional trigger words that might be of interest to him.

"Vaughan offered to make the coffee, Ron. That was nice of him."

"Coffee? Oh, yes, please."

The whole day had gone reasonably well. I gave the children their presents, having spent a happy afternoon at the shops so that Jamie could come with me to the cash machine and choose his money himself. Dillie had wanted a little electronic diary into which you could type your secrets and no one could read them because only you knew how to access it. A bit like my brain, I thought, except that she hadn't forgotten the password yet.

I had been unsure whether I should get Maddy anything. But I happened to stumble upon a beautiful but understated gold necklace after browsing through a number of jewelry shops. And there was a satisfactory moment of tension after lunch when Madeleine unwrapped my present and murmured, "You shouldn't have." I knew she really meant it. I had clearly spent a great deal of time and money choosing the perfect gift. Right now Maddy would have preferred a present from her ex-partner that confirmed how wrong for her I really was.

Jean was very effusive about what a lovely present the necklace was. "What have you got Vaughan, Madeleine?"

"I didn't get him a present, Mum. We're getting divorced."

"He's still your husband till then, dear."

My gift had been more than a casual act of generosity, and Maddy knew it. This was me resolutely defending the moral high ground that I felt I had seized after discovering that she was seeing another man.

So throughout Christmas Day I played the role of attentive husband. Maddy would head off to the airport the following morning at six, and I would be left alone with my children. I had initially worried that my mother-in-law might be indignant that she was no longer required to look after her grandchildren, but Jean thought the idea excellent. "Isn't it wonderful that Vaughan's moving back in?"

"He's not moving back in, Mum; he's staying here while I'm away."

"Still," said Jean, "it'll be lovely for the children to have their father home."

THE grandparents went to bed, and then it was just the four of us around the fire in the family home: mother, father, and the two children.

"Let's play a game," enthused Dillie.

"What about the water game?" suggested Jamie to excited agreement from his sister.

"The water game? I don't like the sound of that."

"You think of a category—like 'football teams'—and one person has the name of a club, say 'Fulham,' in his head. Then he goes around behind everyone, holding an eggcup full of water above their head, and the first person to say 'Fulham' gets a drenching!"

"Okay, why don't you go first, Jamie?"

Jamie chose "*Simpsons* characters," and although I could only recall Bart and Homer, the latter was sufficient to get the water tipped over my head, which the kids thought was hilarious. Now it was my turn to wield the eggcup. I chose "Fruits" and selected "orange" as the detonator.

"Banana," said Dillie nervously.

"Starfruit," declared Jamie tactically. I moved on to Maddy.

"Orange," she said.

There was a split-second pause. "No . . ." and I moved on. I quickly revised my chosen fruit to "apple," but Maddy said that next time round, so I changed it again. Because Dillie was so desperate to have a go, I decided to pour the water over her whatever she said, which looked a bit suspicious when she said "potato." As she was wiping her head with the tea towel, I suddenly had a memory of the four of us together, doing exactly this.

"We played this before. On holiday, by a swimming pool?"

"That's right," said Maddy. "In France. You've had another memory!"

"And instead of tipping the cup on my head," remembered Jamie, "you picked me up and threw me in the pool!"

The room fell quiet for a moment, and then Dillie said, "Can we go back there? All of us. And play the water game by the pool?"

I struggled to find anything to say to fill the heavy silence. Eventually Jamie rescued the situation. "No, stupid. They're getting divorced."

FINALLY came the moment when the children had gone to bed and there was only Maddy and me left downstairs.

"Well, that all went as well as can be expected," I suggested.

"Better than last year, that's for sure."

"Sorry, you'll have to remind me . . ."

"Last Christmas we had a huge row after you drank yourself into a stupor, which you claimed 'was the only way to make this marriage bearable.'"

"Forgive me for asking, but did we ever try counseling?"

"Yeah, but we couldn't even agree on that. I wanted a woman counselor, and you said not having a bloke would tip the scales against you."

I flopped onto the sofa, and she sat down too, filling up her wineglass and offering the last of the bottle to me.

"I thought my drinking was one of the reasons why you didn't want to be with me?"

"It doesn't matter anymore, does it?"

I poured my wine into the potted plant she had just been given by her mother. "Okay, so I'll stop drinking. What else was it?"

"I don't want to have this discussion now."

"No, I have to know, because it doesn't make any sense. What was so impossible for us to work out? You have to give me concrete examples."

"I don't know." Her head stared up at the ceiling. "When you were young, you were so incisive about what was wrong with the world and how we had to change it. But over the years that just turned into general moaning."

"Okay, that's one thing," I noted. "Allegedly—"

"It was so boring! All these unimportant things making you cross." She was in full flow now. "I mean, I didn't mind that your hair turned gray, or the lines on your face. It was the aging of your soul that made you so much harder to love; all the goodness in you that got flabby and unexercised."

I got up and disposed of the wine bottle rather too forcefully. "That's hardly grounds for divorce, is it? You still haven't given me a good reason."

"We weren't happy." She sighed. "We were fighting all the time, and it made the kids miserable. What better reason do you need?"

"But what did we fight about?"

"Lots of things. You'd always encouraged me to do more photography. But once it finally started to take off, you resented having to accommodate me not being home all the time. You talked the talk of a supportive husband, but when it came to it—getting home from school in time, or giving up stuff like fiddling around on Gary's Internet site—you were never there."

"I admit I don't understand why I got involved with YouNews."

"It was just a reason not to be here, wasn't it? And then you couldn't believe that a certain gallery owner could be interested in exhibiting my photography. You said it was just because he fancied me."

"Okay—well, that does sound annoying. Clearly I was jealous of other men. You are very attractive, and perhaps this gallery owner thought so too."

"But it shows you couldn't see me as anything other than a bit of skirt. I mean, why couldn't he exhibit my stuff because I was an interesting photographer? Why did you presume it was only because Ralph fancied me?"

I nearly dropped the empty glass in my hand. "So this 'certain gallery owner' was Ralph? You're saying I shouldn't have suggested he fancied you, and tomorrow he's taking you to Venice?"

"Yes, but back then he was just a professional acquaintance."

"Who fancied you! I was right. Well, at least I was never unfaithful."

"What are you talking about? Neither was I."

"No? Isn't that your suitcase waiting by the front door?"

"That's what this is about, isn't it? You can't accept I might have met someone else."

"No—I can't accept that you won't give our marriage another go when I still don't see why it failed."

EARLY the following morning Maddy crept downstairs to find me already dressed in the kitchen.

"Wow—you're up early!"

"I wanted to get the kids' breakfast things ready. Here—I've made you a cup of tea."

"Thanks. *Did you see that, Ron? He made his wife a cup of tea.*" And the two of us were able to smile in a way that put the previous night's argument behind us.

The darkness outside seemed to add to the illicitness of this encounter—she was about to fly off with her boyfriend, but here she was sharing a half joke with her last partner.

"What was it like sleeping on the sofa bed?"

"It was fine. Except Woody hogged most of the duvet . . ."

Maddy got a text message. "Oh, that's . . . er, the car's outside."

She wheeled her bag to the doorway, and the two of us hovered there for a moment. "Okay—bye." It was clear that I was not to lean in and kiss her. "So, have a great time."

"Thanks." She unlocked the front door and forced an awkward smile.

"Just out of interest," I mused, "did we ever go to Venice?"

"No. You always said you'd take me, but it never happened."

"Oh. Sorry."

"It's okay. I'm going now, aren't I? Bye."

And the door closed, and I heard a muffled man's voice and Maddy's upbeat response and the sound of a car taking her away.

IF THE name of the place was supposed to fill you with excitement and wonder, it didn't work on me. "Splash City?"

"It's like a giant swimming complex with wave machines."

"It's a lovely idea, kids, but the thing is . . ." I stammered. "I don't think I can take you swimming . . . because I don't think I can remember how to swim."

"We'll teach you," squealed Dillie. "Just like you taught us!"

An hour later I found myself standing in a pair of baggy swimming shorts, plucking up courage to skip through the freezing footbath between the changing rooms and the pools. I was struck by the scale of the place. It was an enormous postmodern cathedral. Huge human-swallowing tubes spiraled through the air; children and adults alike were digested one by one, screaming as they disappeared down the fiberglass gullet.

We had agreed to start my lesson in the Little Tadpoles pool, where a sprinkling of under-fours splashed around with overkeen parents. The water came halfway up my thighs, so I decided it might be less embarrassing to squat down as the children debated the best way to proceed.

"We could both sort of hold him underneath while he practiced kicking his feet," said Jamie.

"Or there are some inflatable water wings in that basket."

"I can't wear those!" I protested. "They're for the under-fives!"

"No answering back in the learner pool," declared Dillie.

"Yes, be a good boy, and if you're very brave, we'll buy you an ice cream."

The kids seemed to find this reversal of power hilarious.

"And do not wee in the pool!" said Dillie too loudly.

They were in hysterics now. I was sure that when I had taught them to swim it wouldn't have involved me utterly humiliating them first.

"So how are we going to do this, then?" I demanded as a four-year-old swam confidently past me.

"Well, er . . . why don't you just start kicking your legs and moving your arms and see if you can do it?" suggested Jamie.

"All right! I will. Here goes . . ."

And then I just fell forward into the water. It felt unnatural and foolhardy, but I closed my eyes and found my arms were instinctively sculling and my legs flexing and pushing me onward. I was swimming!

I could hear my two kids cheering and

applauding, but I didn't want to stop, so I swam to the end of the pool in a forceful front crawl. I did a flawless tumble turn and powered my way through the water. Then I became aware of a blowing whistle, and I stood up to see the parents of toddlers in armbands clutching their frightened children and staring at me.

"Oi, mate, this is the children's pool," said the lifeguard. "Use the Olympic pool, you idiot."

I HAD a memorable lunch with my children at the burger franchise within the Splash City fun park. Because families came to this complex for the whole day, the eatery boasted a convenient waterside location at which it was traditional to dine in the ultra-casual dress of soggy swimming trunks.

"So are you going to move back out when Mum comes home?" asked my daughter, finally taking a break from a huge vanilla-chocolate shake.

"I think when couples get divorced they're generally supposed to live apart. I've been looking for a little flat as near to home as possible—they're just very expensive. But wherever I live, we'll still see lots of each other."

"I want you to move back home," said my daughter straight out.

"Well, that's very nice of you . . ." My smile faded as I noticed the thunderous expression on Jamie's face.

"No! No, you can't do that!" he snapped. "Because then you and Mum will just end up shouting at each other all the time again . . ." His plastic white chair fell over as he stood up and stomped off.

"Jamie! Jamie, come back!"

I didn't know whether to run after him or just give him some time to cool off. Dillie took advantage of the opportunity to help herself to his chips.

"Dillie, don't do that. He's upset!"

"If you get down from the table, it means you've finished eating. That's what you always said."

I watched my son march around the perimeter of the big pool, his pace gradually slowing before he sat down on a plastic octopus. I watched him for a while, aware that he was casting the occasional sideways glance in our direction. Then, while Dillie was queuing for a giant slide, I walked around the pool and flopped down next to him.

"You can push me in the pool if you want."

"No. It's all right."

"You know, the whole point of me moving out of the house was so that you and Dillie didn't have to put up with all that stuff anymore."

"Yeah, but then it's just different stuff, isn't it? Mum crying in her room at night. Us having to move house."

When we got back home, I asked Jamie to help me see if I could still ride a bike and, to my amazement, it came back to me instinctively. Jamie clapped and cheered and proudly claimed to have taught his father to ride a bicycle, and I allowed that little bit of distorted history to stand.

THOUGH swimming and cycling had returned easily, it seemed that other skills would have to be relearned. I did my best around the home, but it was difficult because I had clearly forgotten how to use an iron or a vacuum.

"Dad's using the vacuum!" said Jamie. "I've never seen that before."

I felt empowered by discovering that physical memories had been unaffected by my amnesia. So if I can still do all the things I learned before, I reasoned, that means I can still drive. I waited until the children were out at friends' and then picked up the car keys. I must have sat in that driver's seat a thousand times before, I told myself. I'm just going to get in and drive!

Forty minutes later the garage truck arrived to hoist the badly dented Honda off the ornamental wall at the front of number 23. Previously the Parkers' front garden had been separate from the pavement, but now it was all open plan.

"I'm terribly sorry. Obviously I'll pay for all the damage," I said to Mrs. Parker, a very nervous American woman.

"I thought it was a terrorist attack," she stammered.

A couple of police officers arrived. One officer fiddled uncertainly with a laptop on which he was supposed to log the accident details, while the other was perplexed that I tested negative for alcohol and that no calls seem to have been made on my mobile phone.

"So there was no other vehicle involved," continued the older policeman, "and it was broad daylight on a straight road . . . I'm struggling to understand how you managed to crash into a garden wall."

"Well, I sort of forgot how to drive."

"You forgot how to drive?"

"Er, Dave, there's no box for that."

"What?"

"On the new form—there's no box for 'Forgot how to drive.'"

"Let's have a look? Hmm . . . Are you sure you didn't 'swerve to avoid a pedestrian or animal,' sir?"

"Sure. It was completely my fault. I'm sure I used to be able to drive."

"And when did you forget, exactly?"

"The twenty-second of October."

The older policeman looked at me uncertainly. "And are you planning to attempt to drive again?"

"Not until I remember."

The policeman on the computer chuckled at this unintended jest, but immediately dropped his smile when the senior officer shot him a glare. It was time to bring this to a close. "Put that he swerved to avoid a cat."

"Got it," said the second policeman as he ticked the appropriate box, and another little bit of history was made official.

"What were you thinking?" said Maddy on the phone from Italy, when I had decided that it would be best to be completely honest and open about the tiny little scrape on the car. "Why did you imagine you'd suddenly be able to drive?"

"You mean I *couldn't* drive?"

"No! You never learned on principle."

"That's a shame, and it was such a nice car . . ."

"What do you mean, *was?*"

WHEN the Honda was finally delivered back from the garage, I gave it a good clean in the street outside, prompting the raffish neighbor who had borrowed our hedge trimmer to wander across for an extended chat.

"Hello there, Vaughan. Giving the old motor a wash and set?"

"Ha ha!" I chuckled politely. "Yes . . . it wouldn't fit in the dishwasher."

The neighbor thought this was hilarious, and I was unsure about the etiquette of resuming washing the car before the laughter had died down. Suddenly he pounced.

"Arabella was saying that with Maddy away at the moment, you must bring the kids over for their tea one evening."

Behind him I spotted Jamie and Dillie, returning from the Common with the dog. The word "No!" was mouthed over and over again.

"That's very kind," I said, "but I've already planned their meals for the whole week, so another time perhaps?"

I was growing more confident in the kitchen, cooking from recipe books and serving up the kids' favorite dishes by special request. They were incredibly supportive, telling me exactly how it all used to work before. Apparently I always stacked the dishwasher and they weren't expected to do any clearing up because Mum and I were insistent that they watch *Family Guy* "while their food went down."

I knew that they were winding me up, but I let them watch television anyway on the grounds that they'd made me laugh.

I learned that I had put a lot of effort into the renovations. It had been me who had done the refit of the kitchen, who'd made the built-in wardrobes. I had even constructed the wooden summerhouse at the bottom of the garden and the decking outside the kitchen door. This contrasted with all the negative stories that were nothing to do with the new Vaughan.

I was still consumed with the mystery of how this had become a "broken home," so that night, when the children were asleep, I furtively connected an old VHS player to watch some home movies. Seeing Jamie and Dillie as toddlers was thrilling and heart-wrenching at the same time. An angelic little Dillie sang a song in her Brownie uniform, and Jamie was filmed running toward the finish line at his infant school sports day.

I got another couple of beers from the fridge before resuming the home-movie marathon. There was footage of my wife and kids at the seaside. Woody was a puppy, barking at the waves and then running up the beach. The children were fantastically cute, and yet I could see that they were essentially the same people as now. This whole experience was teaching me that memories are continually revised. The view from the divorce courts would have pushed Maddy's negative memories to the fore. I sifted through the films, looking for more positive evidence for the counsel for the defense. And there I was—perhaps just a couple of years ago, judging by the age of the children—in the back garden, tending a barbecue.

"I could always cook the meat in the oven first? And then you could put it on the barbecue to finish it off?" suggested Maddy.

"No, it's getting there," insisted the chef, despite all evidence to the contrary. With the light fading, Dillie did a spoof appeal into the camera lens on behalf of the starving children of South London and Maddy came into shot with a grill pan to transfer the meat to her own domain.

Then the atmosphere turned. "Just let me do it, will you?" I snapped as I took the chicken back. "Why do you have to be such a control freak?"

"I'm not. I'm just making sure the kids get something to eat."

"So dinner is a bit later than usual—so what? You moan that I don't cook enough, and then when I do, you march in and take over."

"What cooking? The chicken is raw two hours after you started."

The footage moved indoors as Jamie, who had been filming, crept away and the domestic rancor faded into the background.

I watched the tape a couple more times, noticing that I'd had a beer bottle in my hand and that there were empties on the table nearby. Dillie's nine-year-old face had a resigned sadness to it, as if she had witnessed scenes like this before.

I lined the tape up to the end of Dillie's comic appeal and pressed "Record." The last five minutes of this story would now be wiped clear.

"Do you remember that lovely evening when we had a barbecue and the coals wouldn't light?" I imagined Maddy fondly reminiscing.

"Oh, yeah—and Dillie did that mock charity appeal to camera?"

"That was a funny evening, wasn't it . . ."

I WATCHED the reedited videos with the children on New Year's Eve, and they were thrilled and delighted to see the way we used to be. Then Dillie fetched a box of photos and the two of them narrated me through the blurred cast of relations and family friends.

"Who's that lady?" I asked, looking at a very old picture of a woman standing alone in some tropical location.

"That's Granny Vaughan. That's . . . your mum . . ."

I held the faded color photo in my hand. She was smiling directly at me, wearing a smart two-piece and clutching a leather handbag over her arm. I wish I could report experiencing some sort of instant bond, but I was only aware of a vacuum where sentiment and longing were supposed to be.

"Are you okay, Dad?" said Dillie.

"Yeah—I'm fine. It's just . . . she looks nice."

"Yeah, she was," said Jamie. "She always gave us chocolate and pound coins and said, 'Don't tell your dad!'"

We found more photos of my mum and dad and of me as a child, and they made me laugh with family stories and tales from the olden days.

"Happy New Year, Dad!"

"Happy New Year."

THE NEXT DAY I took Jamie and Dillie to see their grandfather, and I felt an enormous pride in them being so affectionate toward him, unembarrassed at showing that they cared. His face looked slightly yellow, but Dillie didn't hesitate to lean in and kiss him. She had brought a handmade card, and Jamie lent his grandfather his iPod; he had cleared his own music collection to fill it up with audiobooks. Even though I doubted whether his grandfather would have the energy to listen to an audiobook, the vision of my teenage son taking this much trouble brought me close to tears.

"You are so kind," said my father. The children told him all about their Christmas, and when it was time to go, they hugged him long and hard.

"What lovely grandchildren. Thank you for coming. You must have more important things to do."

"No," said his grandson firmly. "Not more important than you."

THE week passed far too quickly. On the final day I cleaned the house, prepared a dinner, and packed my bags. Maddy arrived alone at the front door and embraced the children as I hovered in the hallway. She had presents for them and an inscrutable smile and a hello for me.

"Wow, it all looks very clean. We should send photos to my mum!"

I had invited myself to stay for dinner by cooking a big casserole, and afterward Maddy and I had the chance to talk on our own.

"So how was your holiday?"

"Oh, one minute I was traveling in great comfort in a gondola; the next I was traveling in extreme discomfort with a budget airline. They sort of cancel each other out."

"Well, it was great being here with the kids. They are so funny and clever and interesting and everything . . ."

"I've been thinking," Maddy announced. "What you said in the courtroom . . . We don't have to get legally divorced, if you really don't want to."

I stood up and gently pushed the kitchen door closed.

"You are so much easier to talk to since your amnesia that I wondered if we could just work something out like adults? If we didn't spend so much on lawyers, we might just be able to hang on to the house."

"For you and the kids to live in without me?"

"Well—this is my proposal. The kids live here all the time, keep their rooms, keep walking to school with their friends. But you and I split the cost of a little flat somewhere cheap and take turns to live in that when it's not our turn to be here. Once the children have grown up and left home, we can sell the house and work out how to split the proceeds. But for the next seven or eight years, we could both have the same second home."

Privately I had to concede that this seemed like a constructive suggestion. I'd get to have every weekend in this house with the children.

"So part of the time you'd be here," she said with a smile, "and the rest of the time it would be me and Ralph."

"So this is Ralph's idea, is it?" I said, feeling my face heating up.

"Not exactly . . . I only meant if Ralph and I decide we want to live together. The kids would have to be cool with it, of course."

"So your great plan is we don't have to

legally get divorced, to save money so that Vaughan lives in a shoebox in the slums while Ralph moves into my half of the double bed here?"

"You're distorting it. Ralph said we shouldn't rush into anything—"

"Oh, well, if that's what Ralph suggests, then that's definitely what we should do! I can't believe you try and dress it up as what's best for the kids, when really it's just your fancy man trying to save on his rent bill!"

Madeleine was still trying to talk to me as I marched to the door and put on my old coat, which was hanging by the door.

"Um . . . that's Ralph's coat," mumbled Maddy.

"What? No, this is mine—I've been wearing it all week."

"No—it's Ralph's. He left it here. It's his. But I'm sure he wouldn't mind you borrowing it . . ."

Chapter 6

"RIGHT, Year Elevens, it's good to be teaching you again. Today we are going to be talking about the causes of the Second World

War," I predicted a little optimistically. "Now Ms. Coney, who I understand was taking you while I was away, has told you all about the Treaty of Versailles—"

"Sir! Mr. Vaughan, sir?"

"Yes, Tanika?" I was pleased to demonstrate my apparently effortless grasp of all their names. It had involved much time staring at school photos.

"Are you a mentalist, sir?"

"I beg your pardon?"

"Dean said you'd gone mental in the nut and didn't know nothin'."

"Well, it is no secret that my absence last term was due to my suffering a rare neurological condition, which in no way affects my abilities to teach you about the fall of the Weimar Republic."

"Yeah, but are you a loony? Do you, like, bark at the moon?"

"No, but I might be in a minute. Since Tanika insists on referring to my memory loss, it's worth asking whether it is possible for whole countries to lose their memory as well. That's why history is so important—"

A few different hands went up.

"Yes—Dean?"

"Did you find them, sir?"

"Did I find what?"

"Your marbles, sir."

"Do you foam at the mouth, sir? Are you afraid of water?"

"Look!" I finally snapped. "This is the easy stuff! The rise of Hitler and the Nazis. This is the easiest history I can teach! So listen or we'll do module four and we'll talk about the repeal of the Corn Laws, all right?"

"Ooooh!" said Tanika, seemingly vindicated. "Boggy Vaughan's gone mental."

AFTER my first lesson with Year Eleven, I reflected on the distressing revelation that I seemed to lack the natural authority required to teach inner-city teenagers. I was not the inspiring, life-changing teacher I had imagined when I had first learned of my occupation.

Perhaps there might be something positive on my online memoir? Perhaps by now former pupils had recalled how I had transformed their lives? When I logged on, I found that a number of students had indeed discovered my Wikipedia page, although their accounts of my past did not smack of rigorous accuracy.

For example, I was skeptical about whether I had indeed been the so-called "fifth member of Abba." I read with interest that I had spent three years fighting alongside Islamic militants during the Second Chechen War, eventually switching sides to the Russian Federation "because they had nicer trousers." I was pleased to learn that I had single-handedly identified the genome of the giant African badger.

I considered taking down the Wikipedia page, but the worthy teacher in me decided that it was providing a valuable outlet for student creativity on the blurred borders of fiction and nonfiction.

DR. LEWINGTON had asked me to come up with some memories that I had recovered and to think of some significant life events that were still out of reach in my memory banks. I duly arrived for another brain scan with a wide selection of episodes from my past life. I was to concentrate on these moments, and my brain activity would be compared to the chemical and temperature changes that occurred when I tried to recall chapters that were still blank.

There was a gentle whir as the conveyor transported me inside the pod of the brain scanner, and it seemed to know when to stop once my skull was in place for the internal mapping to commence. Over the hum of the machine I could hear Dr. Lewington giving me instructions into her microphone, and so I duly summoned up a significant recollection.

It is the summer of 1997, and I am feeling a little nervous in my new suit as I stand outside the nonreligious venue for our marriage service.

"Madeleine's not pregnant," explains Maddy's mother to elderly relatives. "Doesn't she look lovely in red? She didn't want a traditional white dress."

"Mum, it's perfectly normal to want a nonreligious service."

"I just don't want people thinking the church wouldn't have you. Or they might take the red dress as a sign that you were a fallen woman."

"A fallen woman! It's the Nineties, Mum. It doesn't matter if a woman is pregnant when she gets married!"

"Oh, are you pregnant?" says Great-Auntie

Brenda. "Well, it's good you're getting married, dear."

"No, she's not pregnant, Brenda," says Maddy's mum slightly too desperately. "She's just very political—doesn't believe in things."

"Mum, I do believe in things. That's why . . . oh, it doesn't matter."

"Don't let it spoil your day, Madeleine," says Auntie Brenda. "You're still the bride, dear, even if, you know . . ." And after Brenda has done the rounds, Maddy can be overheard politely thanking other relatives for the compliment that she looks "blooming."

LATER moments from the wedding day melted into each other like an edited-highlights package. I thought of Maddy waltzing with my father, as he gracefully led her round the scuffed wooden floor. I could picture a rather drunk Gary remembering every move to "The Birdie Song." And I remembered Maddy giving me a long and meaningful hug at the end of the evening. We could have skipped the service and the party; that embrace was what made me realize that she wanted to be with me always.

One tradition had been upheld during the ceremony, when Maddy and her dad had been the last people to enter the chamber. Her entrance had been delayed outside when a young lawyer had handed her an important-looking wax-sealed envelope that he insisted she must open before she could proceed with her marriage. A flustered Maddy tore open the envelope and pulled out the contents. It was a postcard of a leprechaun saying "Top o' the mornin' to yers!"

The brain scanner hummed and whirred, and Dr. Lewington instructed me to try to think about something significant of which I currently had no remembrance. I tried to picture my mother, searching for the moment when I had learned of her death or the funeral that I must have attended. Now I could see myself standing in a country churchyard, throwing earth onto a wooden coffin. I could have easily convinced myself that this was exactly as it happened, except that I had learned that my mother had been cremated. Even though I knew it was pure fiction, I found it vaguely comforting to have this classic funeral scene to cling to.

Now I was instructed to concentrate on

any episodes I had that were partially recon-
structed. I had deliberately saved the most
negative moment I could recall to contrast
with the bittersweet memories of my wedding. It was the day Madeleine said she
didn't want to be married to me anymore.

*MADDY and I are getting ready for bed one
night. I attempt to suggest that I have had a
tough day at school, but she is not interested.
What I have forgotten is that Maddy has just
had the results of a test for a health scare. She
had found a lump under her arm and had become convinced it was cancer.*

*"You can't diagnose something like that from
looking it up on the Internet," I had said when
she first mentioned it.*

*"A couple of people said my symptoms sound
serious . . ."*

"What people?"

*"I don't know. It was on a blog about
women's health."*

*From the outset she has interpreted my scorn
for online medical chat as lack of interest in her
well-being. Now she gets into bed, as far away
from me as it is physically possible to be, and
starts sobbing.*

"What? What is it?"

"I got the results of my cancer test today."

Two blows strike me almost simultaneously. Firstly, there is the sudden shame I feel at not having remembered, but that counts for nothing as I absorb the far greater blow. Maddy's sobbing tells me that the cancer test must have been positive. Suddenly I see a future in which Maddy will have to endure chemotherapy and the kids might lose their mother.

"It was negative. I don't have cancer. The lump is benign," she weeps.

"Oh, thank God for that!" and I go to hug her, but she pushes me away and now her sobbing seems worse than ever.

"Maddy—it's fantastic news! You had me going there, the way you were crying and everything! God, what a relief."

She wipes her face. "You forgot to ask me about the results."

"Yeah, I know—I'm really sorry, but can I just tell you what happened at school today and you might understand—"

"You didn't even remember to ask! You don't care enough to ask if I am going to live or die, to find out whether I have cancer or not."

"That's just ridiculous. As it happens, I never

thought that you did have cancer, although I could see you were worried about it."

"But you didn't come to the hospital, did you?"

"Because you never asked me to."

"You still should have offered."

"For God's sake, you don't have cancer—why are we arguing again?"

"Our marriage has cancer. Aggressive non-operable terminal cancer. If you can't be there for me when I go through something like this, then I don't think I want to be married to you."

"Look, you're getting this out of proportion. I'll take a couple of days off work, and maybe we should take the kids down to your parents—"

"It's too late, Vaughan. You've never been there for me. It's always been about you, never about us . . ."

And I realize that she wouldn't have sobbed like this about the uncertainty of cancer; she would have been silent and thoughtful. She is crying because she feels that something has died.

LYING in the scanner, I could almost feel my head throbbing as I trawled over that terrible night again, homing in on the tiny details that made it feel so real. The moment when we finished talking and she went to sleep in the spare room, never to return again for all the time that we stayed under the same roof. The broken lightbulb in the bedside lamp. The ache on the back of my skull that kept me company until dawn.

Then, lying inside that machine, I realized I had just had an actual new memory. I had had a blow on the head! The whole time this marriage-ending argument was going on, I could feel a large swelling on the back of my head. I had been concussed. That was what I had been trying to tell her: I had been confronted outside the school by an angry father. He had shoved me over, and I had hit the back of my head on the curb. I had refused to go to hospital, but I knew it had been a pretty bad blow.

That was why I had forgotten Maddy's medical results! It was the first symptom of an amnesia that was later to swallow me completely.

Back in her office, Dr. Lewington showed me the results of the different scans. One image showed lots of blues and reds in the middle part of my brain. And in all the others there were lots of blues and reds in the same part of my brain. "Absolutely no difference whatsoever!" she enthused. "The brain really is such a fascinating enigma." Even the moment when I recovered the brand-new memory revealed no brain activity that was different.

"Of course, we have to be aware that the memories you are recovering may not be all that accurate," she commented cautiously. "You might be regaining memories that were already distorted, and they might have been twisted further in the recovery—they might even be completely false."

"False?" I exclaimed, vaguely offended.

"Certainly. I've had patients with vivid recollections of things that happened when they weren't there. They can become quite angry when their versions of their own past are challenged. Such is the power of memory to affect our emotions!" She made an appointment to see me in a couple of months, and I realized that that would be after I was officially divorced.

"Just as a matter of interest," I said as I

stood up. "Is there any scientific basis for what they say, that 'there's a fine line between love and hate'?"

"Yes, actually. Both emotions occur in the same neural circuits."

"Can you scientifically measure how much you love someone?"

"Well, it might be love. It might be hate. The scans only measure the strength of feeling."

THE memory of my concussion increased the sense of injustice I was already feeling inside. I had to confront Maddy with this new development; she had played the neglected martyr about her health, but at the end of that fateful day she did not have a serious medical condition and I did. I went directly to the house to share my revelation with her. I knew the children would be at school, and I think I was actually looking forward to a really good argument with her. In the fantasy scenario spinning around in my head, she was actually pleading with me to take her back. "No, it's too late now," I told her. "You had your chance, but you threw it away."

Forty minutes later I had worked myself up into a state of indignation as I pressed the entry-phone buzzer. "It's Vaughan! I need to talk to you."

There was a long pause, and then the door lock clicked and I pushed my way in. The dog greeted me enthusiastically, but Maddy did not appear as quickly as my state of excitement demanded. I stiffened in anticipation of the coming difficult conversation. But it would be more awkward than I expected. Coming down the stairs was not Maddy but her boyfriend, Ralph.

I recognized him before he introduced himself. I had already guessed that the man I had seen helping Maddy with the picture frames must have been Ralph. In any case, the confident way he jumped down two steps at a time wearing a toweling dressing gown suggested that he was probably not a burglar. He was maybe a decade younger than me, and indeed Maddy.

"Hi, Vaughan—I'm Ralph! Great to meet you." I felt I had no alternative to accepting the outstretched hand. "Maddy's out at the moment. Sorry about my state of undress— just showered after my run!"

"Ah, right. Hence the dressing gown. 'Hilton Hotels'!" I hadn't intended this to come across like an accusation of theft, but that was how it sounded.

"They were selling them in the Venice Hilton, so I thought, why not?"

I was disorientated by the detail that he had taken Maddy to a luxury hotel. "Yes, Venice, of course. How was that?"

"Amazing! What a city! You ever been?"

"Er, no. Maddy always wanted to go— but, you know . . . Wasn't there some problem with Venice sinking or something?"

"I dunno if they sorted that out or not. But I suppose even if they did stop it sinking, now that sea levels are rising it's going to be back to square one."

"Honestly, if it's not one thing, it's another," I tutted.

The dog yawned, and I knew that it was time to say something about Ralph's relationship with Maddy.

"So . . ." I said ominously, and I saw him prepare himself. "I wonder . . . if they've thought about building, like, a huge tidal barrier across the Strait of Gibraltar? So it could stop the rising Atlantic flowing into the Med and flooding all the low-lying coastal areas?"

"Nah—it's about twenty miles between Spain and Morocco," he said. "I mean, the engineering logistics alone would be insurmountable, before you even considered the political or funding obstacles."

The arrogance with which he dismissed my idea rubbed me up the wrong way. "Well, something's got to be done!" I said, hearing my voice rising.

Ralph might have tried to clinch the argument by pointing out the geopolitical strategic power that control of this barrier would bestow upon Spain or Morocco, but instead he opted for a personal blow below the belt. "So I understand you've been having some mental health issues?"

It was at this point that I felt that my argument for this massive engineering project would become unanswerable if I punched Ralph in the face. I felt my fist clench and my face redden as an alarmed Ralph suddenly took a step back. Only in the last nanoseconds of this thought process did something inside me put the brakes on. I had just remembered how stupid and upsetting the incident with the psycho-dad at school had been. That's why I had come here—to tell Maddy about my concussion.

"Where's Maddy?" I demanded.

When he told me, I knew I wanted to be there too. Failing to bother with the niceties of saying good-bye, I slammed the door on my way out, feeling my hands shaking as I unlocked my bike. It was not a short cycle ride, but it was made considerably quicker by just how fired up I was.

"HELLO, Maddy," I said quietly as I pushed the door open.

"Oh, hi. I didn't know you were coming."

"No, well . . . . Hi, Dad, how you feeling? You're looking a little better."

My father's gaunt face peeked out of the top of the blanket.

"That's for seeing. Your lovely wife!" he suggested breathlessly. "You don't. Normally. Come together."

Maddy and I glanced at one another. "Well, we thought you'd prefer more frequent visits, so we take it in turns," improvised Maddy.

"Yes, that!" I blurted. "But—it's nice to be here together, isn't it, Maddy?"

I was still angry with her and Ralph and realized that there would be nothing she could do if I put my arm around her waist. I felt her stiffen, but I held it there as we stood before the old man's approving gaze.

"Look at you," wheezed my dad. "You still make such a lovely couple."

I gave Maddy an extra squeeze and was contemplating planting a kiss on her cheek, but she quickly sat down and told my father what the children had been up to. I sat beside her, chipping in with inferior contributions.

"Maddy's the daughter. I never had." His breath seemed weaker now; the effort of this visit could not be sustained much longer.

"You have a sleep, Keith," Maddy said. I was startled to see that her eyes had welled up. "I'm just popping to the loo!" she blurted as she dashed out.

Soon the old man was asleep, and I went out and found our family car and waited to catch her there.

"Hi. You okay?"

"Your father is such a wonderful man," she mused, her eyes still red.

"Yeah, I wish I could remember more of what he was like before . . . Look, I need to talk to you, Maddy. Any chance of a lift back?" Madeleine was too grown up to refuse me.

"You didn't have to do the whole lovey-dovey thing in front of him. Do that again, and I'll stamp on your foot."

"Yeah, well, I'll take whatever attention I can get."

Maddy had put her seat belt on and was just checking her texts when she suddenly looked up. "So you met Ralph?"

"Oh—yes. We had a brief conversation."

"What did you say to him? What did he say back?"

"You wouldn't be interested."

"What, my ex-husband and father of my children meets my boyfriend, and you think I wouldn't be interested?"

She had put her ticket in the machine, and the barrier juddered upward.

"Okay, well, he said you could never build a tidal barrier across the Strait of Gibraltar."

She took her eyes off the road to look at me in confusion. "Sorry?"

"Rising sea levels? Venice in Peril? He was actually quite dismissive of my idea of a massive Thames Barrier-type seawall."

"So you didn't talk about anything important?"

"Rising sea levels are important. But, no, we never really talked about the elephant in the room."

"What was the elephant in the room?"

"Well, you, obviously . . ."

Her phone beeped again, and she read the next message at the traffic light. "He says he thought you were going to hit him!"

"What? Over a discussion on sea levels? And as if I'd hit a man in a dressing gown!" This detail embarrassed her, which had been my intention. "From which I am deducing that he's already moved in."

"No! The kids were on sleepovers, so he stayed the night. They don't know he ever stays either, so don't say anything."

"Anyway, I went round there because I wanted to talk to you about something. I had another brain scan today—"

"Okay—back to *you* then."

"It's important. I remembered something. The day you had the results of your cancer test. The thing is, I had a concussion that day—I had been shoved to the ground by an aggressive parent, and I banged my head on the curb. I think it might be related to my amnesia since October."

"Did you tell the doctor?" She was being deliberately obtuse.

"That's not the point. There was a *medical* reason why I forgot to ask you about your test. Remember, it was the final straw for you that I forgot to ask?"

"The point of that phrase is that it takes a lot of other straws as well."

"But the more I remember, the more I see that we didn't need to break up. I knew that from the moment I fell in love with you back in the autumn."

"You didn't fall in love with me. You just loved the idea of being married." She was cross now. "And now I have to put up with everyone saying, 'Poor Vaughan—he can't even remember his own wife!' But you always forgot your own wife—you just took your worldview to its logical conclusion."

The light had changed to green, and a car behind was tooting impatiently.

I was knocked back by the depth of her

resentment, but I had one more line I had prepared and polished and was ready to detonate.

"Have you any idea what it is like to lose your identity? And then to find out who you were, only to have that taken away from you too?"

"Do I know what it's like to lose my identity?" she spat in disbelief. "Before I married you I was 'Madeleine.' Not 'Vaughan's wife' or 'Jamie's mum' or 'Dillie's mum'; I existed in my own right. I was Maddy the photographer, who earned her own money doing something she loved. Then suddenly it was all 'What does your husband do?' and 'How old are your children?' So I do know what it is like to lose my identity. Yes, I do."

"Maddy, you are doing nearly seventy in a thirty-miles-an-hour zone—"

"And now I am doing what I want. I'm going to Venice, I'm working toward an exhibition, and I don't have to compromise my entire existence."

"I think that speed camera just flashed twice—"

"Yeah, well, I'll appeal, explaining that my ex-husband was being really annoying.

You think because you got a bang on the head I am going to go, 'Oh, that changes everything! It was all *my* fault'?" She pulled the car over to the curb. "Why don't you get out here, before you make me run someone over? Or, even better, get out here and then maybe I can run *you* over."

"Oh. But—couldn't you at least drop me where my bike is locked up?"

"Where's that?"

"At the hospital."

It seemed that everything I said was somehow really annoying. I watched Maddy speed off without glancing in her mirror. I stood there in the winter drizzle and eventually crossed the road to catch the bus back in the opposite direction. When nothing came for ten minutes, I began to walk. Eventually I reached Chelsea Bridge.

Around my neck I could feel the dog tag that I had always worn in case my amnesia reoccurred. But so what if I lost my memory all over again? I might handle it all better the second time around. This ID tag weighed a few grams but felt like a couple of kilos; it rubbed against my neck, a constant reminder of my broken brain. I undid the little clasp and then cast it down into the swirling, murky Thames. And then I walked on to face the rest of my life without Madeleine.

Chapter 7

"*I AM never, ever, getting a mobile phone.*"

"*Yeah, you say that now . . .*" laughs my fiancée.

"*No—*" I confirm. "*Come back to me in the year 2000, and even if I'm the last man in Britain without one, I guarantee you will never catch me shouting into a handset.*"

"*It's different for a woman,*" asserts Maddy. "*I might be stuck somewhere at night and be worried about being mugged or something.*"

"*Oh, right, so you make sure that you advertise you have something worth nicking ringing away in your handbag!*"

THIS conversation came back to me twenty years later as I sat in the pub with Gary taking turns to show off the stupid apps on our iPhones. In my defense, when I said I would never get a mobile phone, it was before you could do so many useful things with them.

I had now moved out of Gary and Linda's

flat. Many weeks had passed since Maddy and I had fought in the car.

"So what's the Hi Klass Hotel in Streatham like?" said Gary.

"Well, it's very cheap for me, because I'm the only guest who wants a room for more than half an hour."

"Maybe you should make the most of the convenience. It must be a while . . . When was the last time?"

"I can't remember. The experience has been completely wiped from my brain."

Gary almost fell off his barstool with laughter. "Oh, you know what that means, don't you? For all intents and purposes, that makes you a virgin!"

"Don't be ridiculous. I've got two kids."

"Makes no odds. You're a *born-again virgin*. You do not know what it is like to make love to a woman. Ergo, you're a Virgo!"

I did soon find myself in a situation where some women were interested in me. The night after school had broken up for Easter I accepted the invitation of the younger teachers to go to the pub. My work colleagues had always been cautious not to appear nosy about my medical condition, but after a few bottles of wine, a group of female teachers broached the subject of how much I could remember.

"Can you remember your childhood and stuff like that?"

"Bits of it are coming back. I don't really remember my parents or growing up or going to university or anything."

"It must be weird to have no past," said Sally, the English teacher. "It means you don't quite know who you are in the present."

"Exactly. Though it's made me think none of us really knows who we actually are—we just invent a persona, put it out there, and hope everyone else goes along with it."

The others reflected on this profound thought for a moment.

"And my friend Gary says I'm a virgin because I don't remember having sex!" I joked.

This bewitching detail sent an electric ripple through the group, seeming to instantly elevate me to the status of the most desirable man in all Europe. Suddenly my jokes were hilarious, my anecdotes deeply fascinating, and I was subjected to an hour of intensive flirting from a collection of vivacious women.

I told them about having no memory of my friends and family and then discovering my marriage had failed and that my father was dying.

"Ah, come here—you need a big hug," said Jennifer, who helped late developers with special needs.

"Yes, you are badly in need of a cuddle," agreed Caroline, who taught media studies and drama but seemed keen to expand to adult education.

I realized I was thoroughly enjoying the undivided attention of these women, even though it felt slightly scary.

Eventually I was no longer talking to a group of ladies but to just one. Suzanne was a tall, thin Australian brunette in her early thirties who worked in the PE department. She had been a dancer, and it showed in her impeccable posture and penchant for woolly leggings.

She had seemed fairly attractive at the beginning of the evening, but following several pints of beer and a bottle of red wine, I was even better able to appreciate her stunning good looks and seductive allure. Her account of how she was unfairly passed over for the vacancy of Assistant Principal (Curriculum) seemed positively erotic.

"You know you said you were going to Greenwich Market on Sunday?" I said. "I have a guidebook back in my desk that you could borrow." I was offering up an excuse for her to follow me out of the pub. "A ring-binder one so you could keep the map open on the Greenwich page . . ."

"Oh, that would be really useful, actually, yeah . . ."

There was a moment's silence.

"If you like, you could finish your drink with the rest of your department over there, and I could meet you in school in about ten minutes?"

KOFI and John, the security guards, were well used to teachers coming in at all hours and thought there was nothing unusual in seeing me walk past the reception desk around midnight.

"Hello, Mr. Vaughan, sir. You working too hard, sir."

"Aha, ha, yes, work, work, work! Just picking something up, actually."

I swiped my card to pass through the main

doors and then headed up the stairs. It felt illicit to be in school so late. In my classroom I grabbed the guidebook from my drawer. At that moment the beep of my phone made me jump. The text message read: "Hve bought wine. Am in gym storeroom. S.x."

Now I felt myself physically shaking. "S.x," she had signed the text. It just seemed to put me in mind of something.

SUZANNE was sitting cross-legged on a pile of exercise mats with a bottle of red wine and two plastic cups in front of her. I perched myself on the edge of a low bench and drank my wine far too quickly.

"Are you okay, Vaughan?"

"Yeah, great, fine. Why?"

"Your leg is tapping, like, really fast."

"Oh, sorry. There, it's still now. Do you want some more wine?"

"No, I've still got my first one."

"I'm sure there are rules about members of staff drinking alcohol in the gymnasium after midnight," I joked.

"Who's going to know? Kofi and John never leave the reception desk, and anyway, I can always lock the door." She got up and did so with a suggestively raised eyebrow, and I worried that I may have given a slight whimper.

But still the Rubicon had to be crossed.

She sat beside me, looking directly into my eyes, and I realized that she was even drunker than I was. She kissed me full on the lips.

Okay, we're doing this now, I thought. I wondered how many women I had kissed like this in my previous life. Finally I broke off the kiss, ostensibly to have another glug of wine. I had tried but failed to keep Maddy out of my mind. This woman's body was completely different from that of the mother of my children. And I knew which I preferred. Madeleine had curving hips and tumbling red hair that wasn't cropped short for sport. And then I did something I did not feel proud of. As Suzanne launched her face at mine once more, I imagined it was Madeleine. I closed my eyes and eagerly pulled her close. I kissed her with passion, pretending she was the woman I had told myself that I was over.

Unfortunately, my foot seemed to have gotten tangled in the netting of a large folded-up goal that was propped against the wall, but I wouldn't let that stop me. My foot was not shaking free, however much I tried to wiggle it about. I gave one final tug, and suddenly the whole metal goal frame came crashing to the floor.

"What was that?" She had leaped up in fear.

"Sorry! Sorry! The goal net was tangled in my foot."

"Do you think the guys will have heard that from the reception desk?"

"I doubt it. Don't they normally have the radio on? Shall we just carry on?"

"Did they have a radio on? I don't remember them having a radio on."

"It didn't make that much noise," I claimed, despite the ringing in my head and the fear that my eardrums might now be bleeding. "Shall we just go back to where we left off?"

But the moment had gone. Whereas before her drunkenness had made her adventurous and provocative, now she was excessively paranoid. It was over before it was started.

She suggested I should leave first and she

would tidy up and leave ten minutes later, so that the blokes on the door didn't suspect anything. I gave her a peck on the cheek and headed out.

IN MY imagination, the Easter holidays had loomed as a vast tract of unlimited free time during which I would get on top of all my marking and lesson plans, while also grabbing some quality time with my children and visiting my still-hospitalized father. It was not until I emerged from under the sheets to glance at my bedside clock on Wednesday afternoon that I accepted I might be letting the opportunity slip by. Both my laptop and mobile phone had run out of battery power long ago. It would have been no effort to plug in their chargers, had my own batteries not been so low as well.

I occupied just one side of the double bed, as I always did. I'd only just realized that I instinctively preferred to take the left half of the mattress, subconsciously leaving the other side free. But soon I was staring at a piece of paper that would do away with the need for such considerations.

I had verbally agreed to all the terms in

this document some time ago; now all I had to do was sign where indicated, in front of a witness, return it in the stamped addressed envelope, and my marriage would be history. During four whole days of doing nothing I had still not found the time to do it. It wasn't just the final act of formally ending the marriage that crippled me, but that extra little humiliation of having to ask a witness to watch me sign the form.

I had wondered if I could ask the fat man from the former Soviet republic of Something-astan who ran the Hi Klass Hotel. Except that I sensed he rather resented the way that I paid for my room and then proceeded to sleep in it for the entire night.

Occasionally I thought about that moment in the gym storeroom, but it had clearly left me feeling empty. More significant than the experience of the night with Suzanne was the recovery of my memories of being with Madeleine.

And then I recovered another memory. It was an argument that had begun with Maddy wanting to throw out a plastic shower curtain and me insisting that it just needed cleaning.

"*Just needs cleaning by me, is what you mean*," she says. "*Because it would never occur to you to clean a shower curtain.*"

"*A shower curtain doesn't need cleaning; it has a shower every day.*"

"*Yeah, you take a shower every day and I have a bath, and you said you would clean the shower. Why didn't you clean the curtain as well?*"

But the argument isn't about that at all. We have not so much as touched one another for weeks, and I feel angry and frustrated.

"*You notice a bit of grime on the curtain, but you don't even notice your own husband,*" I say, escalating the conflict.

"*Why are you being so horrible?*"

"*Oh, look, the top is off the toothpaste because Vaughan forgot to put it back on!*" and I run to the toothpaste and make a big show of replacing the top. "*Ooh, look, the toilet seat is up because Vaughan forgot to put it down.*" And I slam down the toilet lid. "*Well, it's better than forgetting you're supposed to be married to someone!*"

I WAS ABLE TO PLACE this incident to about a year before we had separated. I felt ashamed that my frustration had translated into anger. But with hindsight, I understood that sex is so important in keeping a marriage together that it really shouldn't be left to husband and wife alone. We have health checks and visits to the dentist. There ought to be someone who pops round to make sure that married couples are having sex every weekend. "Hmm . . . I see there's a two-week gap at the beginning of the month. You will receive an official letter warning of the dangers of neglecting physical intimacy."

The document from my ex-wife's solicitors had to be signed. I owed it to Maddy. I pulled on my shoes and threw on a jacket before I presented myself to the outside world. My reintegration into civilization seemed to go unnoticed by the rest of society; evening shoppers and busy commuters passed me by. It reminded me of the time before I found my identity, the sense of separateness from the rest of the world, as if everyone else knew the part they were playing but I'd never been given a script. Inside my jacket pocket, however, was the death certificate for my marriage. In my head I was scrolling through all the people who could witness my signature, but somehow I didn't want to admit my final failure to any of my friends.

I found myself at the door of the only person I felt I could ask. Suzanne, the dance teacher, seemed surprised and a little alarmed to see me.

"Vaughan! What the hell are you doing here?"

"I came to ask a favor."

"Er—it's not very convenient . . ." She glanced back down the hallway.

"Who is it?" said a gruff man from inside the flat.

"Just someone from school."

Despite Suzanne's embarrassment, I persuaded her that this wouldn't take a minute and I produced the divorce agreement for her to witness.

"Vaughan," she whispered, "I don't want you to divorce your wife just because of what happened the other night . . ."

"No, I was going to divorce her anyway."

"Brian and I are very happy. I can't leave him for you, Vaughan."

"Really. I just need someone to witness my signature."

"You won't tell anyone what happened, will you?" She glanced nervously in the direction of the lounge. "I mean, it didn't mean anything, did it?"

Her name was hastily scribbled. The deed was done.

I STOOD before the postbox, nervously checking that the envelope was properly sealed and that the stamps would not fall off. Then, in a short ceremony, the Future formally surrendered to the Past and I put the letter in the box. Rather than return to my dismal hotel room, I picked up a newspaper and went into a high-street pub. Even with the sound turned down, the large TV screen was impossible to ignore: images of floods in Bangladesh, the remains of a roadside bomb in Afghanistan, the changes in the stock markets. I finished a third packet of pork cracklings and tied the foil packets into tiny knots. A couple came into the pub hand in hand, and I was disgusted by such an ostentatious public display of passion.

In the toilets I paused to stare at the craggy face of the man whose life I had inherited. "You stupid idiot!" I shouted at my reflection. "You only get one life, and you completely screwed your one up, didn't you, eh? You don't know your own kids! Your wife hates you. You can't even remember people's names, you senile bastard—"

Then a slurred voice spoke up from behind a locked stall door. "Who is this? How do you know so much about me?"

I set off to walk the length of Streatham High Road, the night lit briefly by the blue strobe of a passing police car. Alcohol used to make me excited and up for a laugh, but these days it just made me drowsy. Walking down the uneven pavement, I found myself overcompensating for the sudden appearance of a litter bin and, in trying to give it a wide berth, nearly staggered into some bike racks. Finally I skipped up the steps to the hotel.

As I pushed open the door, I saw Maddy sitting in the chair in the corridor.

"Maddy? What are you doing here?"

"Hello, Vaughan," she said calmly.

Her unexpected appearance at this time

of night alarmed me. "Look, I'm sorry," I blustered. "I posted it today."

"It's not that. We've been trying to ring you . . ."

"What is it?"

"Your father. It happened in his sleep. I'm so sorry."

I could almost feel my body sobering up as I stood there trying to comprehend the news that my father had died.

"But—that's not fair," I heard myself blurting out. "That's just not fair."

"I'm really sorry, Vaughan," repeated Maddy, but I felt too numb to respond. My grief was for something I hadn't had. He'd died before I had gotten to know him properly or before memories of him had returned.

Maddy and I just stood there for a moment looking at one another. Then she put her arms out to embrace me, and I accepted the invitation. Now my emotions were really confused. My only living parent had been taken from me. But the woman I had given up on was hugging me, and it felt right. I raised my hands around her and hugged her back.

MADELEINE SUGGESTED that I should come and stay in the spare room at home so that I didn't wake up on my own and could be with the children in the morning. We stayed up for an hour or two, sharing a bottle of wine and talking about my dad. There was no friction in the air; in fact, looking at her sitting opposite me on the sofa, I couldn't understand how I had ever not been in love with her. Eventually I took a moment to visit the toilet, and looking at the family pictures on the wall, I recovered another memory. I was regaining them every day now, and this one was of a trip to central London with the kids.

WE ARE *in Madame Tussauds. There must have been an era when a visit here was a great family treat, but as far as our own kids are concerned, looking at waxy replicas of has-been celebrities has not been their idea of a thrilling day out. The display of the British Royal Family has singularly failed to excite; in fact, I think it is actually a bonus for our kids that a couple of the figures have been removed for refurbishment. After an increasingly fractious hour or so, we are close to abandoning the whole trip, when a little* light goes on in my wife's eye. Just as a group of tourists is about to join us in the room, Maddy steps over the velvet rope and strikes up a pose on the empty pedestal, where she stares into the middle distance.

Dillie and Jamie are already thrilled at her mischievousness, when some foreign tourists join me as I stare hard at the apparent wax model.

"Dad—who is this model of?" says Dillie pointedly.

"That's Princess Rita. Of Lakeside Thurrock . . ."

Maddy's expression does not alter one iota.

"What relation would she be to the Queen?" asks an American lady.

"Princess Rita is not actually related to the Queen. Rita is the bastard offspring of the Duke of Edinburgh and, um, Eleanor Rigby," I explain.

"Eleanor Rigby? Like the Beatles song?"

"Yeah, that's why she was so lonely—the Duke wouldn't leave the Queen for her. He couldn't afford the alimony."

"Oh, I never knew—that's really interesting! Thank you."

And then as they walk away, their teenage

daughter lets out a scream. "Dad! Dad! Princess Rita just winked at me!"

WHEN I rejoined her in the kitchen, Maddy was putting the wineglasses in the dishwasher and turning off the downstairs lights.

"When did you stop doing stupid stuff?" I asked her.

"Stupid stuff?"

"You know, pretending to be a statue at Madame Tussauds. Making announcements on the train. You were always making us laugh with daft stunts like that, but somehow they just petered out."

"Yeah, well . . ." She shrugged. "I think life probably knocks the fun out of us all in the end."

Ten minutes later I was lying in the dark in the spare room, reflecting on what she had said and thinking of my father, a shadow of the man I had seen in photos. Is that how people die? I wondered. Incrementally? Maddy's spirit had diminished since our marriage had crashed; a part of us both must have died with every disappointment.

This little room where I now lay had once

been Dillie and Jamie's nursery. Luminous stars still glowed on the ceiling from where they had been stuck by a younger, optimistic father. I stared at the random constellations, thinking of the centuries that seemed to have passed in between me putting up the stickers for my newborn baby and this lonely moment.

I recalled how delighted Maddy was when she saw what I'd done. I remembered a few years later how thrilled Dillie was when I'd shown her the stars and we both just lay on our backs in the dark, pointing at the magic of the tiny lights on the ceiling.

Now I was surprised to feel an emotional geyser building up inside me. So much had been lost, so many moments gone forever. I pictured the old man I had gotten to know on the hospital bed. And I thought of Dillie and Jamie visiting him, and that final hug they gave him, understanding that he would soon be dead. Now I wept out loud at the simple sadness of it all—at the hollow sense of loss: disappearing childhoods, irrecoverable decades, a family I had taken for granted but one that I now understood could not be there forever. And when at last I was quiet, I could hear Maddy crying on the other side of the bedroom wall.

In the morning I hugged my daughter long and hard as she wept for the loss of her grandfather. Dillie wore her emotions on her sleeve. Her brother, on the other hand, attempted to play the stoic young male, but he too crumbled when I asked him for a hug. Maddy herself could not help but break down as she watched them. Then the group hug was joined by the excited dog, who jumped up and wrapped his front paws around my jeans.

The kids switched from grieving for their grandfather to eating their cornflakes in front of the television, and Maddy and I tidied up. Maddy's mobile phone got a text with a comical ringtone.

"Ralph?"

"Yes. He was saying he was sorry to hear about your father. He said he lost his own dad a few years back so he knows what you're going through."

"I doubt that." I wiped down the surfaces, perhaps a little too vigorously.

"You know, it's okay. I don't expect you to like him."

"No, he was fine." I pouted. "I just thought he wasn't very 'can do,' that's all. He came across as one of those people who sees the problems first."

Maddy laughed out loud. "Because he foresaw difficulties in building some massive dam?"

Without realizing it, we were unloading the dishwasher in tandem, Maddy doing the glasses, me doing the cutlery as I had always done. Madeleine could have been angered by my criticism of Ralph, but she actually found it quite amusing. Still, the subject of her new partner hung in the air, and I felt the need to show a little humility.

"So, is Ralph going to move in here?" I asked. "I mean, have you got a timetable in your head for it or anything?"

Maddy let out a long sigh. "Oh, I don't know. We had a big fight. He's filled his gallery with awful abstracts by this new painter. I think it's just because he fancies her."

"Oh, dear," I lied.

"Maybe I was never meant to be with anyone. I'll be one of those old ladies with seventeen cats and a council injunction about the smell."

Inside I wanted to punch the air in triumph, but I remained determined to carry on as normal. I announced that I should be on my way and thanked her for letting me stay the night, and added that it had been good to have someone to talk to. Maddy avoided eye contact, embarrassed that she had revealed more than she had intended. She wanted to leave me with a clear signal that we had to move on.

"You know what you need, Vaughan? You need a girlfriend."

Even though I had my coat on, I began stacking the dirty plates into the dishwasher. "Hmm. I don't think I could handle the emotional involvement."

"It doesn't have to be Miss Right straightaway. Just someone to make you realize that there are plenty of other women out there."

"What, you'd like me to have a fling?"

"Well, it's nothing to do with me. I just think it might help you move on."

"Actually, there was this woman from school—"

"What woman?"

"Suzanne. She's a dance teacher, Australian."

"And you fancy her?"

"In the cold light of day, I can't say I do, really."

She had stopped the housework and just stood there looking at me.

"But I had a one-night stand with her. Like you said—just to try to help myself move on."

"Oh." Suddenly it seemed her eyes didn't know where to look. "A dance teacher? Skinny, is she?"

The dirty mugs were being placed in the dishwasher with more force than was strictly necessary.

"Yeah, not really my type. I mean, I wasn't seeking it or anything. Suzy just happened to come along."

"Oh, she's called 'Suzy'? It's all right—*I'm* stacking the dishwasher. It doesn't take two of us." And we both pretended not to notice that she had just chipped Kate Middleton's face on the Royal Wedding mug.

SUDDENLY I was responsible for all sorts of legal duties and tasks that took me the entire week. I learned that I was the executor of the will, that it fell to me to register the death, choose the hymns, book the cremation, and decide on the appropriate number of sliced carrots for the hummus dip.

Who was I supposed to invite to the funeral anyway? I settled on writing to all the names that had not been crossed out of my father's address book. And so, shortly after his death, I stood at the top of the drive of a suburban crematorium, ready to fulfill my duty as the chief mourner and only son of Air Commodore Keith Vaughan.

The first guests to turn up were a couple of elderly ladies from the rest home where my dad had spent his last years. They were followed by a reasonably young man in an RAF uniform, who marched straight past without making eye contact. Then my heart lifted as I saw Maddy and the children.

"Are you okay, Dad?" asked Dillie, giving me a hug.

Maddy told me that I didn't have to stand outside waiting for everyone, and once her parents had arrived, we all went inside to take our seats.

Our host for the afternoon led the traditional mumbling of the hymns and did an impressive piece of reading from the Bible, in which he managed not to change the emphasis of his voice by one iota for the entire passage. My mind drifted off; then I heard the vicar say, "And now Keith's only child will say a few words about his father." Surely I imagined that? But there was the vicar, gesturing to me to come up and share a lifetime of recollections of my dad, unaware that I had none. I saw the elderly mourners looking at me in anticipation. I made eye contact with Maddy, who looked slightly panic-stricken on my behalf.

"So," he repeated with a firm smile, "Vaughan, if you would—"

"Oh, no, I er . . . I can't. I mean . . ." I mumbled.

"Obviously it can be very difficult," said the vicar.

You have no idea, I thought as I slowly walked to the pulpit. I took a deep breath. My legs felt unreliable behind the lectern as I gripped on tight.

"What can I say about my dad?"

I gave a long, significant pause. One retired RAF colleague nodded meaningfully.

There was a wheezy cough from the back row.

"Well, there's so much to say it almost seems wrong to attempt to sum it all up in a few minutes . . . but obviously I'm going to have to. He had a distinguished career in the Royal Air Force, rising to the very senior rank of Air Commodore and serving his country with distinction. Er, he was posted all over the world, but always wanted his family with him." Time just to start making stuff up. "Because he was always a great father and a wonderful husband to my late mother . . ." This prompted a few nods. I saw Dillie looking up at me admiringly.

"But he was a wonderful grandfather too. I remember on family holidays in Cornwall"— I chuckled to myself at the memory of it— "he was always so patient with his grand-children." There was another cough. "He and my mother made very powerful home-made wine." A few smiles at that. "And he had a long and distinguished career in the Royal Air Force . . ." I realized I'd already said that. I could feel a bead of sweat run down my back. In my panic, I could think of no other course but the lowest one available. I clutched my thumb and forefinger to the bridge of my nose and just said, "And I'm going to really miss him."

In fact, having resorted to this posture, I realized that I did really miss him. He had always been so delighted to see me and made the world seem such a positive place, lifting my spirits when I was supposed to be lifting his. As I glanced up, I saw the ladies who had been the first to arrive clutching their tissues to their noses. And right in front of me sat Maddy with tears streaming down her cheeks.

Witnessing Maddy so upset suddenly flicked a switch inside me. "My dad really thought the world of Maddy," I said, looking directly at her and starting to speak with a fluency that had been absent till now. "When he was in the hospital at the end, her regular visits were the highlight of his day. He pointed out her kindness and intelligence to me, as if to warn me against the risk of ever losing his beloved daughter-in-law. He was not to know that he was too late. With him being so ill, we took the decision that he should be protected from the bleak truth that his son was unable to hold a marriage together in the way that he had done.

"Maddy brought his grandchildren to see him one last time, and I think we all knew that he would never see them again. He refused to let a little thing like his own imminent death get him down. 'What a lucky man I am,'" I said, impersonating him, 'to have such a wonderful family!'"

The crowd recognized Keith's optimism and smiled at the memory. I had stumbled on my thesis now and was conveying it with a missionary zeal. "And maybe the best way we could all remember my father is for each of us to take that worldview and try to remember Keith whenever we are feeling sorry for ourselves. My wife and children don't live with me anymore. But what a lucky man I am to be able to recall so many wonderful times together and to have so much to look forward to as they grow up.

"Believe me when I say that I wish I'd had a bit more time with him. It's made me determined to spend every possible moment with my own family, to grab every memory that I can—even though I can't be there as much as I would like and Maddy now has someone else."

"No," interjected Dillie. "She dumped him."

The heckle had not been a loud one. The children were in the second row. It was more a mumbled point of order than a public declaration. But I had heard her clear enough. So Maddy and Ralph had broken up. Madeleine avoided eye contact, but I looked at her mother, and the undisguised satisfaction on her face confirmed that this was indeed the case.

"What a lucky man I am!" I said, but I didn't qualify this any further. "That's what I think." And I sat down, trying to hold back a beatific smile.

Now I understood the therapeutic value of a funeral, because the world seemed like a better place as the coffin set off on its short journey to the sound of the Carpenters. They had been Dad's favorite band, although in retrospect I realized that "We've Only Just Begun" was probably not the best choice of song to mark an old man's demise.

"Don't sing along, Vaughan," whispered Maddy behind me.

"Sɪʀ, Mr. Vaughan, sir, why weren't you in on Friday? Were you in the loony bin, sir?"

"That's enough, Tanika."

"Have you been admitted, though? Do you have a padded cell?"

"Tanika, you are on a first warning. Any more disrespect and failure to focus on today's lesson outcomes and you will be one step away from removal from this classroom, detention, and a telephone call home." I had relearned the official script and was hoping that my most difficult pupils would recognize the magic words and change their behavior.

"Are you a serial killer, sir? Do you eat your victims?"

"Second warning, Tanika!"

"Sir, do you bury your victims under the patio? Is that where you was on Friday? Burying a victim?"

"If you must know, I was burying someone."

The moment I said it, I felt it was probably

a mistake, but the room fell into a stunned silence that demanded some further explanation.

"Well, it was a cremation, actually. I was at my father's funeral, okay? He died during the holidays, so that's why you had a substitute teacher on Friday, for which I apologize."

The teacher-baiting stopped after that. They cooperated with the lesson, answered the questions, and wrote down their homework assignments at the end. In fact, I was wondering if I could get away with announcing a family bereavement at the start of every class.

After the students had all filed out, I noticed Tanika hanging back.

"I'm sorry about your dad, sir. I didn't mean to disrespect him."

"That's okay, Tanika. Only . . . let's drop it with the 'mentalist' thing, eh? I didn't have all my memories of my father back before he died, so I do have some sort of mental condition that can be quite difficult at times."

"Sir? My dad died . . ."

I had never seen Tanika drop her cocksure

guard before. "I'm very sorry to hear that, Tanika. Was that recently?"

"No, it was when I was three. He was shot."

"Shot!" I exclaimed, unprofessionally revealing my alarm.

"It was on the London news and that. They said it was a drug-related murder, but it wasn't. Would you like to see a picture of him?"

She had already gotten a photograph from her wallet. Through the misty plastic was a toddler version of Tanika standing next to a tall man smiling for the camera.

"He looks like a very nice man."

"It wasn't drug-related, though. They just said that to make everyone feel better. If people see a picture of a murdered black man and then the newspaper says it was like 'drug-related,' all the posh white people think, 'Oh, that's all right then, it won't happen to me.'" This was a level of analysis that I had not witnessed in Tanika before.

"Losing your father at three is much, much harder than losing your dad at my age. I can't imagine what you must have gone through."

She was no longer staring at the floor but making direct eye contact with me. There wasn't any sadness or emotion there; instead I understood the hard shell that had grown over her to make her top dog in the classroom.

"Tanika? You know you have to do an independent history module for your coursework? Why don't you set the history straight on your dad?"

"What?"

"Why don't you gather all the records of your dad's murder—in the newspapers, online, or whatever—and then set about correcting them with the true story of what really happened?"

"Are we allowed to do that?"

"What you said about how things get distorted to make people feel more comfortable has to be part of it. That's how history gets rewritten."

I was already worrying that I should have reflected upon this perilous idea before suggesting it, but Tanika's education was going to end soon unless I could find a way of getting her engaged.

"Anyway, have a think about it," I said,

and she nodded blankly, put the photo away, and headed out.

AFTER school I sat at the computer screen in my classroom. Gary's user-generated news site had a front-page story explaining how the BP oil spill in the Gulf of Mexico had been deliberately staged as part of a white supremacist conspiracy between Buckingham Palace and the American military-industrial complex to destabilize Barack Obama. Surprisingly, none of the major news outlets had picked up on the YouNews exclusive. It made me feel marginally less guilty for having told Gary I didn't want to resume my involvement in YouNews.

I had not looked at my online Wiki-biography for a week, following a session when I had methodically reversed all the facetious edits, deleting claims that I could "talk to animals" and that I had "discovered France." In the time since I had last corrected the document, no further changes had been made. Clearly the young writers had gotten bored reinventing Mr. Vaughan's life and had now moved on to other things. I couldn't help but feel a little hurt.

But then I noticed a new paragraph under "Career." It said: "Mr. Vaughan was the best teacher I ever had. When I left school to work in JD Sports, he kept coming into the shop to persuade me to come back. I would never have gone to university if it wasn't for Mr. Vaughan."

This one comment from a former pupil utterly changed my mood. There *had* been a time when I had transformed lives. "Now I am manager of JD Sports," boasted my former pupil.

Despite the accumulating evidence and recovering memory, I still found myself regarding the negative side of the old Vaughan with a dispassionate objectivity. The marital breakup was an event that had happened to another man. And the Maddy before the fugue was a fictional character from some half-remembered domestic drama; the other was a living, breathing woman who seemed to understand me better than I did myself. But what was so irrational about this Maddy was that she kept getting the two genres mixed up. She resented real-life Vaughan for things that fictional Vaughan had done. I was different now; she acknowledged as much; but I was not to be allowed to forget things I couldn't remember.

I had found myself pondering how much my brain wipe had altered my actual character. I suggested to Gary that this question raised all sorts of issues about the relationship between memory and experience. We were sitting in a busy pub, probably not the best setting for a debate.

"What I'm trying to say is: Is it possible that all the character-defining experiences of my life were wiped along with the memories of them? Do I still have the mental scars of a failed marriage and all the other disappointments and unrealized ambitions, whatever they may have been?"

"Well, you were lousy at football before and you are now."

"I'm about average at football, actually—"

"You run like a girl . . . can't drive a car . . . can't hold your drink . . . appalling dress sense—"

"All right, you don't have to list them. I'm just saying, surely we don't have to remember something to be affected by it? None of us can recall everything that's happened to us, yet all of it helps shape our personalities."

"Nah," Gary said, taking a sip of his beer.
"You were always into all that philosophical
bollocks. Can I eat your crisps?"

But even Gary's rhinoceros sensitivity was
gradually being affected by the outside world.
The photo on his iPhone was from the scan
of his unborn child. He even had an idea
about a possible girlfriend for me.

"Do you know who I thought you ought
to ask out on a date? Maddy!" he declared,
as if this was the brain wave of a genius.
"You've got loads in common—and I've
a hunch you've still got a bit of a soft spot
for her."

"Wow! Thanks, Gary. I'll bear that in
mind."

Deep down, I feared that as more memories of my marriage came back, I might re-
acquire some of the bitterness and cynicism
of my prefugue incarnation. I could now recall various stages of our marriage. The
power struggle in our home seemed to have
escalated like a small regional war. I had
been insistent that the shelves above the
television were the historic homeland of
my vinyl LP collection, and demanded an

immediate end to the provocative settlement of scented candles and framed photos in the disputed territories. Madeleine upped the tension with the infamous July 10 massacre of all the history programs stored on the video recorder.

We ended up fighting about all sorts of stupid things. And the tension following any fight would continue for days, with a coded war of attrition fought on a dozen different fronts. Maddy's critical appraisal of detective thrillers on the television became unreasonably sympathetic toward the deranged wife who murdered her husband. Traditional little kindnesses disappeared: favorite treats were no longer placed in the supermarket trolley; just a single cup of tea was made at any one time. Years earlier the news of other couples splitting up would have been recounted in the same tones as a car crash. Now the reporting of such events sounded more like an innocent person being let out of prison.

None of this, of course, featured in this Wiki-memoir that I had pulled together, where I had taken care to be as neutral and objective as I could be. In any case, I was

uneasy about trusting my own memories of
the marriage; in the narrative I had recon-
structed in my mind, the unhappy ending
still didn't seem to work. I could remember
the Maddy who had been my companion,
my best friend, my soul mate. Was a bitter
divorce always going to be the final chapter
in this case?

Over the past months I had spent many
hours wanting to understand why this relationship had fallen apart as it did. Then in a
flash I saw what was wrong. I was only thinking about me. Could it be that the problem
with my marriage had been that I had approached it as an individual, not as one half
of a pair?

Feeling inspired by this flash of insight, I
created a new document and wrote at the
top: "The life story of Madeleine R.
Vaughan." Then I deleted that and put in
her maiden name. In no particular order, I
began to recall everything I knew about her
story. Her family background, her interests,
and with all the objectivity I could muster,
details of boyfriends before me. I took care
to write as much as I could about the struggle of being a professional photographer. I

recalled the excitement she had felt when buyers began to be interested, and the indignant fury she had sometimes expressed when she suspected me of regarding her job as less important than my own.

I attempted to chronicle our own entire relationship from her point of view. Memories I was unaware I had recovered poured out of me. I wrote about her pregnancy and the birth of Jamie. I wrote about the time she was called up at home by a telemarketer and she pretended to be really stupid. "Yer wha?" she grunted to every question.

My fingers were still pecking away at the keyboard two hours later. Even if I did not agree with what I understood to be her analysis of my own faults and mistakes, I recorded them. I was determined to see our two lives from her point of view. My first draft of Maddy's biography ended with her splitting up with Ralph and then grieving for her father-in-law.

In just a couple of hours of trying to see the world through her eyes, I felt as if I had discovered an extra hemisphere in my brain. I didn't pretend that now I completely understood Maddy's psyche, but I had found a way in.

We used to have stupid arguments about nothing. "What's wrong with you?" I would finally ask. "If there's something wrong, tell me what it is."

"I shouldn't have to tell you. You should just know."

Now I think I understood what she had meant. It was Maddy-speak for "Did you ever once stop to look at the world from my point of view?"

She had seemed so quiet after the funeral, pensive and distracted. Obviously she was upset about my dad, and splitting up with Ralph must have been distressing, but there was something else going on in her mind. At one point I had caught her on her own in the kitchen and had asked her if she was all right.

"I just don't know what I think anymore" had been her enigmatic reply.

"Don't know what you think about what?"

"About anything," and I thought for a moment she might be about to put her head on my shoulder.

I didn't get another chance to talk to her

after that; there were just a few words about practical arrangements as she left. I had wanted to be her counselor and confidant, but instead I was watching her car drive away while I was forced to listen to an old man in a beret explain that he had been stationed with my dad at Northolt.

Sitting in the empty classroom on my own, I felt a deepening worry on Maddy's behalf. I glanced at the time in the corner of my computer screen and realized it was now too late to go round there and just check that she was all right. I should have rung her over the weekend, I thought; I should have gone round to see her. Maybe I could go past in the street and just see if any lights were on? No, it was ridiculous. I was making something out of nothing. She was probably completely fine. I shut down my computer and hurried out the door.

Even before I was close, I could see that lights were on all over our house, which struck me as quite unlike Maddy. Even the outside porch light was still glowing like a beacon. I climbed up the steps and hesitantly reached for the button. I was relieved to see movement from the other side of the glass; it wasn't Maddy, though, but her mother, looking anxious.

"It's not her!" Jean called back into the house. "It's Vaughan!" She urgently beckoned me in. "I was going to ring you if we didn't hear from her this evening. It's been two days—we've been worried sick."

"What? What is it? Where's my wife?"

"She's disappeared, Vaughan. She's completely vanished."

Chapter 8

MY FIRST thought was that Madeleine had experienced the same sort of neurological breakdown that had befallen me. This was not such a fantastical notion; one of the early theories put to me by Dr. Lewington was that I had contracted viral encephalitis— perhaps Maddy could have literally caught this amnesia virus off her ex-husband? She might be in a hospital somewhere labeled "unknown white female."

Then I wondered: If she had been struck with retrograde amnesia, would this manifest itself in the same way? Would she now fall in love with me all over again? Isn't that

John O'Farrell

every middle-aged couple's fantasy—to feel that white-hot passion burning as fiercely as when they first fused together?

But the more I heard about Madeleine's disappearance, the less likely it felt. If Maddy's brain had suddenly wiped all memories, it was a convenient moment at which to do so, on the Saturday morning both children had left for the school's skiing trip. It occurred to me that this would have been the first time in twenty years that she'd had her home to herself. At least it would have been, had her mother not insisted that they stay for the week. Maddy's disappearance had occurred at the end of a period of enormous stress: she'd had her ex-husband disappear and then resurface wanting to turn back the clock; she'd gotten involved with another man and then broken it off; she'd taken her children to their grandfather's funeral.

Enduring all that and then having her mother in her house, focusing on her twenty-four hours a day, might be more than any sane person could be expected to endure. "I can't comprehend why Madeleine would just disappear like that. Can you comprehend it, Ron? It's incomprehendible—"

"Incomprehensible . . ."

"It is! Ron, will you phone the police? It's nine-nine-nine."

"Let's not phone the police just yet," I counseled.

"It's all right, I'd forgotten the number anyway," said Ron with a twinkling smile toward me. He had clearly come to the same conclusion as me: that his daughter's disappearance might not be so mysterious after all.

"The thing is, Jean," I said, "perhaps Maddy just needed a bit of space?"

"She's got lots of space. You had the loft converted, didn't you?"

"No, I mean headspace—from all the pressures she's been under recently. You know, some time on her own."

I assured Jean that Madeleine would call soon, but privately I remained worried. To leave her parents alone in the house without so much as an explanation was unlike the Maddy I thought I remembered. She was always so ultraconsiderate.

I knew where she kept the family passports. If she had really wanted to flee abroad for a few days, that would be an obvious clue.

I slipped upstairs to the large Victorian bureau beneath the bedroom window. I slid open the little drawer for essential documents. My hunch had been correct. Maddy had stolen herself away; the person who had always put herself second had emerged from her cocoon of commitments and responsibilities and flown.

I imagined her hastily packing a bag while her parents were out walking the dog. I wished I could have seen it as a spontaneous declaration of independence. But she had left no note, no text message; it smacked of a moment of crisis, a woman at the end of her tether. Then I sat on the edge of the bed and tried to imagine where she might possibly be.

Putting myself back into Maddy's mindset, this is the sequence of events that I finally projected onto her.

IT WAS unseasonably hot for April, and I pictured her skipping over some rocks to where the water was deep enough to dive in. She would have stopped and just inhaled the sense of space that was her favorite beach in the world. In the distance a few sheep populated the gray-green hills that sur-rounded the bay, but no cars came along the coast road.

I saw Maddy positioning her bag and towel, and then an unhesitant leap and a splash. The grace of her dive would probably have been undermined by her surfacing and swearing loudly about the iciness of the At-lantic Ocean in springtime. But Maddy was a strong swimmer, and I saw her doing a powerful front crawl across the bay. She would have checked the tides and stayed close to the shore, and maybe she had spot-ted a local collecting wood at the far end of the beach, who might be keeping one eye on the mad swimmer.

I could see her hauling herself back onto the rocks. She knew she could climb out here—she had never forgotten that swim on this beach all those years ago, the shared bottle of wine and the snugness of the tent before the storm pulled it from its moorings. Now the light spring breeze felt like an icy wind, and her towel seemed inadequate as it wrapped around her shoulders. The figure at the far end of the beach had lit a fire, which sent a plume of white smoke up over the dunes. She wanted to go and warm herself by its flames, but she could hardly wander up to a strange man in her wet swimming costume. Then again, this was Ireland; to wander over and chat would be a perfectly normal thing to do here.

She walked barefoot along the length of the dunes. It was hard to see in all the smoke whether the man was still there or not, and she was quite close before she attempted a friendly good afternoon.

"Good afternoon," replied an English accent she recognized. And then the smoke changed direction, and right before her stood her ex-husband, smiling warmly, holding out a canvas bag. "I brought your cashmere hoodie," I said.

Once I became certain that this would be where Maddy had gone, it had been easy to follow her. I had already done the difficult journey: getting to the point where I understood her. Now Maddy looked at me as if too many thoughts were racing through her head for her to articulate any one of them.

"And I just made a fire to warm you up. But I know you probably came here to get a bit of space, so I'll be on my way. If you fancy meeting up for a drink later, it's up to you," and with that I turned to head back up the beach.

She took quite a few bewildered seconds to call after me, and I started to worry that she was actually going to let me just walk away.

"Wait! How did you . . . How come . . . Are Mum and Dad all right?"

Now I stopped and turned. "They're fine." I laughed. "See, you can't help it. You can't help thinking about other people."

"How did you guess I'd come here? How did you find me?"

"Well, I remembered that whenever you couldn't hear yourself think, you'd always say, 'I wish I was at Barleycove.'"

"You remembered that?"

"I saw your passport was gone, but then I saw that you hadn't taken your cashmere, and I thought, Oh, she's going to want that."

She had already pulled it on, and her sea-scrubbed cheeks were glowing in the warmth of the fire.

"And I've got some sausages, by the way, if you fancy a sandwich?"

To Madeleine's post-swim appetite, these

bonfire-roasted Irish sausages were the best meal she'd ever eaten, and when I brought out a small bottle of wine and a plastic cup, I think she had to stop herself from hugging me. We sat on the dunes looking out at the blurred horizon, chatting and laughing as the tide went out and our shadows lengthened.

Madeleine explained that she had decided to disappear abroad without saying anything to her mother, as the only other option would have been to bludgeon her to death with a saucepan. "Mum thought she might cheer me up by listing all the things that her lucky daughter had that *she* hadn't had when she was bringing up children. So I thought I would slip away." Maddy had spotted a cheap flight to Cork and realized that she could make that flight and ring her parents later. "But then my phone was out of battery and the telephone box was broken."

"Don't worry—we'll say that you rang me and asked me to tell them. But then my dodgy memory wiped any trace of it."

"Good idea. On second thought, that's exactly what *did* happen!"

We watched a distant tanker disappear around the headland and threw our crusts to a slightly scary seagull. When she offered to fill up my glass, she noticed I wasn't drinking.

"Why? Are you driving?" she joked, then looked as if she regretted being so unkind.

"Well, actually, I am. I've got a little rented car up the hill . . ."

"You learned to drive?"

"Yes. I did this intensive course and haven't demolished a single garden wall yet. I can chauffeur you back to Crookhaven later if you like."

She didn't say anything; she just looked at me long and hard as if she was processing this new person she had known all her life.

When the fire had faded and the temperature had dropped, we headed back to the village and Maddy tried not to grip onto the passenger seat too obviously as we weaved around the coast road. We had a drink at the pub where she had booked a room, and we both got an excited skiing update text from the children. Maddy rang her parents and apologized.

I asked Maddy about her work; then she

asked me about mine, and I went on for far too long about the breakthrough I had had with my most difficult pupil, finding myself getting carried away: ". . . and then Tanika stood up in front of the class and talked about how her father's death had been mis-represented in the media, and you should have seen it, Maddy—I was so proud of her. She did this really impassioned speech, and it was all the stuff we'd talked about in History—how getting the past wrong will send you off into the wrong future. And she's written to the *South London Press* to ask them to print an article setting the record straight, and the class was cheering her, and she shouted that she was going to *kill the lie:* 'Me and Mr. Vaughan are going to kill the lie,' she repeated over the cheers, 'and I know my dad is looking down from heaven, saying thank you.'"

"So you've remembered why you loved teaching," Maddy said with a smile. "You used to talk with that sort of passion often in the old days. I always loved that about you . . ."

Eventually Maddy went up to her room, and since the pub had a couple of other rooms free, I took the cheapest of those. An hour later I was still wide awake.

Something momentous had occurred. The two of us had forgiven one another. Eventually I felt the adventure of the day catching up with me: the flight, the anxious drive, and most of all the worry that she would be utterly appalled that I had followed her. But it had gone far better than I had dared hope. Then my door opened and Maddy whispered, "Budge up!" and climbed into bed beside me.

I wanted to hug her, but something told me she'd prefer it if I just shifted across the bed and made sure there was enough quilt for my ex-wife. Or my wife, maybe? I couldn't be sure.

"How did you know which room I was in?"

"I didn't—I tiptoed into the room opposite first. Anyway, I don't think finding the right door is quite as impressive as the feat of mind reading you pulled off today." She put her head on my shoulder. "You knew I'd come here!" she said in amazement. "You just knew!"

And we didn't talk anymore, but just lay

beside one another, my arm around her. I had remembered things I never would have remembered before my amnesia. I had remembered her favorite place; I had remembered that she loved to swim but never took warm enough clothes; I had remembered that she'd said that sausage sandwich we'd shared on that perfect beach had been the best meal she'd ever had.

And I had also remembered her Gmail log-in so I could check where she had booked her flight and accommodation—but it didn't seem the moment to mention that right now.

IF A historian had to put a date on the absolute low point in our marriage, it would most likely be 11:15 p.m. on February 13, eight months before the sudden onset of my amnesia. On that night I had come home late to discover that Maddy had actually carried out her threat to change the locks on our front door. She would not answer the phone or come to the door; indeed, she pretended not to be at home, and in my anger I struck my hand against the front panel, smashed the glass, and ended up taking myself to Accident and Emergency, where I had a few stitches, the precise number varying with the level of injustice I felt at the time of recounting the episode. I refused to speak to Maddy for weeks after that, until I had gotten divorce proceedings under way.

The undignified exit from my marriage was not a new memory to me; but this morning the memory came back to me again, lying in bed with Madeleine in West Cork. I had heard the sound of broken glass being swept up outside, and the episode leaped into my consciousness. I glanced down at Maddy and was glad the noise hadn't jolted her awake.

After I woke that morning, there had been a surge of elation as I remembered how Maddy had tiptoed to my bed the night before and cuddled up next to me. And there she still was, her dozing head on the Madeleine-shaped dip below my shoulder as in a previous life. I was stroking her hair as she dozed, but now I could not get the memory of February 13 out of my head. I recalled feeling utterly humiliated as I stood on my own front doorstep, screaming through the letter box to be let in. It had felt like she was stealing my whole life from me. She had actually changed the locks on the house where I lived with my children! I felt my indignation rising as I thought about the injustice that had been done to me. I climbed out of bed, thinking I might go and have breakfast alone, but she opened her eyes and smiled dreamily at me.

"I seem to be in your bedroom . . ." she said playfully.

"Yes," I mumbled coldly.

"Why don't you come back to bed?"

"No, I'm, er—"

She was wearing my T-shirt, which I understood was quite significant in the complex code of marital diplomacy. She looked at me with a coy smile and pulled it over her head.

"Oh . . ." I groaned a few minutes later. "You are so beautiful . . ."

Now the case of the lock changing was re-examined and found to be inconsequential.

AFTER breakfast we walked by the port. Only the Post Office and General Store was open. In the height of summer the quayside buzzed with local boys hurling themselves into the sea and tourists emerging from the pub, but now the village felt ghostly.

"Do you want to go back to Barleycove for one last swim?"

"No, thanks, I'm not risking pneumonia a second time. Anyway, it's nice here—we could walk up to the headland maybe?"

"You're right, it's a lovely spot. We should have stayed at that pub when we were students instead of camping."

"Well . . . Some things take you twenty years to learn."

Now that the words were out, it seemed to demand some sort of clarification about where the two of us stood. We stared out at the bobbing yachts.

"I came out to West Cork to decide something," Maddy said finally. "And yesterday, at Barleycove, I came to a conclusion."

I felt my heart accelerate. "What did you decide?"

She took both my hands in hers as she looked me in the eye. "That next time I go swimming in the Atlantic in April, I'm buying a wet suit."

"Seems reasonable . . . I might not always be there with your cashmere."

"That was the other thing." She looked back out across the water. "It would be quite nice if you were."

A couple of seagulls seemed to laugh together in the distance. After about twenty seconds Maddy said, "Can you stop hugging me now as I'm having trouble breathing?"

We walked out of the village and toward the cliffs. Finally we were looking down on the bay, sitting on a weathered bench that a bereaved husband had erected in memory of his late wife.

"Look at those dates," I said. "Fifty-five years they were married. Do you think we could stay together fifty-five years?"

"Depends. You might go off and have an affair tomorrow, and then I would have to kill you . . ."

"Really? Is that the very worst thing?"

"No, actually. If you immediately confessed, I might just forgive you. But if you didn't tell me and then I found out, well, I would kill you slowly and post the video on YouTube."

We reminisced fondly about the first time

we had come on holiday here; how we had hired bicycles and eaten pub lunches and swum on deserted beaches. We delighted in parading these liberated memories; during the years of fighting, such stories had been officially suppressed, as they had done nothing to help the war effort. Now these folktales were being positively encouraged as part of the ongoing peace process; we were writing a new history of our marriage, one that suited the new ending of the happy, loving, divorced couple.

"So, tell me, are we legally divorced yet?"

"No, there's one last court thing, but we're not expected to go to it."

"Well, maybe we should go?" I half joked.

"Yeah! I could wear my wedding dress again—and we could have confetti outside and a big reception afterward?"

"Oh, fantastic!"

"Fantastic?"

"Yeah—you're up for doing stupid stuff again!" I took her hand and got down on one knee. "Madeleine Vaughan, would you do me the immense privilege of becoming my ex-wife? Will you divorce me?"

"I would be honored!"

WE BOTH ACCEPTED it would be far too complex and expensive to try to reverse the whole process now, so we resolved we would have a different kind of decree nisi with a big party to celebrate that we were going to live happily ever after now that we were finally divorced.

"I'm sorry I couldn't just take you back after your fugue. But I had to be really sure that you wouldn't walk out on us again."

I was shocked by how distorted her version of our split was.

"Erm . . . it seems a shame to drag this up now, but . . . it was you who changed the locks, if you remember?"

"Changed the locks? What are you talking about?"

"You changed the lock on the front door. That was the moment I realized I had to start divorce proceedings."

"I didn't change the locks, you stupid idiot!"

"Yes, you did. And you pretended to be out—even after I cut my hand on the glass in the door."

"What? That was you? We thought someone had tried to break in! I'd taken the kids to stay at my parents to give them a break from all the fighting—I left you a note and everything. When I came back, the window was smashed and you weren't there and wouldn't return my calls . . ."

"Yeah, because you'd gone and changed the locks!"

Maddy turned to look directly at me. "Had you been drinking? When the key didn't work in the front-door lock?"

There was a long pause. "Look, er, if you like, I can move my vinyl LPs out of the lounge . . ."

IT WAS spring, when a middle-aged man's fancy turns to divorce. Maddy and I entered the court arm in arm and walked ceremoniously down the central aisle. Madeleine was unmistakably a bride, in the crimson-silk, three-quarter-length dress she'd worn for our wedding, clutching a bunch of roses that matched the single rose in her coquettish hat. I complimented her that after two children and fifteen years she could still get into it.

Despite giving up alcohol, I failed to fit into the suit I'd worn on my wedding day, which was just as well considering the size of the shoulder pads. But I hired a smart gray morning suit and wore a rose in my buttonhole, and we stood side by side in the Principal Registry of the Family Division, ready for the judge to pronounce us man and ex-wife.

The judge himself initially checked that we weren't in the wrong court. Both our long-suffering lawyers were present, finding some sort of common cause in the obstinate refusal of this impossible couple to follow the traditional script of bitter acrimony. The judge's day had been brightened up by this unconventional couple. "Are you certain, Mr. Vaughan, that you wish to divorce this woman?"

"Oh, yes, your honor." I looked lovingly at Maddy, who smiled back. "I've never been so sure of anything in my whole life."

The judge then declared that the decree nisi was granted, and my lawyer mumbled sarcastically, "You may now kiss the divorcée." So I did.

As Maddy and I emerged hand in hand, a small gathering of friends and family showered us in tiny colored bits of tissue paper.

Our children were particularly generous with the confetti, tipping boxes of the stuff onto their parents' heads, before asking if they could ride in the white Rolls-Royce that had been booked to drive their parents to the reception. And so the whole family climbed inside and pulled away to the applause of the crowd.

For Jamie and Dillie's benefit, the Rolls-Royce took a scenic route, and by the time we pulled up at our home, most of the guests were already sipping champagne in the marquee that took up most of the garden. Our friends had happily dressed up in their best wedding outfits to mark the occasion. Only Madeleine's mother struggled to process the irony of the thing, explaining that we would probably get married again like Richard Burton and Elizabeth Taylor.

Most of our social circle had been delighted to learn that one of their favorite couples were back together. There was a sense of real euphoria among the friends gathered here on this special day. "This is so romantic!" said the heavily pregnant Linda. "Why can't we get divorced?"

Today Gary was taking the role of best

man, or "worst man," as he enjoyed telling everyone. In his waistcoat pocket he checked that he still had the wedding rings we had not worn for months but would later place on one another's finger in front of everyone we knew and loved.

Eventually it was time for the mock ceremony, and Gary guided people toward the raised decking in preparation for the service. For this special "second time around" ceremony we had resolved that we should still publicly commit to one another, but with revised, more realistic vows. "I promise to pretend to listen to you going on about stuff, when really I am thinking about something completely different." "I promise to love you in an everyday, familiar, best-friend sort of way, but not expect gushing declarations of devotion every five minutes." And "I promise to tolerate your imperfections and varying moods as you tolerate mine, and not to use these as private justification for entering my old girlfriends' names on Google."

Gary reminded the guests once again what a special occasion this was. "Earlier today Vaughan and Maddy finally took the big step that so many of us have often thought about but never quite had the courage to do, and finally got themselves divorced." A big drunken cheer went up from the crowd.

"Now, Maddy and Vaughan appreciate that some of you came to their wedding fifteen years ago and brought them some lovely gifts, which they now feel morally obliged to return to you . . ."

One lone voice heckled, "They've bought them back off eBay?"

"Mark and Erena," he continued, "with a heavy heart they are returning the twenty-two-piece dining set you gave them, which after one particularly fierce argument is now a ninety-two-piece set." Slightly nervous laughter greeted this; the audience was unsure if it was acceptable to refer to past marital difficulties at a divorce party. "Pete and Kate—to you they are returning the set of six crystal wineglasses, which is now a set of eleven crystal wineglasses, as Maddy and Vaughan buy their petrol from the same garage as you."

Gary was milking this chance to perform to a generous crowd, but after a while, though I could hear his voice, I ceased to hear the actual words. I closed my eyes and felt the warmth of the sun on my face, the swirling sunspots floating me somewhere else. When suddenly it happened—an entire sequence of memories arrived in my head uninvited.

I had had an affair. Her name was Yolande, a twentysomething French language assistant at school, who had eventually returned to France. But for a month or so I had seen her secretly after work, and eventually I had been bold enough to gate-crash a school trip to Paris, creeping into Yolande's hotel bedroom after the other staff and students were asleep.

I felt appalled. I remembered that the affair had come at a point in our marriage when normal communication had broken down. But if I'd felt that there had been any moral justification, why had I kept this secret locked up so tightly that it was one of the very last memories to reemerge?

Details of my affair were churning in my brain. I remembered the first time I had come home after it had begun, wondering if Maddy would be able to tell. But there was too much hostility in the air for Maddy's antennae to detect any suppressed contrition. Nor could I possibly tell her. If she knew, it would only make everything worse.

But that was then. Standing here now, surely she had to know the truth before the two of us began our new life together? If not now, then when? When is the best time to tell your wife you've had an affair—before or after you make a set of vows in front of friends and family? "If you immediately confessed, I might just forgive you . . ." That was what she had said.

Gary had finished his speech, but before the climax of the afternoon's entertainment Maddy just wanted to say a few words. She wanted to thank all the people who had helped make today's party possible: she thanked her mother and father, Dillie and Jamie, thanked Gary for being so entertaining; in fact, she was thanking so many people there was a chance the marriage would run its natural course before I had the chance to come clean.

"Gary!" I whispered, gesturing him to step back inside the kitchen. "Listen—I just remembered something." I lowered my voice to almost inaudible, "I had an affair a couple of years ago."

"Bloody hell, Vaughan. Why are you telling me this now?"

"I only just remembered it. I have to tell Madeleine before the vows!"

The two of us looked at Maddy out on the makeshift stage.

"Are you insane? Don't tell her now. Don't tell her ever, but especially not now. Don't throw it all away, you idiot."

"But it has to be before we commit. Withholding it is deception."

"Deception is fine. Deception is normal. You should never, ever be completely honest with your wife. That's the worst thing you can possibly do."

"But she said she'd forgive me if I told her *immediately*."

"Don't ruin her big day. 'Cause this whole thing is actually like a wedding," observed Gary, as if this was a perceptive insight.

Now the moment had come for the spoof ceremony and the symbolic (and unironic) exchange of rings. I stepped back outside with Gary, who seemed less assured than he had before and stammered and mumbled his explanation of the next section of the proceedings.

I caught Maddy's eye, and she raised her eyebrows at me with a slightly coy grin. This might possibly be the last smile I ever got from her, I thought. Which was better: a happy marriage based on a lie, or the risk of no marriage because I'd told the truth?

"Maddy!" I whispered behind Gary's back. "There's something I have to tell you. It's about before we split up. I've only just remembered it, but you have to know now." With just a gesture of my head, I indicated that we move back from the exposed stage, and, looking perplexed, Maddy stepped inside.

"So what's the big deal?" she whispered.

"You know when I went to Paris with the school? It wasn't just with the school. I went because there was another woman."

No amount of blush or lipstick could hide the color draining from Maddy's face. "What do you mean? How . . . who is she?"

"She was a French language assistant at

school. It was over in a month. I'm really, really sorry, but I had to be honest with you. It'll never happen again, I promise. Maddy, say something."

But Maddy had nothing to say, though her mascara was being diluted and a dark line ran down her cheek.

"So Vaughan and Madeleine, step forward, please!" demanded Gary, the unconvincing clergyman. We hovered on the other side of the open doors for a second. "Come on, come on, don't be shy!" said Gary, ushering us back out into the open air. "So, if any person or golden retriever knows of any just impediment why this man and this woman should not be disunited in unholy divorce, let them speak now or forever hold their peace."

I glanced at Maddy, who seemed stunned.

"Jack Joseph Neil Vaughan, do you take Madeleine Rose Vaughan of this parish to be your legally separated ex-wife, to live with in sin from this day forth? Will you notice when she's been to the hairdresser's and accept her choice of driving routes as a reasonable alternative?"

"I, um . . . I will." I glanced at her; at least the crying seemed to be at a minimum.

"And Madeleine Rose Vaughan, do you take Jack Joseph Neil Vaughan to be your legally separated ex-husband, to live with in sin from this day forth? Will you tolerate him and humor him? Will you laugh at jokes you've heard a hundred times before?"

A silence followed.

"She's forgotten her lines, ladies and gentlemen—it's a very big day . . ." Gary had been aware of us whispering inside and feared the worst. "Just say 'I will,'" he whispered to her.

"She's changed her mind!" shouted a drunken heckler, whose wife then slapped him on the arm because she realized that maybe Maddy had.

"Take your time, Maddy—it's a big decision . . ." The humor had gone from Gary's voice, as if he was speaking to her sincerely now.

Finally Maddy seemed ready to speak. "You . . . you . . ." She was staring directly at me. "You BASTARD!" And now she really did burst into tears as she threw her bouquet at my face. "I never want to see you again for as long as I live." And then she ran off the stage into the house, until the stunned crowd heard the front door slamming behind her.

Chapter 9

APPARENTLY the party went downhill a bit after Madeleine left. Gary tried to do one or two of his prepared jokes, but even he soon realized that perhaps the moment had gone. I ran out after Maddy, but she'd grabbed the car keys and sped off.

The party guests drifted off, mumbling embarrassed thank-yous to me and saying that most of the party had been very enjoyable. Later that evening Jean came round to collect a few things of Maddy's, explaining to the children that their mummy was going to stay with her mummy for a night or two and that she would ring them later.

"Could you tell her that I need to talk to her?" I pleaded.

"She just needs a bit of *headspace* at the moment, Vaughan. Every relationship goes through this . . ."

I was pretty sure that every relationship did not go through this. Husband and wife split up, he has a mental breakdown resulting in total amnesia, eventually sees his estranged wife as if for the first time, changes his mind about getting a divorce, eventually wins his wife back, then at the party to celebrate their new beginning remembers that he was unfaithful, tells her, and she breaks up with him all over again.

In fact, Maddy stayed away for more than a couple of nights, and now I was the stressed single parent, getting the kids off to school, dashing on to work, then rushing back and cooking and failing to be of any assistance with their math homework.

Maddy rang Jamie's mobile every night, and he grunted his few words before passing the handset to Dillie. I had texted and emailed Maddy, but she couldn't bring herself to speak to me just yet.

I offered to move out if Maddy wanted to be back at the house with Dillie and Jamie, but she interpreted this as me not wanting to be responsible for the children so that I would be free to chase female members of staff.

Gary and Linda had me round for supper, and I learned that they had talked to Maddy about me, pointing out, in my defense, that I had at least told her the truth.

"Okay, it was wrong, he admits that," Linda had said. "But not every bloke would have owned up—"

"I wouldn't have," Gary had chipped in brightly. But now Gary had reasons of his own to be depressed. He reported to me that he had finally decided to close down YouNews. "User-generated news doesn't work. People were just making stuff up."

"What, unlike tabloid journalists?"

It felt like everything went wrong in the end.

I HAD a final appointment with Dr. Lewington. When she asked me if I had regained any more significant memories, I said, "No. None at all." The curious thing that I should have shared with her was that this was the first memory I had regained and then subsequently lost again. I clearly recalled the moment it all came back to me, but the details of Yolande and Paris were now a vague blur.

Finally she announced, "Well, I don't think there is anything else we can do for you. You can walk out of here and get on with the rest of your life."

ON THE fourth day of limbo, I was surprised to receive a call from Maddy's father. Ron wanted to meet me and suggested the café at the British Library at Euston. I was reassured by his choice of venue. If he wanted to punch me in the face for betraying his daughter, the British Library did not seem the most obvious place to do it.

Ron was already waiting for me when I arrived; he was seated at a booth and got up to shake my hand. I felt too embarrassed to look him in the eye.

"How's Maddy?"

"She's been staying in her old room. Her mother puts plates of food beside her bed, then takes them away again later . . ."

"Right. So . . . this is a long way from home."

"Yes, I've been commuting to London to do a bit of research on your medical condition. I hope you don't mind?"

Inside I felt a pang of disappointment that

this was what he had come to talk about. I had hoped he might have a message from Maddy.

"I think I may have unearthed some interesting case studies," he said. I gave a neutral nod. I'd already read everything there was to read on retrograde amnesia and dissociative fugues.

At the next table a young student couple were staring at one another, too in love to have separate drinks, their two straws intimately sharing the same iced mocha.

"Now I'm not saying that this applies in your case, but it's something I think you should be aware of." He indicated the pages he had photocopied from various reference books and old journals. "In 1957, this businessman in New York had exactly the same thing as you. He had been under great stress as a chief executive, with millions of dollars riding on his decisions, when one day he disappeared and was found a week later with no knowledge of who he was. Like you, this gentleman gradually regained all his memories, and the board voted to reinstate him."

The student took his straw out of the cup

and presented the foam on the end for his girlfriend to lick off.

"But at the moment when he returned to his old life, he suddenly remembered that he had defrauded the company. He was racked with guilt, confessed, and resigned."

"Sorry, Ron—but I don't quite see how that helps me now? I remembered all the worst stuff last as well."

"I think this might have some bearing on your indiscretion in Paris."

I blushed. "The funny thing is, I don't even remember that anymore. It came back to me as clear as anything on the day of our party. But it's the first memory I have regained and then lost again."

"But that's one of the symptoms!" said Ron excitedly. "Look, this is the interesting bit. His company investigated his confession, and *it wasn't true*. There had been no fraud; it was a false memory!"

"A false memory? How does that work?"

"Deep down he was frightened of returning to the challenges of his old life and subconsciously needed an excuse not to make that final leap."

"Where did you get all this from?"

"From books. These examples are from years back, long before online medical journals and suchlike. It is amazing what you can find in libraries."

"You mean there are others?" Only now did I look properly at the photocopied pages on the table.

"Yes—look. This was in a 1930s book about psychiatry. A local alderman in Lincoln confessed to killing a woman who, it transpired, was still alive."

"I don't get it."

"The sufferers aren't pretending to have these memories; they really do believe they did these bad things."

I hurriedly scanned the dense print of the photocopied book. The psychiatrist's theory was that this handful of individuals had experienced false memories for the same reason that they had suffered their original amnesia. Unable to cope, their brains had created an extreme solution: wipe all memories of the stressful life or create new memories that would make a return to that stressful life impossible.

"When I told a language teacher at school the reason Maddy and I had split up again, he said that Yolande never went on the Paris trip. He said she'd already left at that point. I thought he must have gotten it wrong."

"Well, it seems like your brain has been playing tricks on you again."

"Oh, Ron, this is fantastic! I feel like I've been let out of prison. I *didn't* have an affair! Does Maddy know about this?"

"Yes. She suggested I came to tell you."

"Right. Was she happy?"

"She said, 'So Vaughan may not be an adulterer, he's just a total nutter.'"

"Will you tell her that Yolande didn't even go to Paris? That proves my innocence, doesn't it? Will you tell her and get her to call me?"

"You're not really mad at all, are you? You're just mad about Maddy," he said with a smile. "But then, who wouldn't be?"

A FEW hours later I was seated in the hall at my children's school, saving the empty seat beside me. Jamie and Dillie were appearing in the school production of *South Pacific*. I had texted Maddy to say that I would leave her ticket at the desk. The nerves of all the children on the stage were nothing compared to those of one of the adults watching them.

The band struck up the overture, and Jamie looked as though he wished his guitar were big enough to hide him. All the parents were looking directly ahead except one, who kept looking round. It was at that moment that a body slipped quietly in beside me and I heard Maddy whisper, "Hi."

I felt a surge of elation. What better time for my wonderful wife to make an appearance than during the chorus of "There Is Nothing Like a Dame." I turned to her and exclaimed, "Maddy!" so loudly that several parents glared at me for interrupting. "You haven't missed Dillie yet," I whispered.

She said nothing else to me for most of the first act, which made me anxious and distracted throughout "Some Enchanted Evening" and "A Cockeyed Optimist." Finally, during "Younger than Springtime," I whispered, "I spoke to your dad."

"Yeah, he called me immediately afterward."

"Isn't it fantastic?"

"What's fantastic about it?"

"Shhh!" said a couple of teachers in front of us.

I tried to establish how her father's discovery could be anything other than positive, but every time I whispered loud enough for her to hear, heads would turn.

"Can you please stop talking!" came the harsh whisper from behind us.

There was a round of applause for the end of the song, so Maddy gestured to me to come outside. At that moment Dillie made her entrance. Just in time to see both her parents getting up and scurrying to the exit.

The two of us stood and talked in the school corridor. I tried to fathom why Maddy was still so cool with me.

"Look, I remember Yolande being at the school, but it's like I hardly knew her. I don't understand why you aren't pleased. I *didn't* sleep with the French language assistant!" The group of teenage girls in grass skirts rushing down the corridor gave me a strange look. I gestured to hug Maddy, but she did not accept the invitation.

"So why did you imagine you had an affair with this Yolande woman?"

"You're not going to hold it against me that I *imagined* I had sex with another woman, are you? That's every male in the known universe . . ."

"The first question is, did you imagine you had sex with Yolande because you fancied her?"

"Of course I fancied Yolande. Everyone did—she was gorgeous. What's pathetic is that my subconscious believed that a stunning young thing like Yolande would ever have an affair with an old fart like me! It's ridiculous."

At that moment the double doors of the hall burst open and the audience swept toward the dining room, where the catering students would be selling interval drinks. Maddy and I went through with the rest of the crowd, feeling mortified when someone congratulated us on Dillie's performance.

"Maddy—come home with me, Jamie, and Dillie tonight. They've really missed you. I miss you. You were all set to give our relationship another go until I tried to be honest about something that had happened in the past. Well, now you've got the best of both worlds: I *wasn't* unfaithful, but you know I'd tell you if I had been."

"It's not as simple as that."

"It is as simple as that."

Other families we knew joined us, and I didn't get another chance to talk with Maddy before we returned to our seats. Finally, during the applause for "Happy Talk," I grabbed my opportunity.

"You said the *first* question is did I fancy Yolande. What was the second question?"

"Why did your mind need to create a false memory?" she said.

"I dunno."

"Because at some deep level, you don't want to commit. Your brain invented a reason not to be with me because it doesn't want to be with me."

"But—"

She put her fingers to her lips as the room fell quiet. All the way through "This Nearly Was Mine" I wanted to scream at the unfairness of it. My memory was like some involuntary muscle: acting independently, wiping files, making up stuff, while I was held to account for the way it was trashing my past and future.

"But I *do* want to be with you. In sickness

and in mental health. Remember our wedding vows."

"Yeah. Except we got divorced."

Now Dillie was on stage again, and we clapped loudly, making sure she could see us in the audience. Only at the end did we have another opportunity to talk. During the repeated curtain calls, while we waved enthusiastically to our children on stage, we tried to work out whether their mum and dad were going to stay together.

"You have a psychological condition," sighed Maddy. "And your psyche doesn't want you to be with me. That will manifest itself sooner or later, and I'm not going through all that again."

"This is so unfair. I want you back home, okay? The kids want you back home, I didn't sleep with anyone else, and now you know you can trust me to tell you if I ever had. What else do I have to do?"

"Dillie's waving—wave back!"

I waved at my daughter, then gave two thumbs-ups to Jamie.

"Oh God, I don't know," sighed Maddy. "I spoke to the lawyers before this false-memory stuff came up. Under the terms of the divorce, you have to vacate the house and I have to allow you access to the children every weekend. They're waiting for me to direct them to instruct you."

"No, Maddy, think about it. Give us another chance."

"Look, we can't put the kids through another breakup. I'll go back to Mum and Dad's, and I'll be in touch, okay?"

FOR two days I waited for any message from Maddy. I had sent her a long email listing all the reasons why I felt that we should be together, but heard nothing back. I didn't dare leave the house in case she came round.

On the third day a solitary letter landed face up on the doormat, and in that moment I feared the worst. A formal letter, addressed to me, from her lawyer; that could only be an official instruction to vacate the house and adhere to the terms of the divorce.

I was not sure where I wanted to be when I opened this emotional letter bomb. I took it into the kitchen, but decided I didn't want to read it there. I wandered into the lounge and then back to the hallway. I held the letter up to the light, but the envelope was too expensive to see through. And finally I ripped it open to have my fate confirmed to me.

Inside there was no letter from the lawyers. Just a tatty green postcard featuring a cartoon leprechaun saying "Top o' the mornin' to yers!"

"SHE'S beautiful; she's absolutely perfect!" I said, looking at the newborn baby in Maddy's arms, or possibly at Maddy; I never actually specified.

"Would you like to hold her, Vaughan?" suggested Linda from the hospital bed, and Madeleine passed the baby over.

Linda's birth plan had specified a traditional birthing experience, which Gary had taken as his cue to play it like a 1950s husband and remain in the pub the entire evening. He only just made it in time.

But now, incredibly, here the new baby was. And here was Maddy with our own children, marveling at the miracle of a whole new life.

I looked into the unfocused eyes of the tiny baby, feeling some sort of vague affinity with this new arrival. And Maddy smiled as she looked at the baby staring up in the direction of her newborn man.

"Does it take you back to when you first held our two?" said Maddy.

"God, yeah, I'll never forget that—"

"Again . . ." heckled Jamie.

Linda took the baby back, and we headed home.

Family life had quickly reverted to normality after Maddy had returned. The children found it irritating that their parents were trying really hard to be nice to one another, and shouted, "Get a room!" every time we so much as cuddled. But they obviously appreciated having both their father and their mother around to tell them to do their homework, tidy their rooms, and clear the dinner table. It was just at such a profound level that the children wouldn't have realized quite how much they appreciated it.

But Madeleine and I hadn't gotten back together for the sake of our kids. Maddy told me she realized that I was, in fact, "the light of her life." I was amazed to hear her being this romantic, until she added, "Okay, so the light flickers a bit, and the bulbs don't last five minutes, but frankly I can't be bothered to get another bloody light now."

Despite our kids' outwardly confident and contented manner, I worried about how much they might have been affected by our original breakup. I'd been particularly worried about how Jamie might react to the reunion. I was still haunted by his outburst at the swimming pool.

I contrived an opportunity to walk Woody on the Common with Jamie to give me a chance to have a grown-up talk.

"I won't let it ever get like it was before," I said.

"You can't promise that," he said, like the admonishing parent.

"Well, I can promise that I've changed."

"We'll see," said Jamie, which is what adults always say when they don't want to agree to something. We walked on in awkward silence for a while. Then from nowhere he piped up, "Still, at least it means we won't have to see Ralph anymore."

In the distance a tractor chugged and rattled, and the delicious aroma of fresh-cut grass mingled with the smoke of the first summer barbecues. Then Maddy and Dillie were spotted, approaching on their bicycles, my daughter puffed and pink-cheeked from racing to catch up with us.

"We thought we could all go to the band-stand and get an ice cream."

"Great idea. Get me a coffee," I said as they cycled ahead.

It was just a perfectly ordinary scene, a family sitting outside a café in a London park, spooning the chocolate froth off their parents' coffee or sharing a taste of each other's cones. But as I chatted and laughed along, I felt myself detach, like some lab scientist gazing down in wonder at the whole incredibly unlikely scenario. How fragile a thing was human happiness. This might turn out to be the best moment ever, right here, right now.

Maddy was so beautiful, her face showing the creases of forty years of smiling at everyone. Jamie was quiet and dignified, always so judicious when he did choose to speak. Dillie glowed with enthusiasm and unshakeable trust in the goodness of people. And there was I in the middle of them all, consciously recording this precious memory. I felt like a born-again father, an evangelical family man.

Maddy had told me something remarkable about our quiet, contemplative son. During that terrifying purgatory when Madeleine had been staying with her parents in Berkshire, she had answered the front door to see Jamie standing there in his school uniform, clutching the present of a chocolate orange. And while he was supposed to be in double math, mother and son sat on a bench in a pretty back garden in the country, sharing his gift.

"Me and Dillie were talking," he had said. "We just thought you should know that whatever you do, it should be what you want, not what you think we want. Because what we want is what you want."

"Well, that's no good," she told him, "because all I want is what you two want, so now we're completely stuck!" And she kissed the top of his head so he couldn't see that she was crying. I later noticed that Maddy kept the packaging of that chocolate orange in her bedside drawer.

As for the leprechaun postcard, that was officially decommissioned and put on display in the public gallery that was the downstairs toilet. It had become a bit battered and faded down the years, but the little leprechaun's upbeat message still made me smile every time I looked at it.

THE day after Gary finally became a father I offered to take my old friend out for a celebratory lager, or, in my case, sparkling mineral water. Gary took the last empty table, dangerously close to the dartboard.

"Well, here's to your new arrival!"

"I'll drink to that . . . Gazoody-baby!"

"A girl! Now that's two people in your home you won't understand."

"Talking of which—how are things with Maddy?" ventured Gary.

"Great! Really great. It's early days, but I think we're both really happy."

"That's good." He took a large sip of beer. "So she still hasn't twigged that her father forged all that false-memory bollocks?"

"What?" My mouth hung open.

"He did a good job, old Ron, with his phony photocopies and made-up psychiatrists."

A dart bounced off the board and just missed me.

"You mean . . . So I did commit . . ."

Gary burst out laughing at my intense mortification. "I tell you one thing that has never changed. You were gullible when I first met you, and you're just as gullible now!"

"Bull's-eye!" came the cry from behind us.

"Ah, you should see your face!" laughed Gary. And I affected a good-natured smile, using muscles normally intended for screaming.

THE next morning in school, I found myself wandering off the curriculum during my last lesson with Year Eleven. "So all this history we have done over the past year—is it all true, do you think?"

"Yeah, 'cause if it's not true, it's not history."

"But who's to say what's true? Is 'true' what everyone thinks happened? Tanika's letter to the *South London Press* about how her dad really died has changed the official history, hasn't it, Tanika?"

"Yeah, and we're planting a tree and we're going to put a notice underneath. Will you come, sir?"

"I'd be honored."

Six months ago an exchange like this would have prompted jeers to the effect that Tanika loved Boggy Vaughan, but all that had been left behind.

"You see, it's all a question of perception. Sometimes we think we remember something but have actually reinvented it, because the fictional memory suits us better. And the same is true in history. We all put our own angle on everything that happens to us, consciously and subconsciously. Governments, countries, and individuals—"

"So what you have been teaching us all year might be a load of old bull?"

"I wouldn't put it quite like that. I'm just saying that history is not what definitely happened. History is . . . well, history is just old spin."

THAT evening Maddy and I sat out on the wooden decking as the light gently fell away.

"Linda and Gary took the baby home today."

"Blimey! I wonder how their marriage will cope."

"Oh, I'm sure they'll get through it," said Maddy. "Gary's probably got a special app for it on his iPhone."

"Ha! I could have used one of those. GPS technology to tell me where I'd gone wrong in my life . . ."

"I think the secret is just to find what it is that really makes you happy. And then drink a few glasses of it every evening." She took a sip.

"I must tell that to my Year Eleven class. We had a really interesting discussion today. About the nature of history. They so want to be certain about what definitely happened."

"Yeah, well, you might not be the best judge of all that . . ."

"Fair point. But having completely lost my past, it makes you realize how all that stuff can actually get in the way. Countries go to war over distorted versions of history; couples get divorced from accumulating bitterness about stuff that never quite happened the way they remember it."

"So everyone should get chronic amnesia?"

"No, I'm just saying that you've got *your* version of the past, and now I've got mine back, and we should each respect the differences."

She went to pour some wine into my empty water glass, but I covered the top of it with my hand.

"Not drinking anymore—remember?"

"Oh, yeah—old habits die hard." But the end of the bottle somehow knocked my fingers, and the glass fell and broke in two.

"Sorry! I thought I had it."

"No, that was me—I knocked your hand."

We burst out laughing at ourselves, and I picked up the broken glass.

"Give it a few months, and I'll remember that was definitely your fault."

"In ten years' time I'll say you smashed the glass. After you threw it at me."

"Ten years' time! Do you think we'll still be together in ten years' time?"

"Maybe. Maybe not." She put her bare feet up onto my lap. "Who knows what the past will hold?"

And then I recovered perhaps my final unreclaimed memory.

A STRIKING REDHEAD *walks into the Students' Union bar. I have never seen anyone so beautiful, and once she sits down, I place myself in an empty seat nearby and hope she might notice the fellow first-year directly in her sight line. I pull my brand-new textbook from the bookshop bag but decide it will look more impressive if I open it somewhere near the final chapter. I can't help glancing up every few minutes to catch her eye.*

"That's a very scholarly sounding book," she says eventually.

"This? I'm just reading this for pleasure; it's not part of my course."

"Hmm . . . Do you mind me asking, why are you starting at the back?"

"That's just how I prefer history." I feel myself blushing at having been caught out. "I can never wait to find out what happens at the end." I glance down at the final page and exclaim, "Oh, no! The Romans win!"

"Oh . . . . Now there's no point in me reading it."

"Sorry about that. I'm Vaughan, by the way."

"I'm Madeleine . . . Sociology."

"Unusual surname."

"Yeah—Russian or something . . . Are you here for the Experimental Poetry Performance?"

"What? Er, yeah. I love that stuff. Oh, you just made that up, didn't you?"

And she grins, and that is the moment I decide this is the woman I want to marry. Then a couple of Maddy's friends arrive at the table, and she invites me to join them. "This is Vaughan, everyone. He's studying history," she explains. "Backward."

RICHARD PAUL EVANS

Richard Paul Evans has been inspiring readers for more than twenty years, and it's no surprise that he has a very active Facebook page. In fact, that's where the idea for *The Mistletoe Promise* originated.

Evans posts daily, and one February, he asked his fans if they had any special Valentine's memories. One woman posted about when a man she barely knew approached her; he had no valentine and asked if she would pretend to be his. She was surprised but said yes, and for a week he wrote her notes and sent her candy and flowers.

Tracy Evans

Evans felt there was a story there, and he set it at another time of year when loneliness is often felt acutely. He hopes that people will feel warmed and loved when they read it.

JOHN O'FARRELL

When asked about the initial spark of inspiration behind *The Man Who Forgot His Wife*, John O'Farrell explained, "I had seen contemporaries get divorced and be just as miserable afterwards, and I spent ages trying to think of a way in which a protagonist might look at his life with fresh eyes. I think both partners in a marriage can start to take each other for granted and forget how special their other half is."

However, his own marriage is quite different. O'Farrell gushes about when he met his wife, saying he thought she was one of the smartest women he'd ever met. He is married with two children, who both attended Lambeth Academy. They all currently live in Clapham in South London.

Joseph M. Mascia

Helping to enrich the lives of thousands of visually impaired individuals every day
www.rdpfs.org

Reader's Digest Partners for Sight is a non-profit foundation established in 1955 by DeWitt Wallace, co-founder of Reader's Digest. Originally created with the purpose of publishing high-quality reading material for the visually impaired, the Foundation has helped to enrich the lives of thousands of visually impaired individuals.

Now, through its program of carefully directed charitable grants to qualifying organizations, the Foundation is also a vital source of support on local, regional, and national levels for the blind and visually impaired community. **Partners for Sight** is also the co-sponsor of the helpful online resource VisionAware.org.

If you would like to contact the Foundation, write to: **Reader's Digest Partners for Sight Foundation, Inc.,** 118 North Bedford Road, Suite 100, Mt. Kisco, NY 10549.